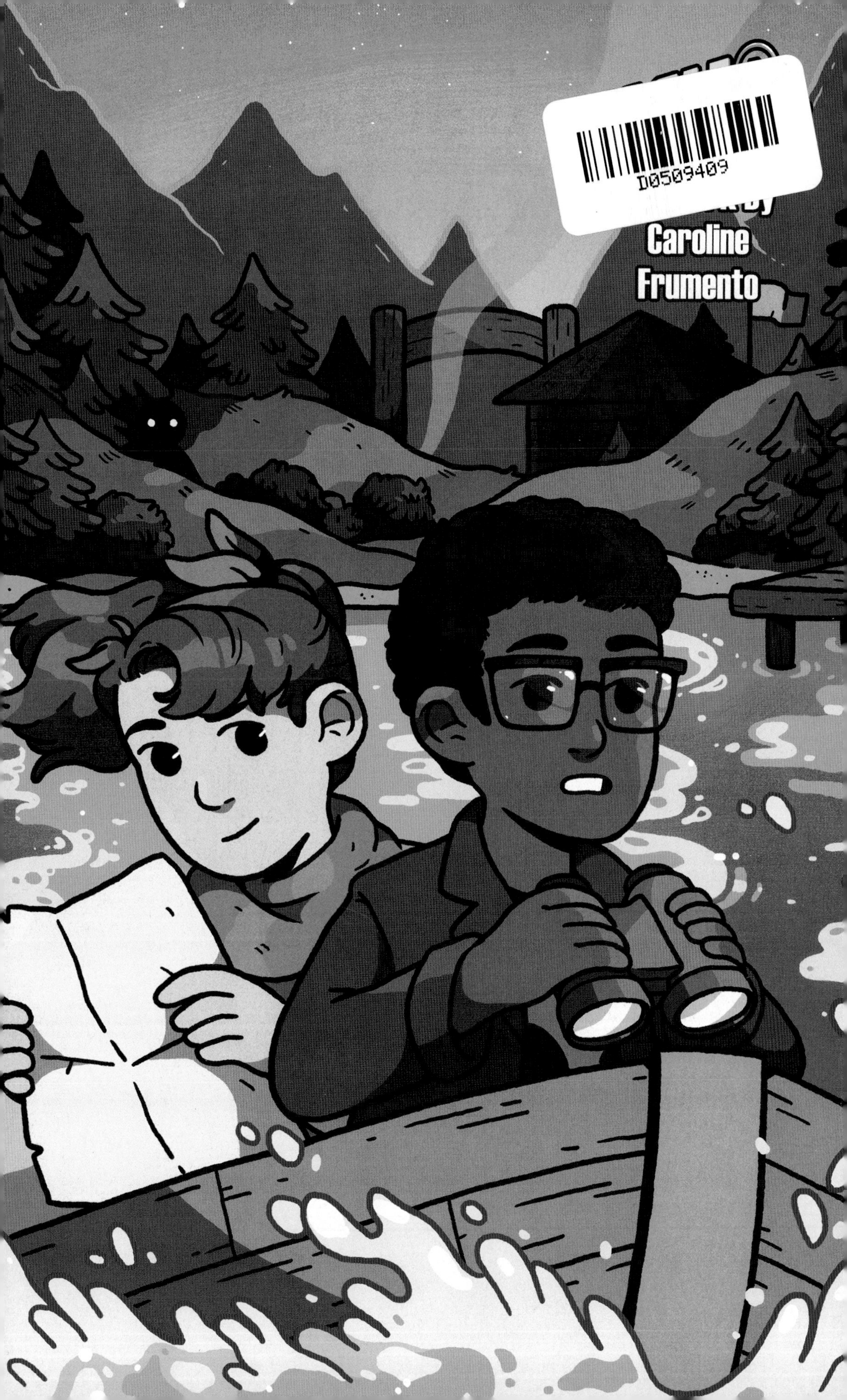
Caroline
Frumento

CASH + CARRIE

CREATED BY
SHAWN PRYOR & GIULIE SPEZIANI
FRONT COVER BY
CAROLINE FRUMENTO

CONCEPTUAL DESIGN & LOGO BY
PENNY CANDY STUDIOS
BACK COVER BY
VALENTINE BARKER

CHAPTER ONE:
BIG FOOT, SMALL SNEAKERS
WRITTEN BY GIULIE SPEZIANI
ARTWORK BY MARCUS KWAME ANDERSON
LETTERS BY JUSTIN BIRCH

CHAPTER TWO:
BULL'S-EYE!
WRITTEN BY GIULIE SPEZIANI
ARTWORK BY MARCUS KWAME ANDERSON
LETTERS BY JUSTIN BIRCH

CHAPTER THREE:
LUNCH LADY HAS THE LAST LAUGH
WRITTEN BY GIULIE SPEZIANI
ARTWORK BY MARCUS KWAME ANDERSON
LETTERS BY JUSTIN BIRCH

CHAPTER FOUR:
COOK'D BOOK
WRITTEN BY SHAWN PRYOR & CHRIS & GIN
ARTWORK BY CHRIS & GIN
LETTERS BY CHRIS & GIN

CHAPTER FIVE:
MASON MIDDLE MESSENGER: SUMMER EDITION
WRITTEN BY SHAWN PRYOR
ARTWORK BY TRESSINA BOWLING
COLORS BY DANNY BOWLING
LETTERS BY JUSTIN BIRCH

BRYAN SEATON: PUBLISHER/ CEO
SHAWN GABBORIN: EDITOR-IN-CHIEF
JASON MARTIN: PUBLISHER-DANGER ZONE
NICOLE D'ANDRIA: MARKETING DIRECTOR/EDITOR
JESSICA LOWRIE: SOCIAL MEDIA CZAR
DANIELLE DAVISON: EXECUTIVE ADMINISTRATOR
CHAD CICCONI: FINGERPRINT DUSTER
SHAWN PRYOR: PRESIDENT OF CREATOR RELATIONS

ISBN NUMBER 978-1-63229-491-3
CASH & CARRIE BOOK 2: SUMMER SLEUTHS, SEPTEMBER 2019.
© COPYRIGHT SHAWN PRYOR, 2019. PUBLISHED BY ACTION LAB ENTERTAINMENT.
ALL RIGHTS RESERVED. ALL CHARACTERS ARE FICTIONAL. ANY LIKENESS TO
ANYONE LIVING OR DEAD IS COINCIDENTAL. NO PART OF THIS PUBLICATION MAY
BE REPRODUCED OR TRANSMITTED WITHOUT PERMISSION, EXCEPT FOR
SMALL EXCERPTS FOR REVIEW PURPOSES. PRINTED IN USA. FIRST PRINTING.

CROWNTAKER
STUDIOS

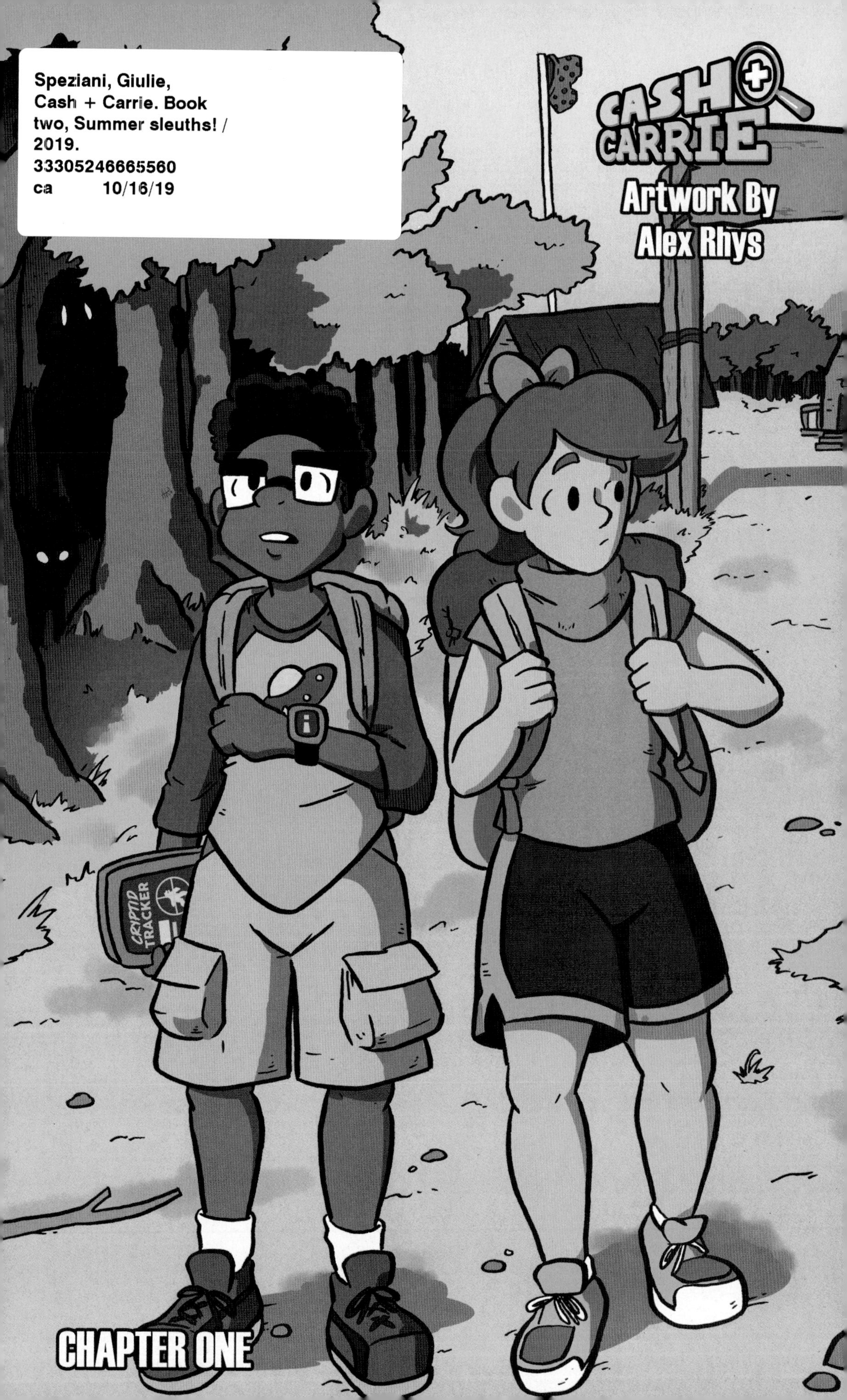
CASH + CARRIE
Artwork By
Alex Rhys
CRYPTID TRACKER
CHAPTER ONE

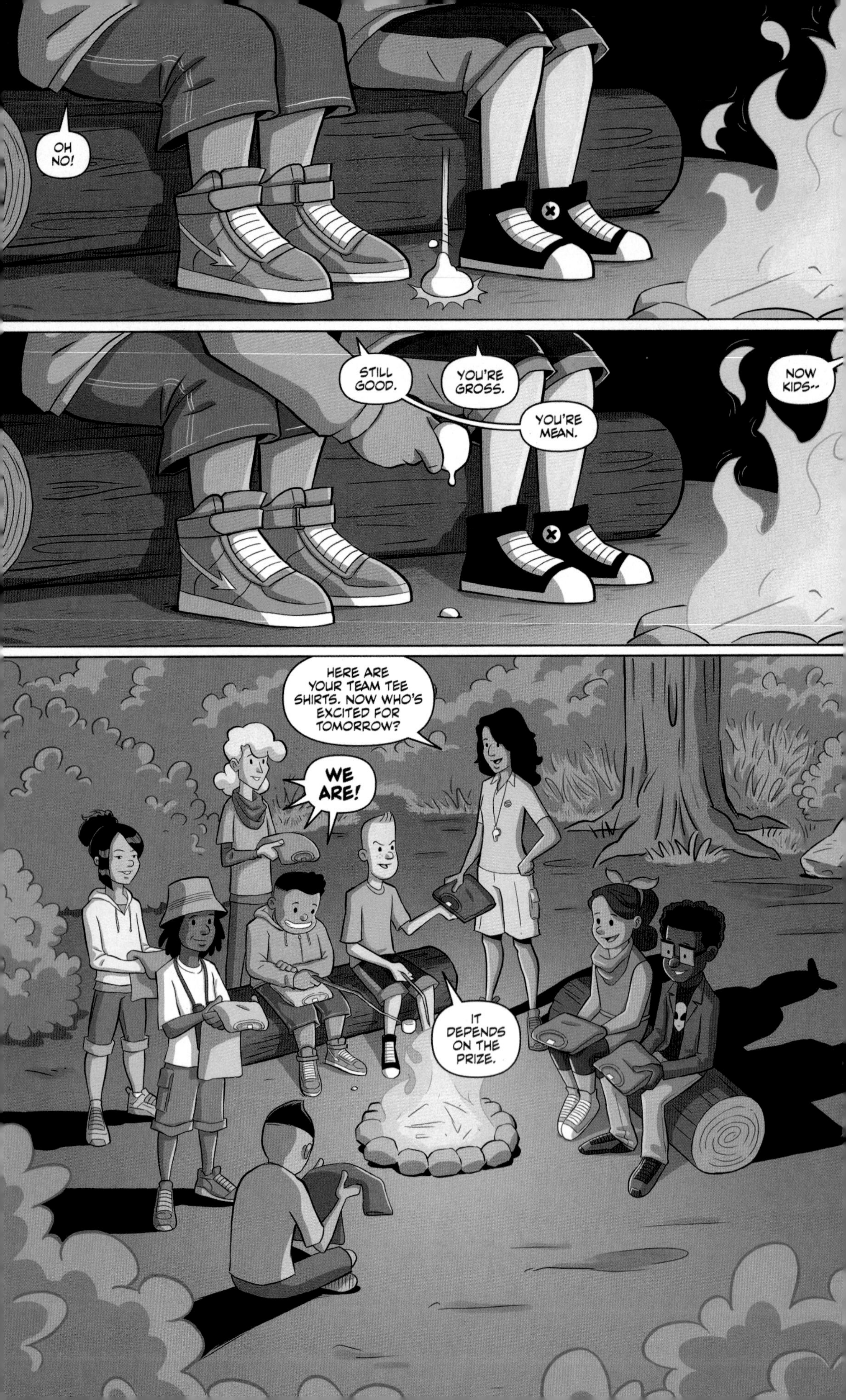
OH NO!
STILL GOOD.
YOU'RE GROSS.
YOU'RE MEAN.
NOW KIDS--
HERE ARE YOUR TEAM TEE SHIRTS. NOW WHO'S EXCITED FOR TOMORROW?
WE ARE!
IT DEPENDS ON THE PRIZE.

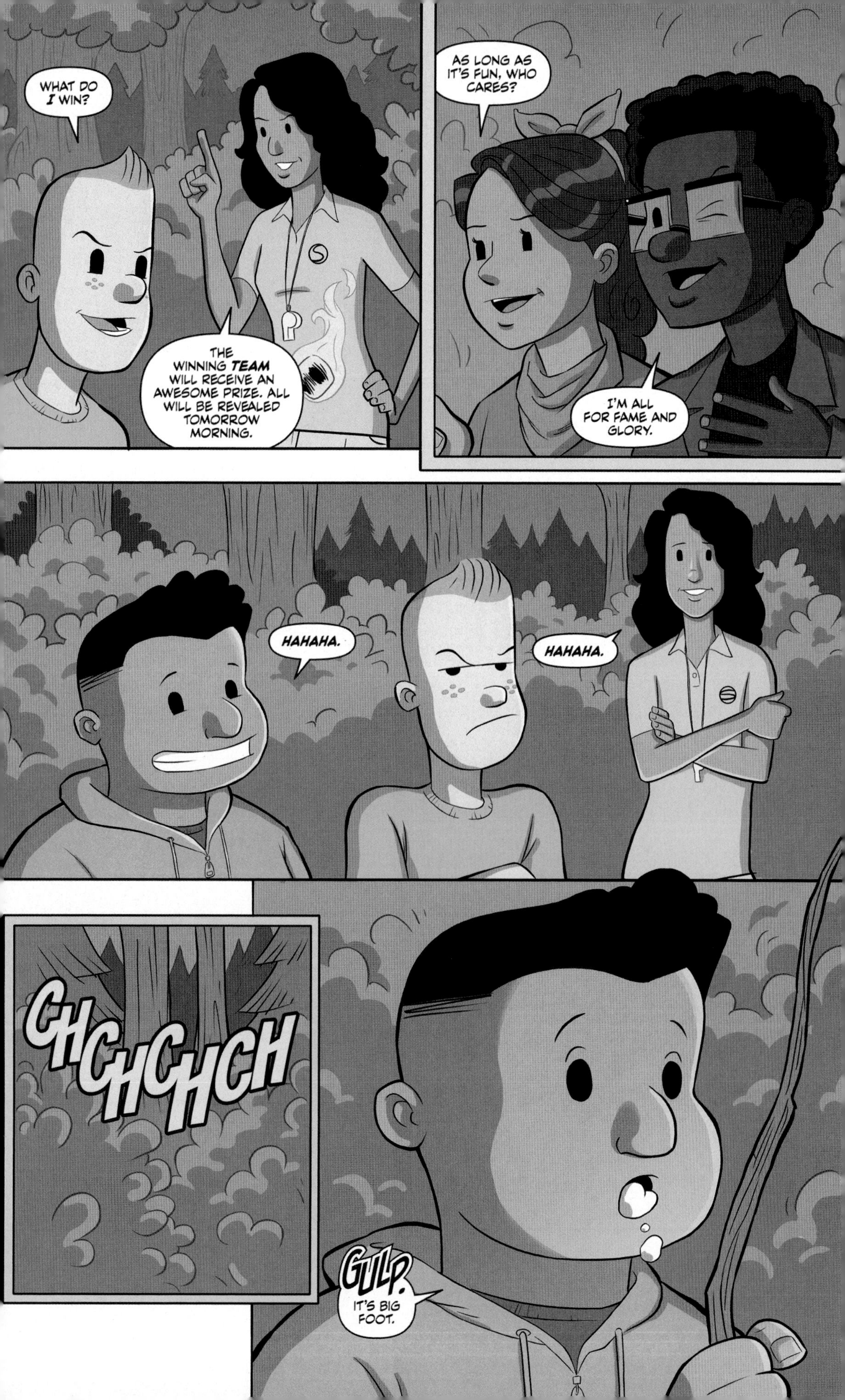
WHAT DO *I* WIN?
THE WINNING **TEAM** WILL RECEIVE AN AWESOME PRIZE. ALL WILL BE REVEALED TOMORROW MORNING.
AS LONG AS IT'S FUN, WHO CARES?
I'M ALL FOR FAME AND GLORY.
HAHAHA.
HAHAHA.
CHCHCHCH
GULP.
IT'S BIG FOOT.

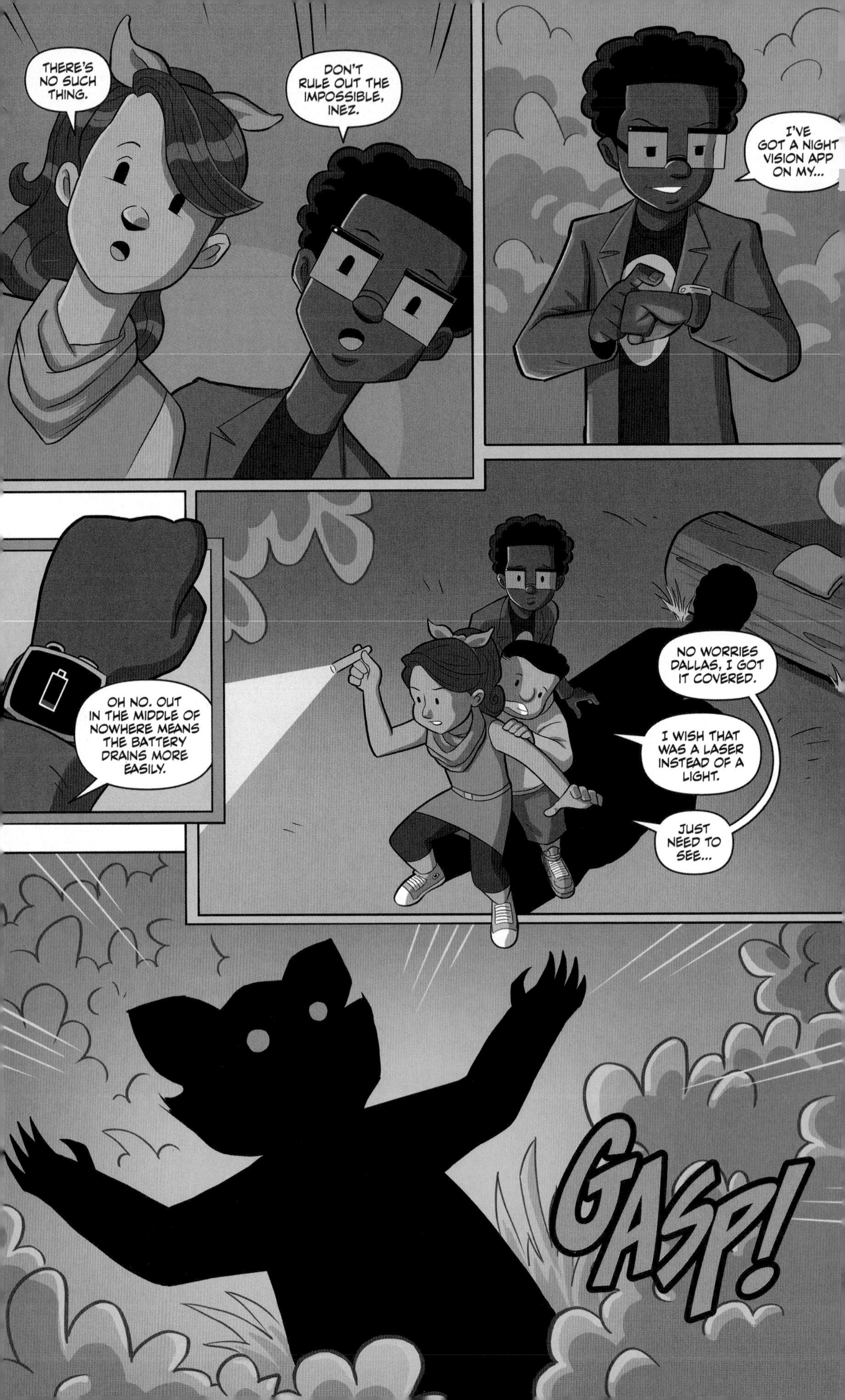
THERE'S NO SUCH THING.
DON'T RULE OUT THE IMPOSSIBLE, INEZ.
I'VE GOT A NIGHT VISION APP ON MY...
OH NO. OUT IN THE MIDDLE OF NOWHERE MEANS THE BATTERY DRAINS MORE EASILY.
NO WORRIES DALLAS, I GOT IT COVERED.
I WISH THAT WAS A LASER INSTEAD OF A LIGHT.
JUST NEED TO SEE...
GASP!

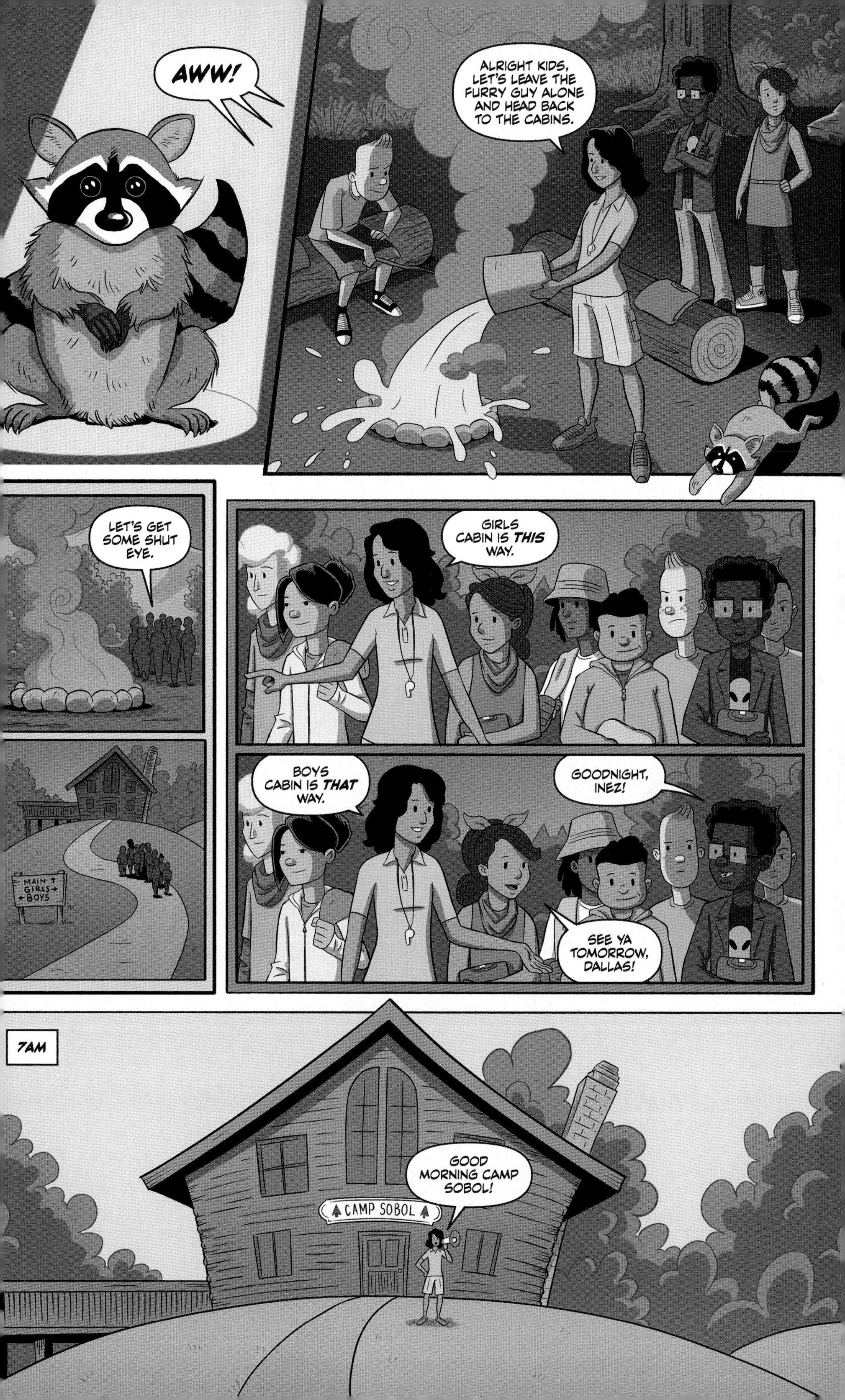
AWW!
ALRIGHT KIDS, LET'S LEAVE THE FURRY GUY ALONE AND HEAD BACK TO THE CABINS.
LET'S GET SOME SHUT EYE.
GIRLS CABIN IS *THIS* WAY.
MAIN ↑
GIRLS →
← BOYS
BOYS CABIN IS *THAT* WAY.
GOODNIGHT, INEZ!
SEE YA TOMORROW, DALLAS!
7AM
CAMP SOBOL
GOOD MORNING CAMP SOBOL!

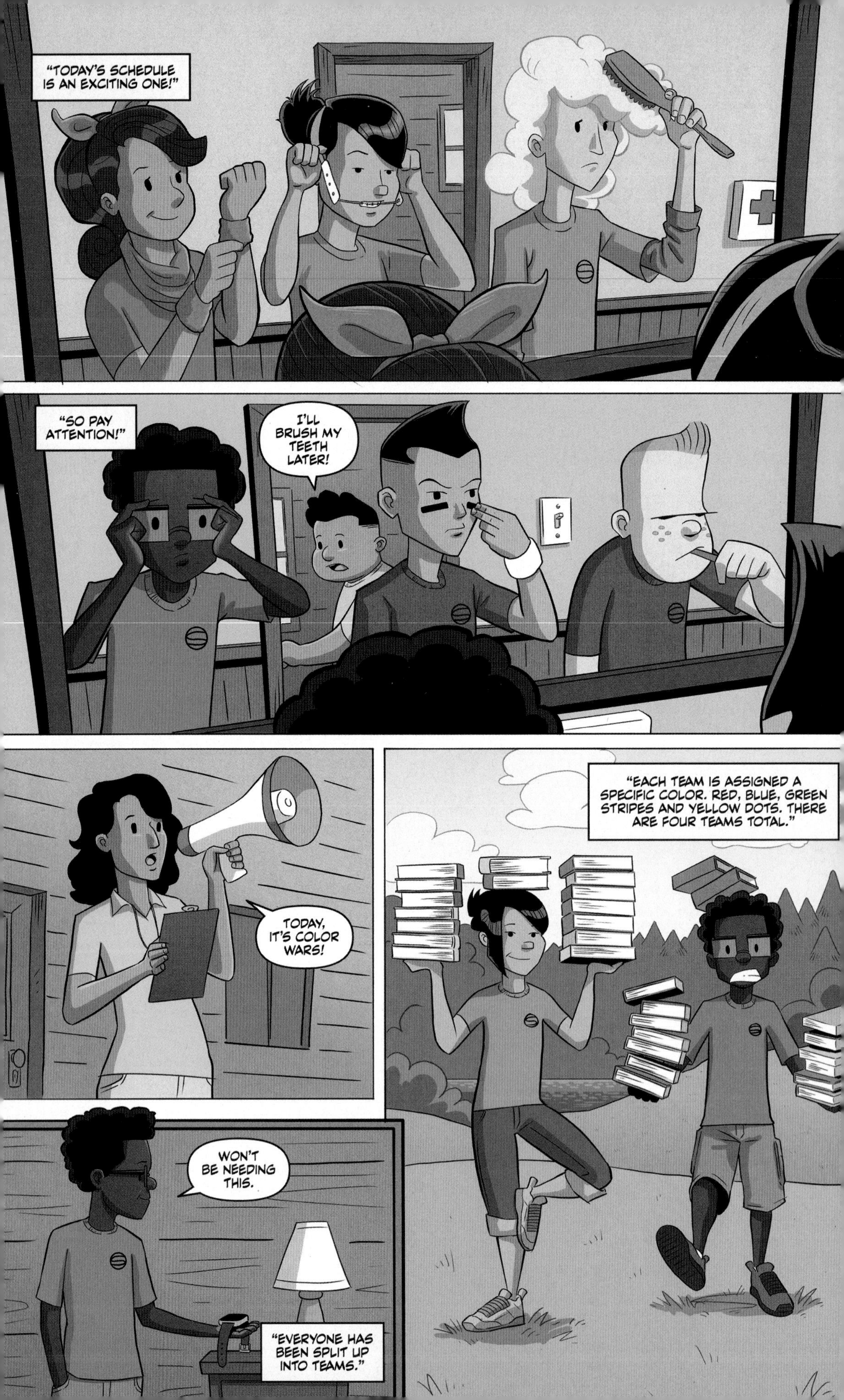
"TODAY'S SCHEDULE IS AN EXCITING ONE!"
"SO PAY ATTENTION!"
I'LL BRUSH MY TEETH LATER!
TODAY, IT'S COLOR WARS!
WON'T BE NEEDING THIS.
"EVERYONE HAS BEEN SPLIT UP INTO TEAMS."
"EACH TEAM IS ASSIGNED A SPECIFIC COLOR. RED, BLUE, GREEN STRIPES AND YELLOW DOTS. THERE ARE FOUR TEAMS TOTAL."

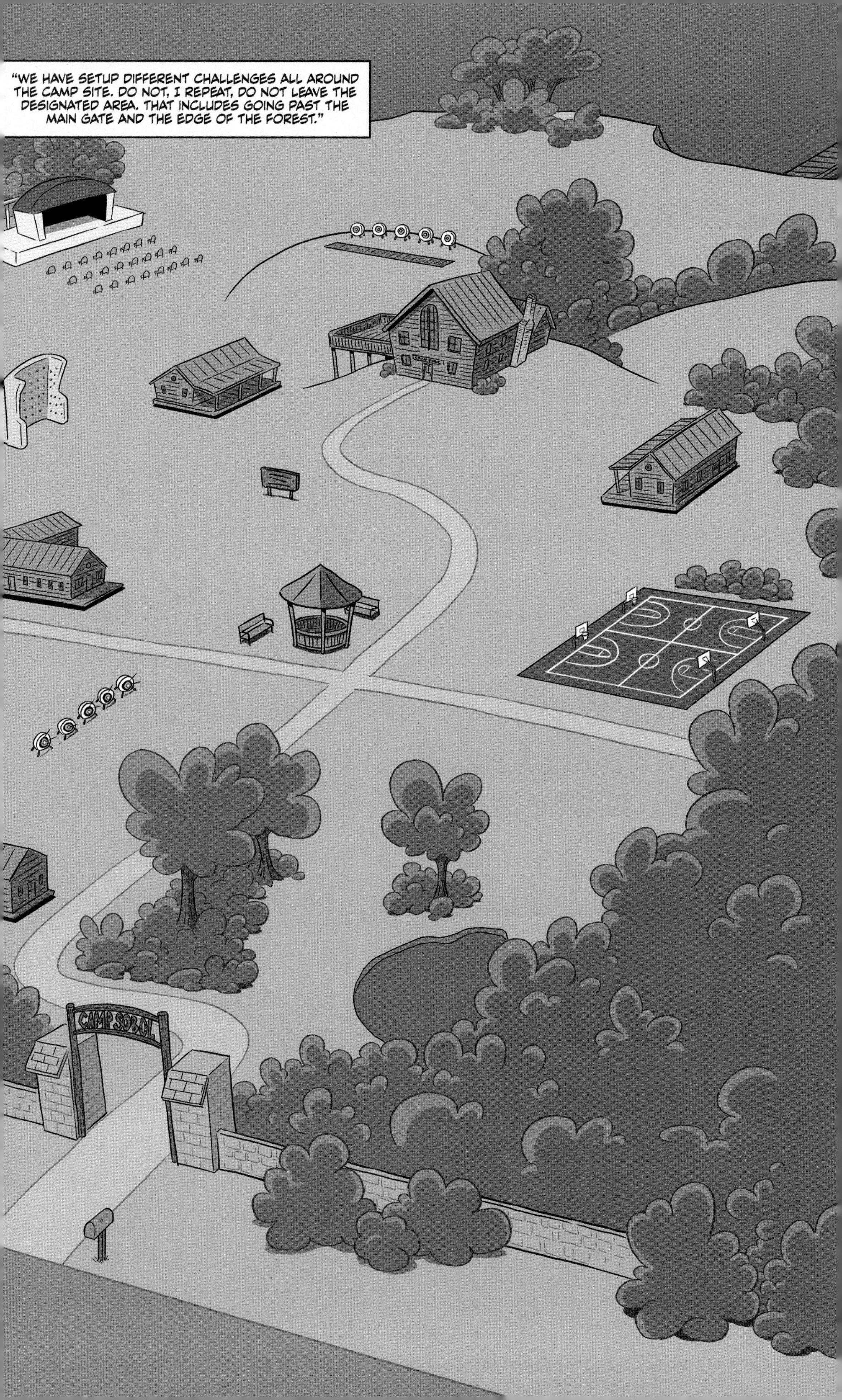
"WE HAVE SETUP DIFFERENT CHALLENGES ALL AROUND THE CAMP SITE. DO NOT, I REPEAT, DO NOT LEAVE THE DESIGNATED AREA. THAT INCLUDES GOING PAST THE MAIN GATE AND THE EDGE OF THE FOREST."
CAMP SOBOL

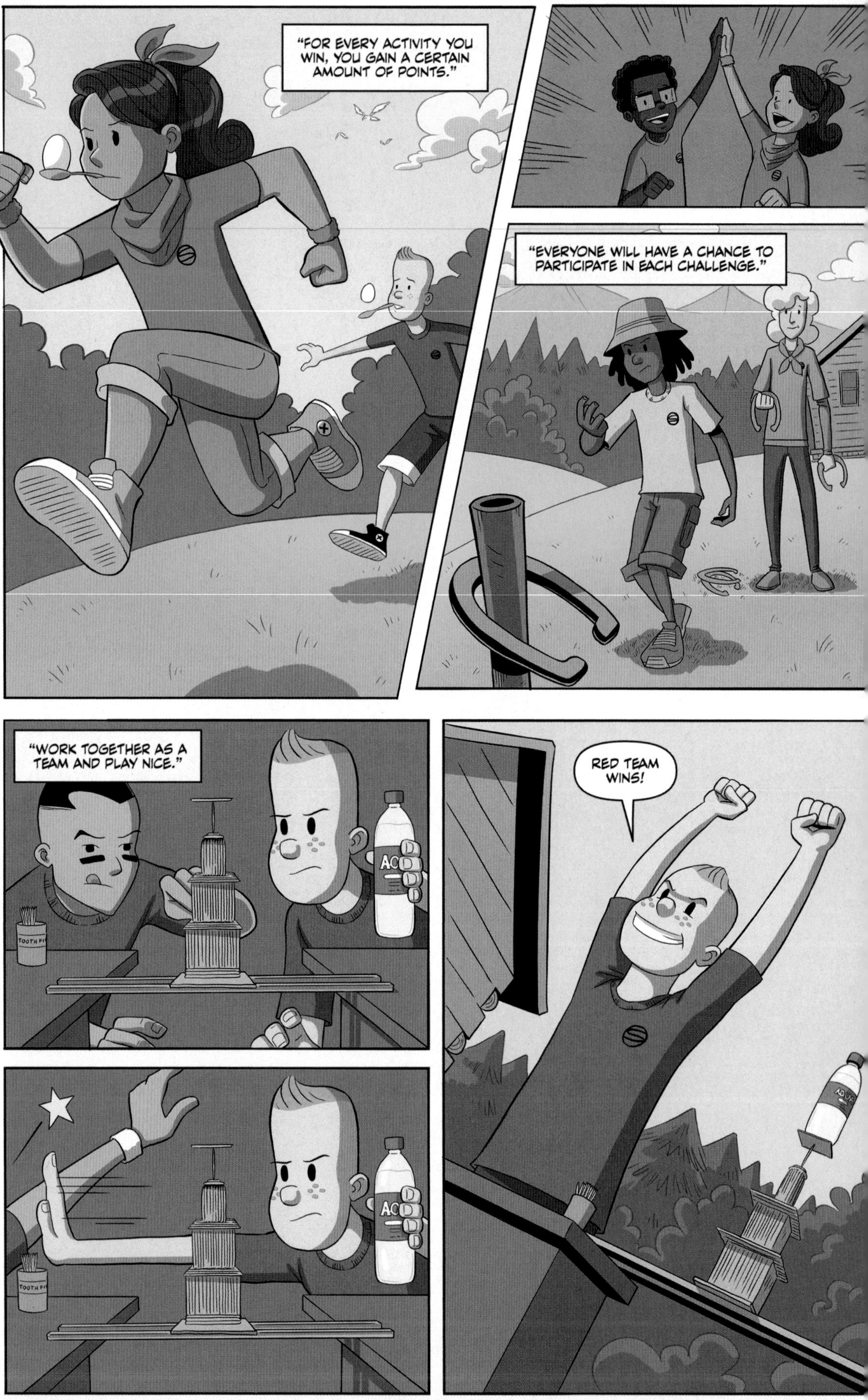

"FOR EVERY ACTIVITY YOU WIN, YOU GAIN A CERTAIN AMOUNT OF POINTS."
"EVERYONE WILL HAVE A CHANCE TO PARTICIPATE IN EACH CHALLENGE."
"WORK TOGETHER AS A TEAM AND PLAY NICE."
RED TEAM WINS!

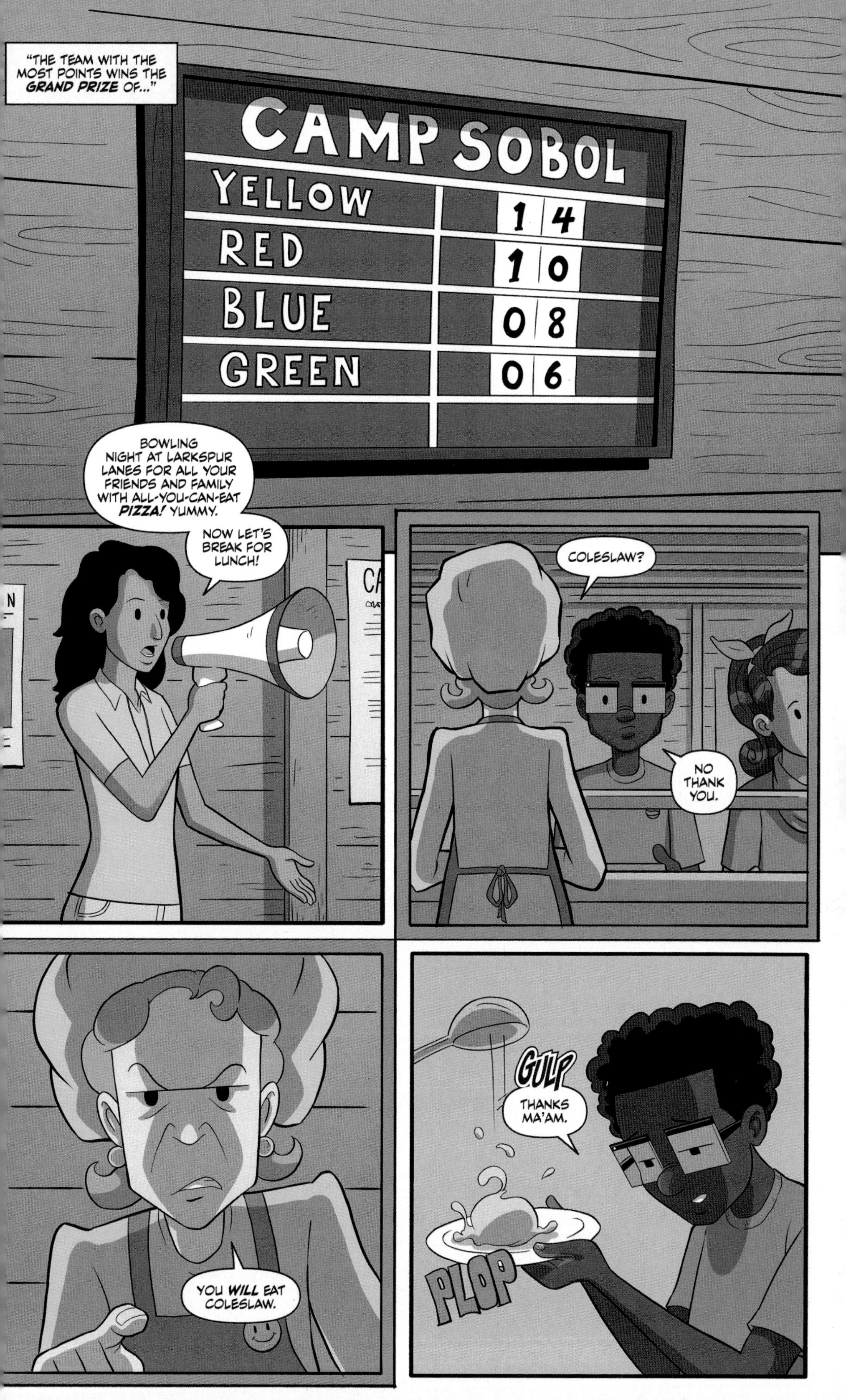

"THE TEAM WITH THE MOST POINTS WINS THE GRAND PRIZE OF..."
CAMP SOBOL
YELLOW 14
RED 10
BLUE 08
GREEN 06
BOWLING NIGHT AT LARKSPUR LANES FOR ALL YOUR FRIENDS AND FAMILY WITH ALL-YOU-CAN-EAT PIZZA! YUMMY.
NOW LET'S BREAK FOR LUNCH!
COLESLAW?
NO THANK YOU.
YOU WILL EAT COLESLAW.
GULP
THANKS MA'AM.
PLOP

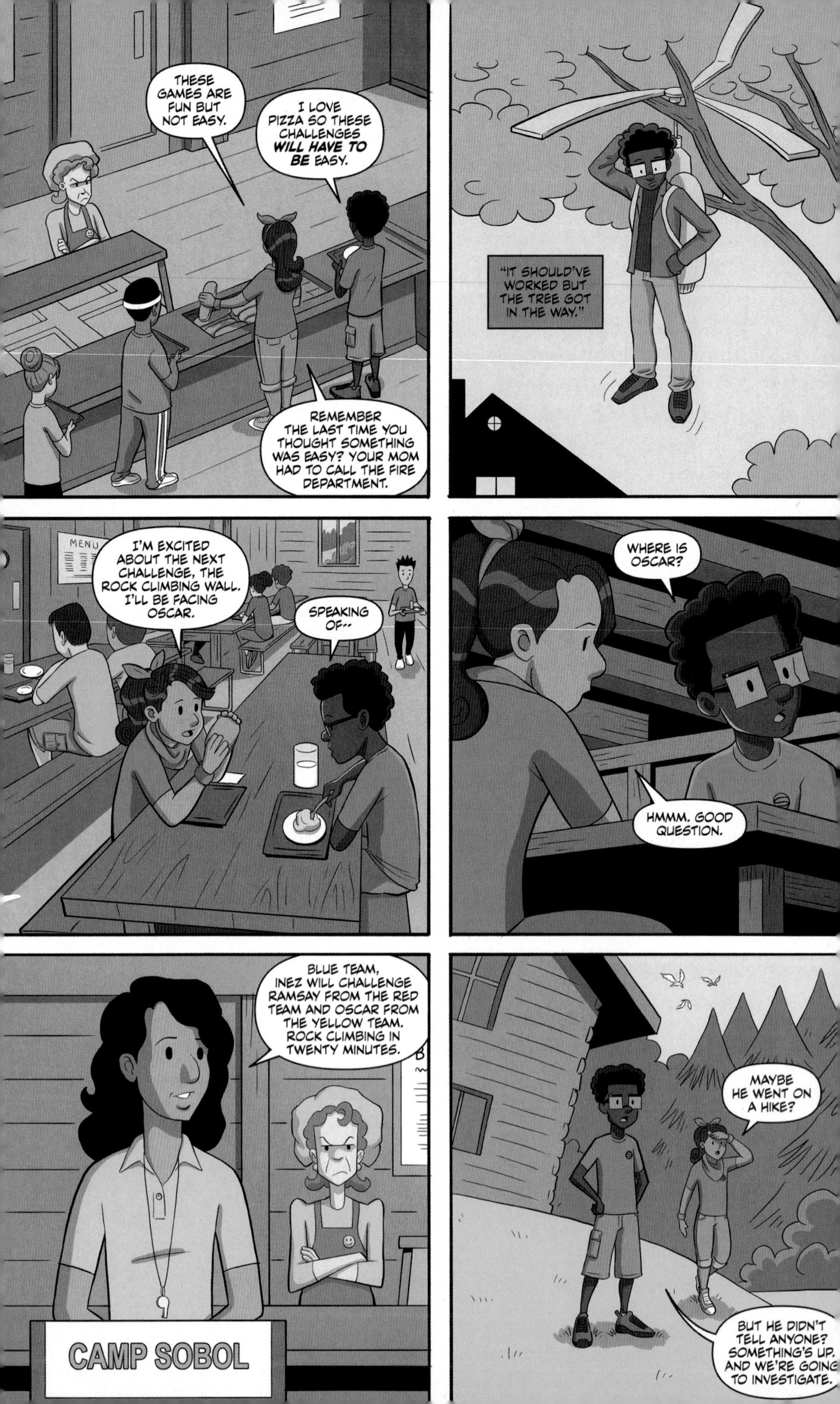
THESE GAMES ARE FUN BUT NOT EASY.
I LOVE PIZZA SO THESE CHALLENGES **WILL HAVE TO BE** EASY.
REMEMBER THE LAST TIME YOU THOUGHT SOMETHING WAS EASY? YOUR MOM HAD TO CALL THE FIRE DEPARTMENT.
"IT SHOULD'VE WORKED BUT THE TREE GOT IN THE WAY."
MENU
I'M EXCITED ABOUT THE NEXT CHALLENGE, THE ROCK CLIMBING WALL. I'LL BE FACING OSCAR.
SPEAKING OF--
WHERE IS OSCAR?
HMMM. GOOD QUESTION.
BLUE TEAM, INEZ WILL CHALLENGE RAMSAY FROM THE RED TEAM AND OSCAR FROM THE YELLOW TEAM. ROCK CLIMBING IN TWENTY MINUTES.
CAMP SOBOL
MAYBE HE WENT ON A HIKE?
BUT HE DIDN'T TELL ANYONE? SOMETHING'S UP. AND WE'RE GOING TO INVESTIGATE.

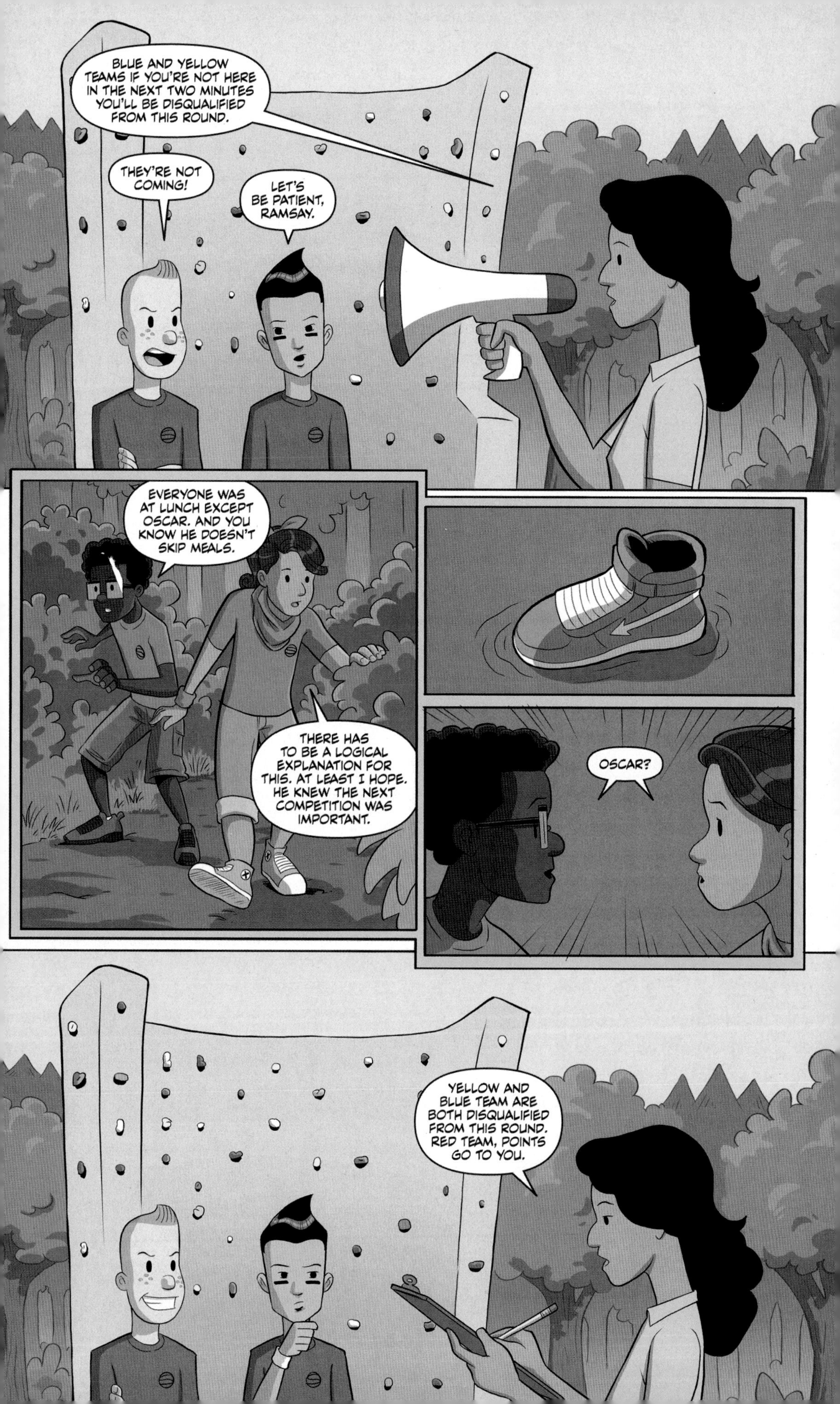

BLUE AND YELLOW TEAMS IF YOU'RE NOT HERE IN THE NEXT TWO MINUTES YOU'LL BE DISQUALIFIED FROM THIS ROUND.
THEY'RE NOT COMING!
LET'S BE PATIENT, RAMSAY.
EVERYONE WAS AT LUNCH EXCEPT OSCAR. AND YOU KNOW HE DOESN'T SKIP MEALS.
THERE HAS TO BE A LOGICAL EXPLANATION FOR THIS. AT LEAST I HOPE. HE KNEW THE NEXT COMPETITION WAS IMPORTANT.
OSCAR?
YELLOW AND BLUE TEAM ARE BOTH DISQUALIFIED FROM THIS ROUND. RED TEAM, POINTS GO TO YOU.

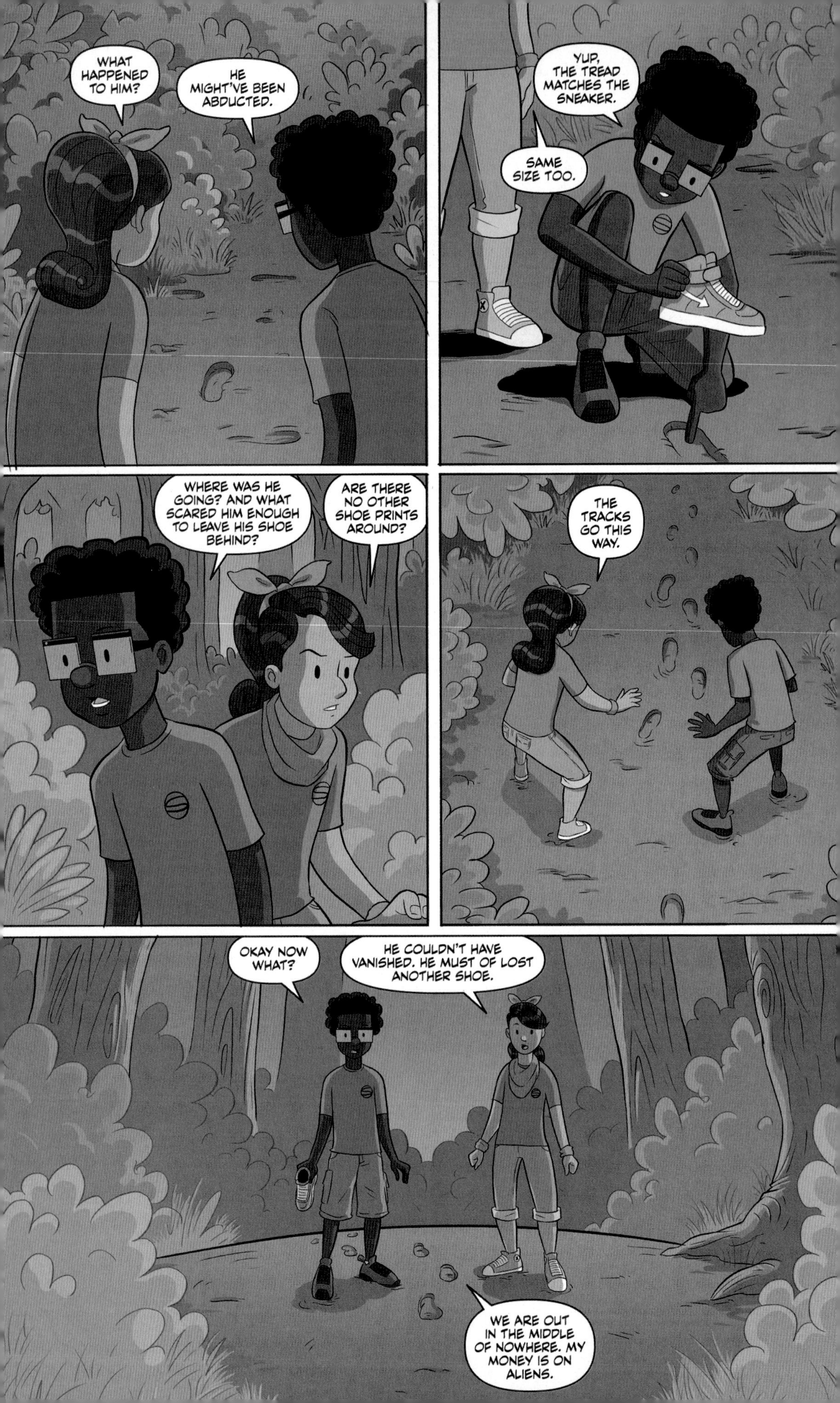
WHAT HAPPENED TO HIM?
HE MIGHT'VE BEEN ABDUCTED.
YUP, THE TREAD MATCHES THE SNEAKER.
SAME SIZE TOO.
WHERE WAS HE GOING? AND WHAT SCARED HIM ENOUGH TO LEAVE HIS SHOE BEHIND?
ARE THERE NO OTHER SHOE PRINTS AROUND?
THE TRACKS GO THIS WAY.
OKAY NOW WHAT?
HE COULDN'T HAVE VANISHED. HE MUST OF LOST ANOTHER SHOE.
WE ARE OUT IN THE MIDDLE OF NOWHERE. MY MONEY IS ON ALIENS.

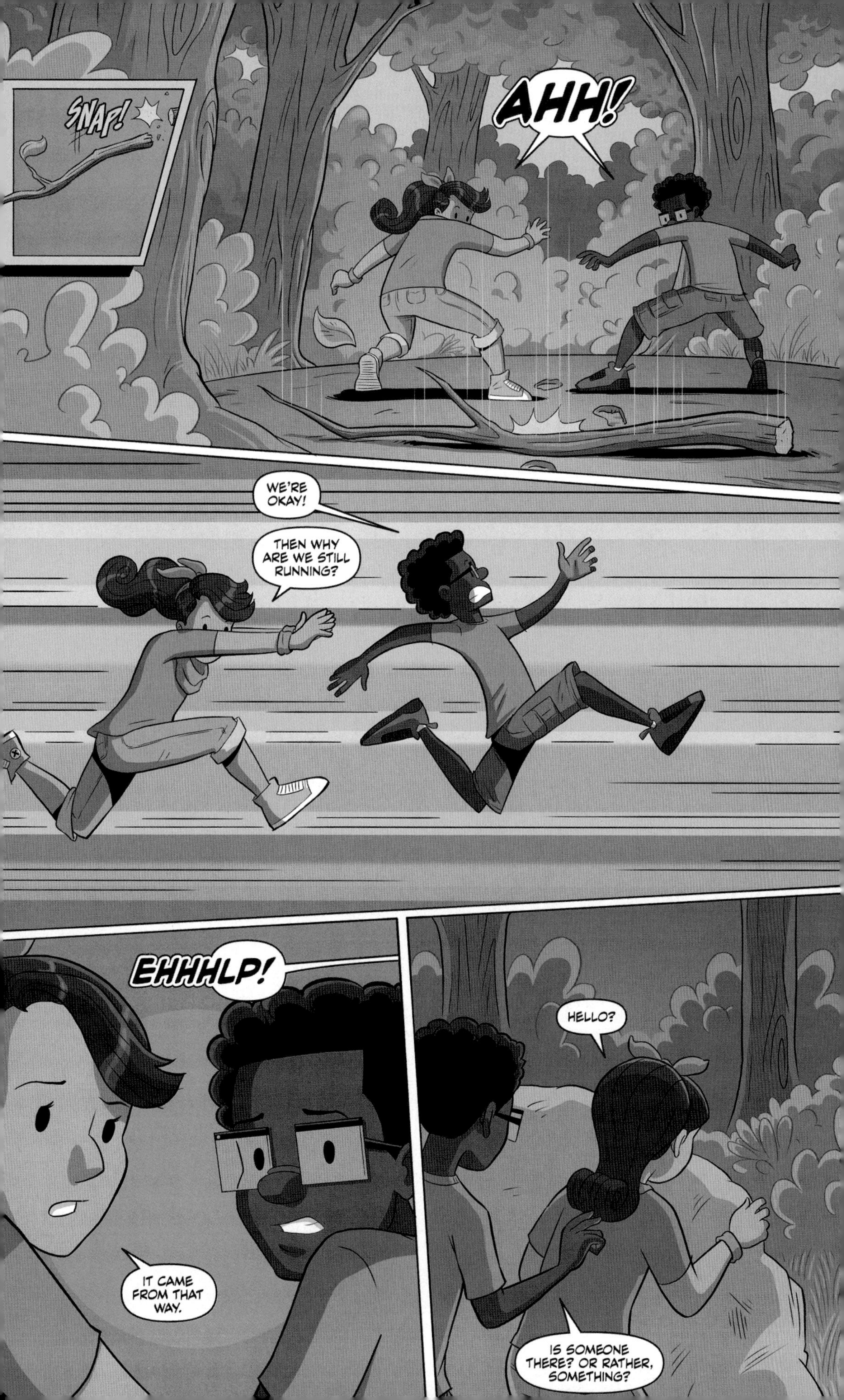
SNAP!
AHH!
WE'RE OKAY!
THEN WHY ARE WE STILL RUNNING?
EHHHLP!
IT CAME FROM THAT WAY.
HELLO?
IS SOMEONE THERE? OR RATHER, SOMETHING?

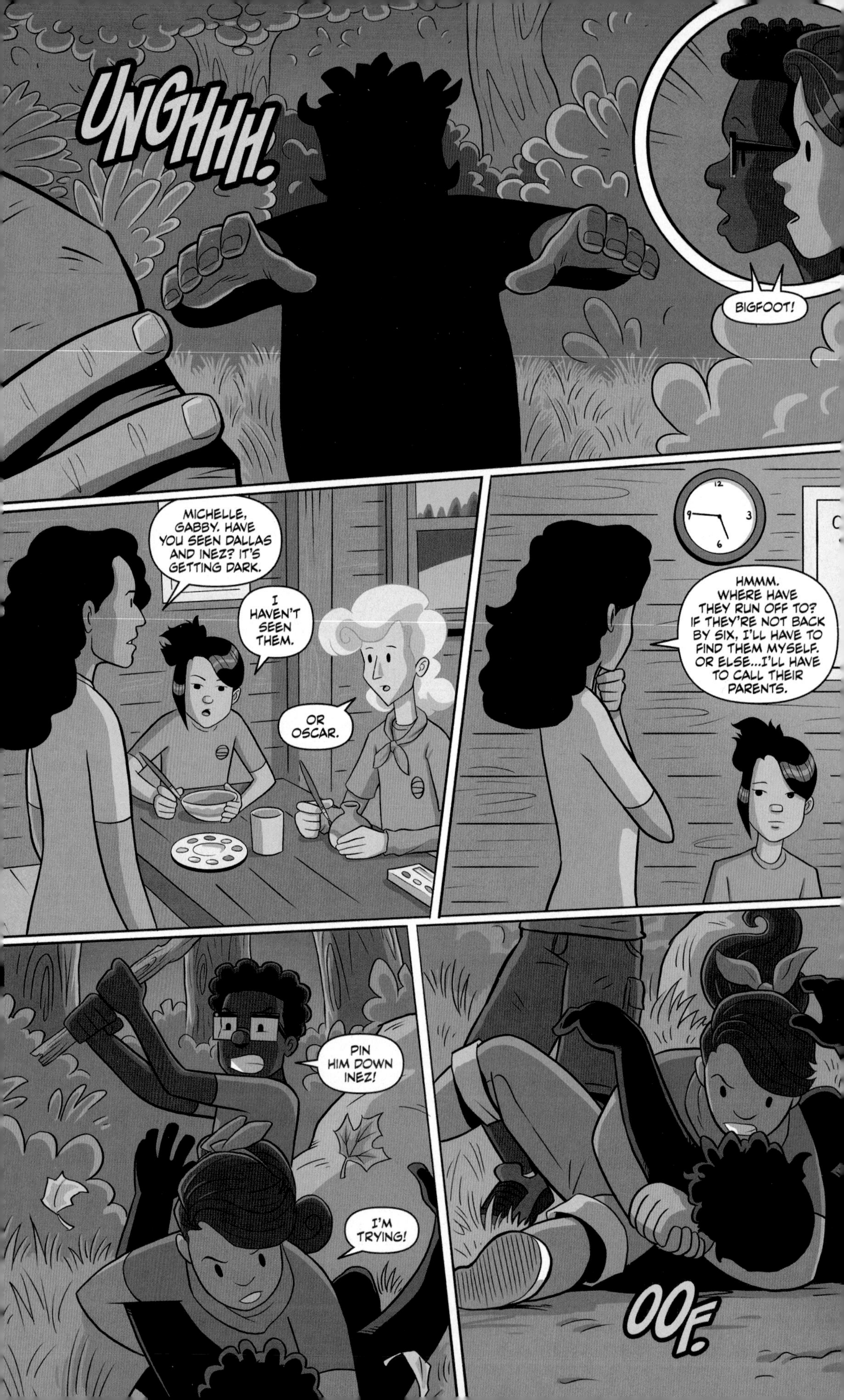
UNGHHH.
BIGFOOT!
MICHELLE, GABBY. HAVE YOU SEEN DALLAS AND INEZ? IT'S GETTING DARK.
I HAVEN'T SEEN THEM.
OR OSCAR.
HMMM. WHERE HAVE THEY RUN OFF TO? IF THEY'RE NOT BACK BY SIX, I'LL HAVE TO FIND THEM MYSELF. OR ELSE...I'LL HAVE TO CALL THEIR PARENTS.
PIN HIM DOWN INEZ!
I'M TRYING!
OOF.

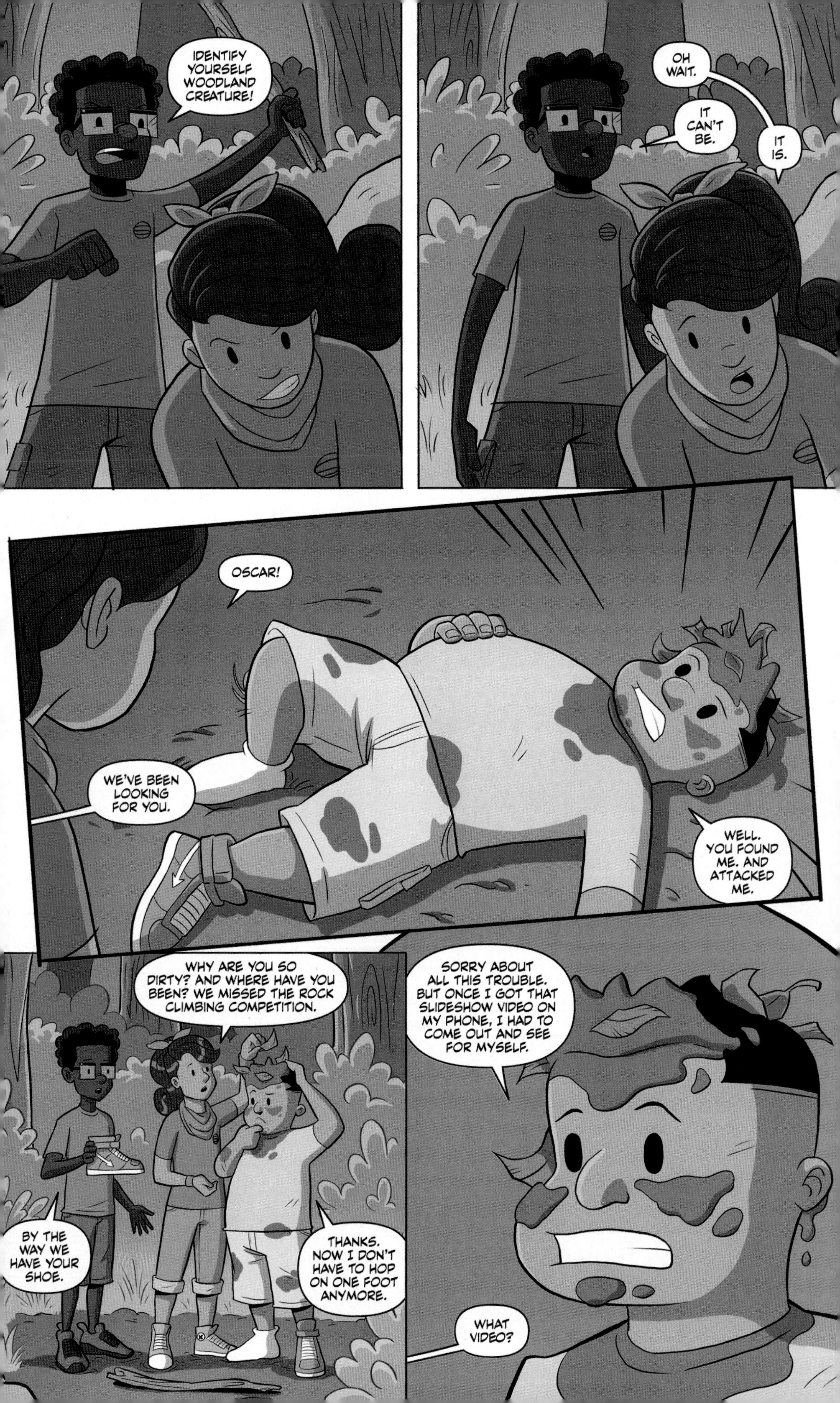
IDENTIFY YOURSELF WOODLAND CREATURE!
OH WAIT.
IT CAN'T BE.
IT IS.
OSCAR!
WE'VE BEEN LOOKING FOR YOU.
WELL. YOU FOUND ME. AND ATTACKED ME.
WHY ARE YOU SO DIRTY? AND WHERE HAVE YOU BEEN? WE MISSED THE ROCK CLIMBING COMPETITION.
BY THE WAY WE HAVE YOUR SHOE.
THANKS. NOW I DON'T HAVE TO HOP ON ONE FOOT ANYMORE.
SORRY ABOUT ALL THIS TROUBLE. BUT ONCE I GOT THAT SLIDESHOW VIDEO ON MY PHONE, I HAD TO COME OUT AND SEE FOR MYSELF.
WHAT VIDEO?

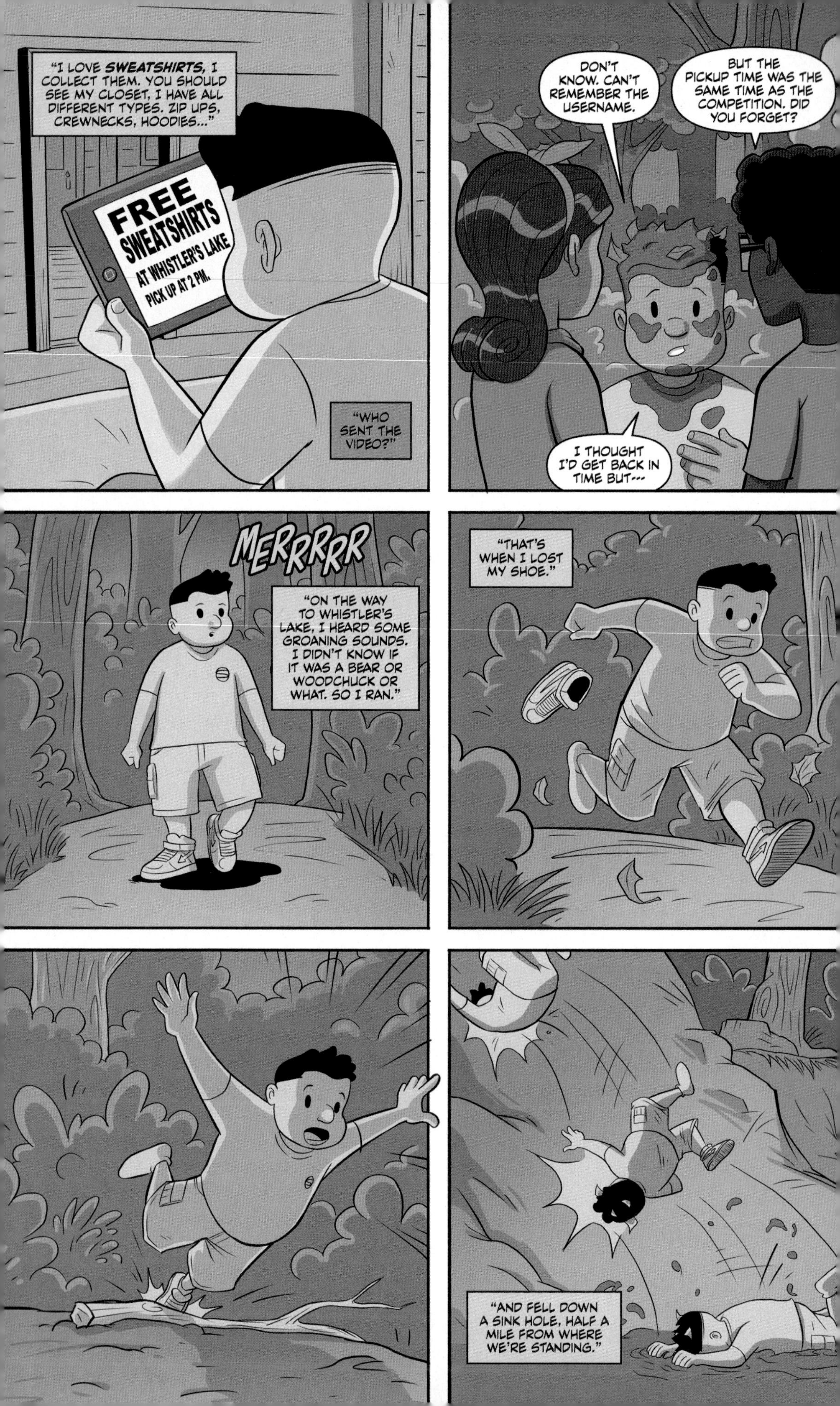
"I LOVE SWEATSHIRTS, I COLLECT THEM. YOU SHOULD SEE MY CLOSET, I HAVE ALL DIFFERENT TYPES. ZIP UPS, CREWNECKS, HOODIES..."
FREE SWEATSHIRTS AT WHISTLER'S LAKE PICK UP AT 2 PM.
"WHO SENT THE VIDEO?"
DON'T KNOW. CAN'T REMEMBER THE USERNAME.
BUT THE PICKUP TIME WAS THE SAME TIME AS THE COMPETITION. DID YOU FORGET?
I THOUGHT I'D GET BACK IN TIME BUT---
MERRRRR
"ON THE WAY TO WHISTLER'S LAKE, I HEARD SOME GROANING SOUNDS. I DIDN'T KNOW IF IT WAS A BEAR OR WOODCHUCK OR WHAT. SO I RAN."
"THAT'S WHEN I LOST MY SHOE."
"AND FELL DOWN A SINK HOLE, HALF A MILE FROM WHERE WE'RE STANDING."

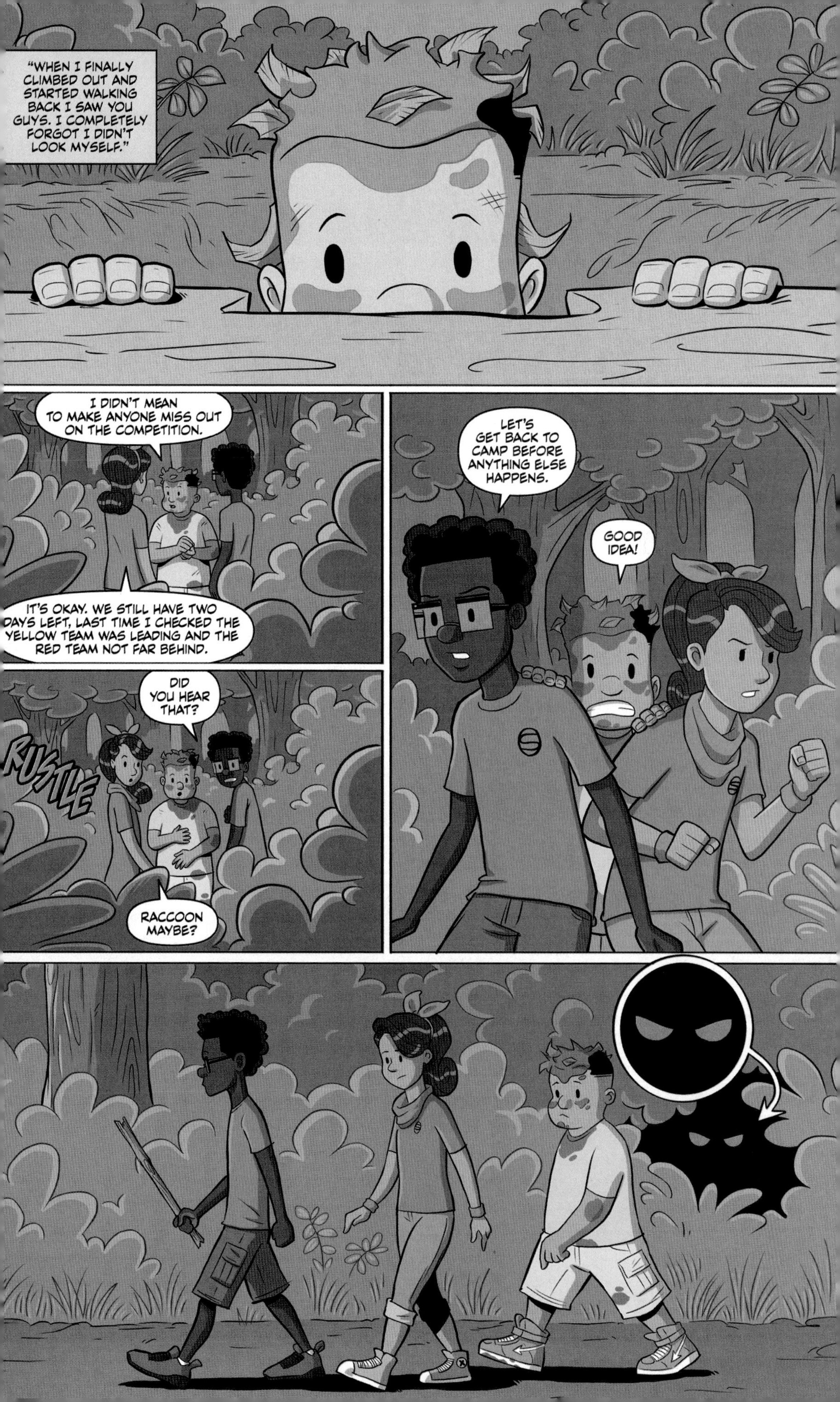
"WHEN I FINALLY CLIMBED OUT AND STARTED WALKING BACK I SAW YOU GUYS. I COMPLETELY FORGOT I DIDN'T LOOK MYSELF."
I DIDN'T MEAN TO MAKE ANYONE MISS OUT ON THE COMPETITION.
IT'S OKAY. WE STILL HAVE TWO DAYS LEFT, LAST TIME I CHECKED THE YELLOW TEAM WAS LEADING AND THE RED TEAM NOT FAR BEHIND.
RUSTLE
DID YOU HEAR THAT?
RACCOON MAYBE?
LET'S GET BACK TO CAMP BEFORE ANYTHING ELSE HAPPENS.
GOOD IDEA!

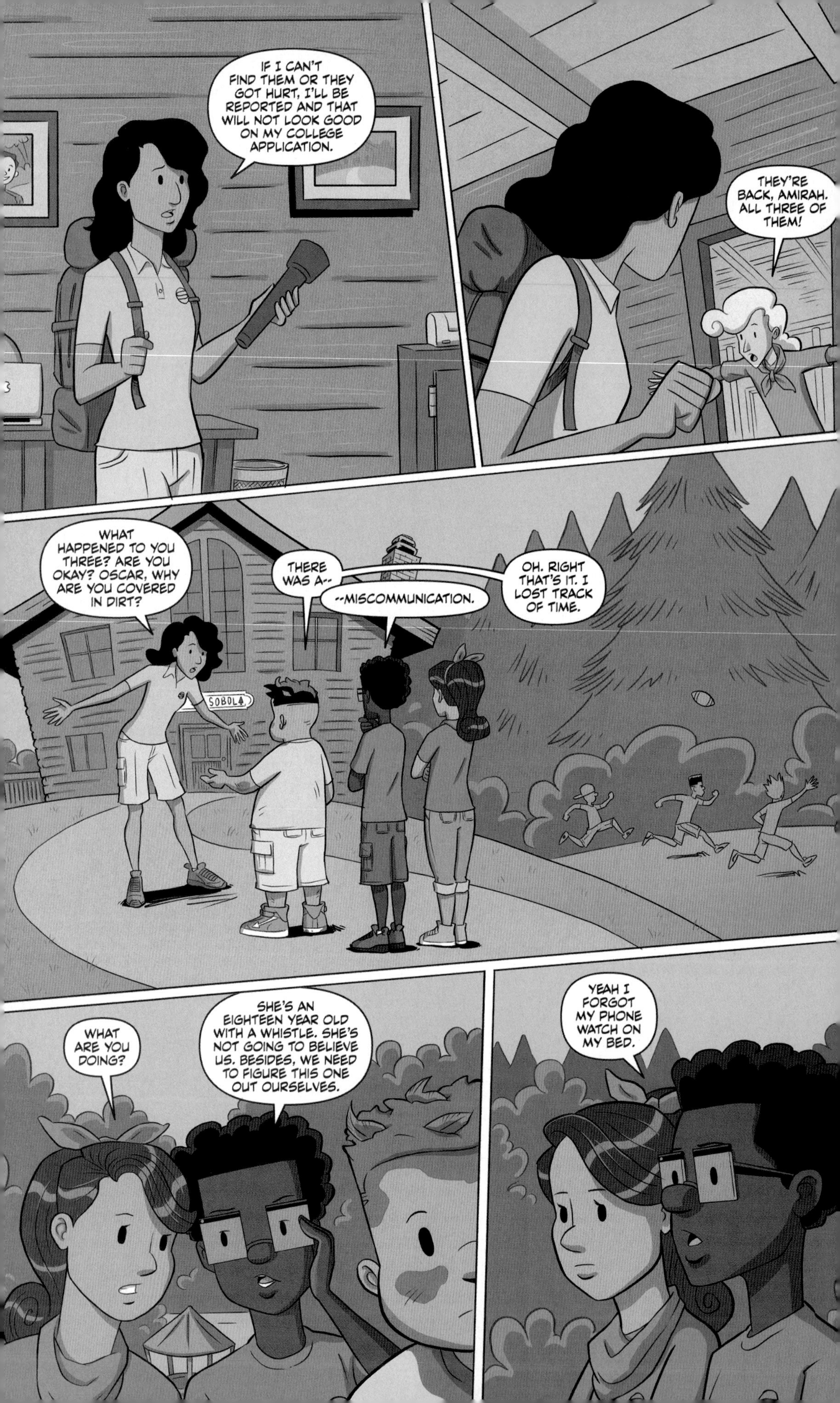
IF I CAN'T FIND THEM OR THEY GOT HURT, I'LL BE REPORTED AND THAT WILL NOT LOOK GOOD ON MY COLLEGE APPLICATION.
THEY'RE BACK, AMIRAH. ALL THREE OF THEM!
WHAT HAPPENED TO YOU THREE? ARE YOU OKAY? OSCAR, WHY ARE YOU COVERED IN DIRT?
THERE WAS A--
--MISCOMMUNICATION.
OH. RIGHT THAT'S IT. I LOST TRACK OF TIME.
SOBOL 4
WHAT ARE YOU DOING?
SHE'S AN EIGHTEEN YEAR OLD WITH A WHISTLE. SHE'S NOT GOING TO BELIEVE US. BESIDES, WE NEED TO FIGURE THIS ONE OUT OURSELVES.
YEAH I FORGOT MY PHONE WATCH ON MY BED.

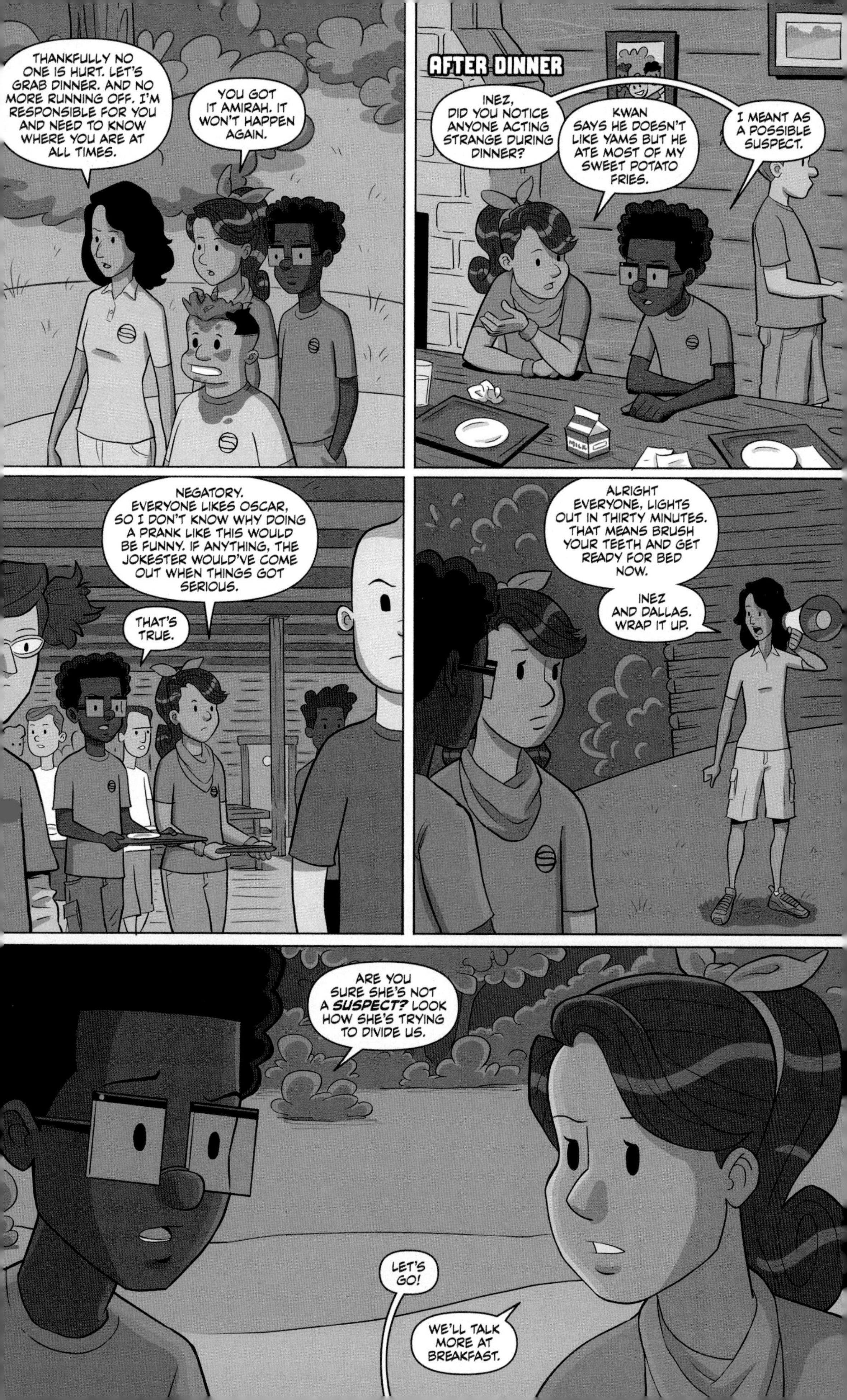
THANKFULLY NO ONE IS HURT. LET'S GRAB DINNER. AND NO MORE RUNNING OFF. I'M RESPONSIBLE FOR YOU AND NEED TO KNOW WHERE YOU ARE AT ALL TIMES.
YOU GOT IT AMIRAH. IT WON'T HAPPEN AGAIN.
AFTER DINNER
INEZ, DID YOU NOTICE ANYONE ACTING STRANGE DURING DINNER?
KWAN SAYS HE DOESN'T LIKE YAMS BUT HE ATE MOST OF MY SWEET POTATO FRIES.
I MEANT AS A POSSIBLE SUSPECT.
MILK
NEGATORY. EVERYONE LIKES OSCAR, SO I DON'T KNOW WHY DOING A PRANK LIKE THIS WOULD BE FUNNY. IF ANYTHING, THE JOKESTER WOULD'VE COME OUT WHEN THINGS GOT SERIOUS.
THAT'S TRUE.
ALRIGHT EVERYONE, LIGHTS OUT IN THIRTY MINUTES. THAT MEANS BRUSH YOUR TEETH AND GET READY FOR BED NOW.
INEZ AND DALLAS. WRAP IT UP.
ARE YOU SURE SHE'S NOT A SUSPECT? LOOK HOW SHE'S TRYING TO DIVIDE US.
LET'S GO!
WE'LL TALK MORE AT BREAKFAST.

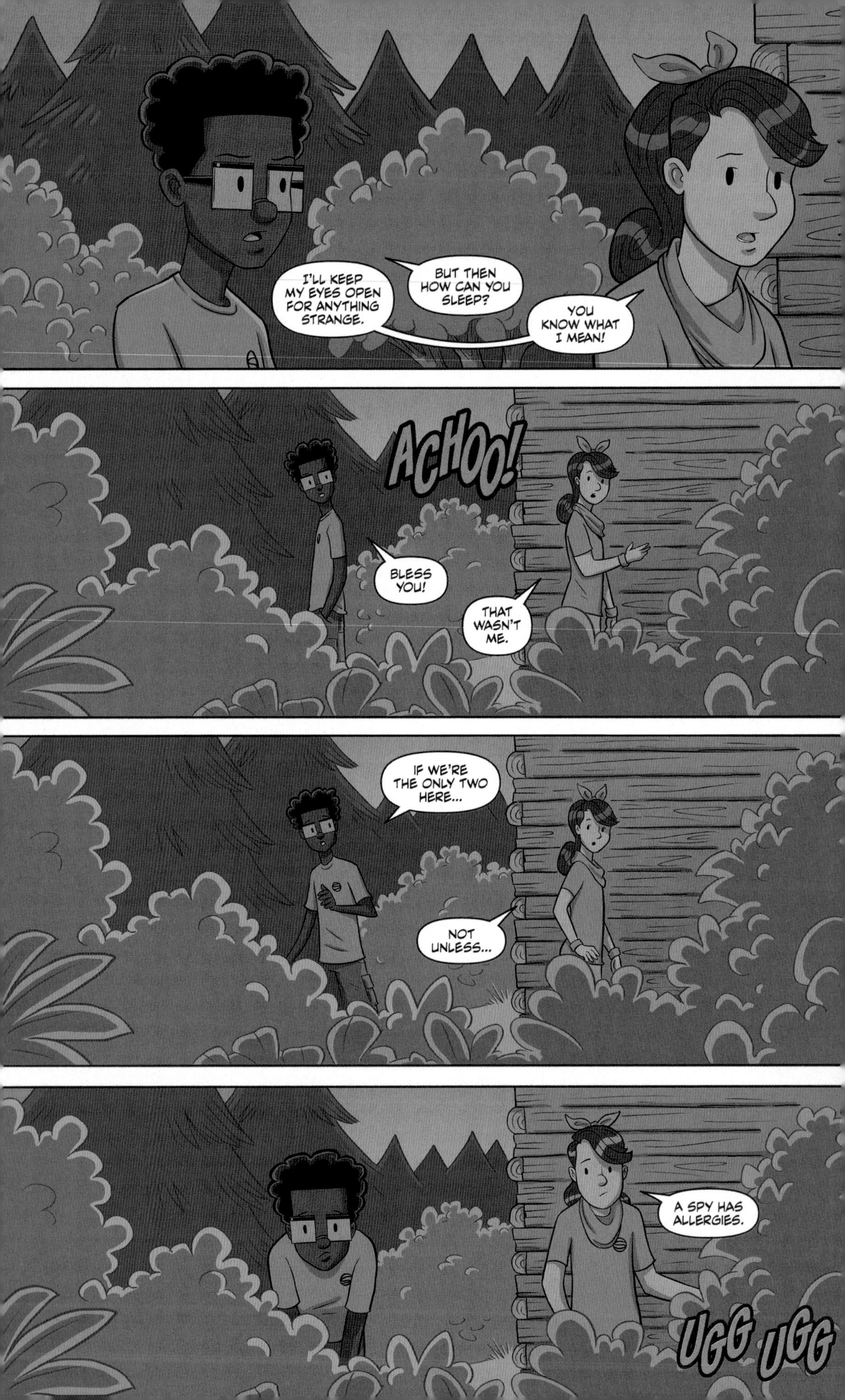
I'LL KEEP MY EYES OPEN FOR ANYTHING STRANGE.
BUT THEN HOW CAN YOU SLEEP?
YOU KNOW WHAT I MEAN!
ACHOO!
BLESS YOU!
THAT WASN'T ME.
IF WE'RE THE ONLY TWO HERE...
NOT UNLESS...
A SPY HAS ALLERGIES.
UGG UGG

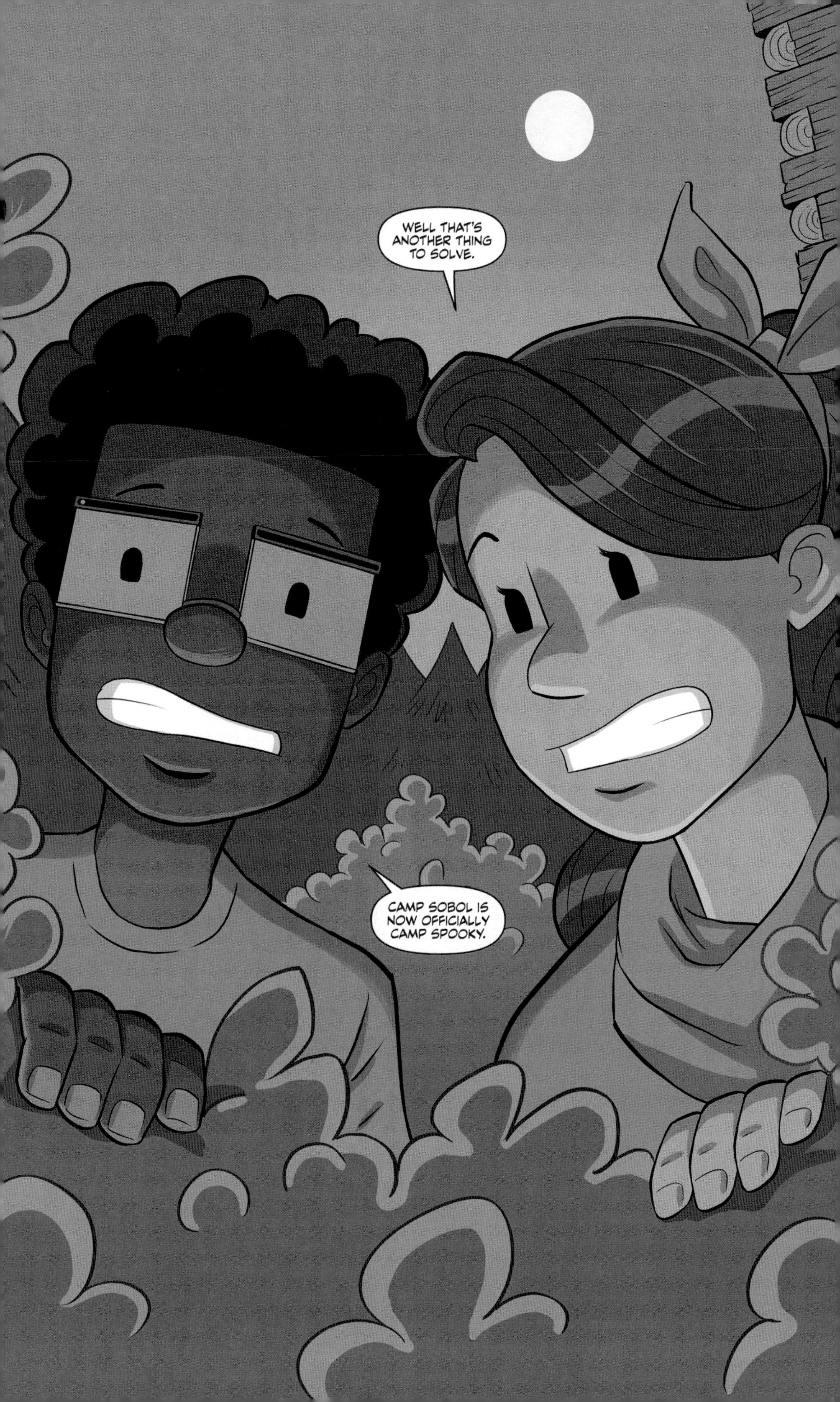
WELL THAT'S ANOTHER THING TO SOLVE.
CAMP SOBOL IS NOW OFFICIALLY CAMP SPOOKY.

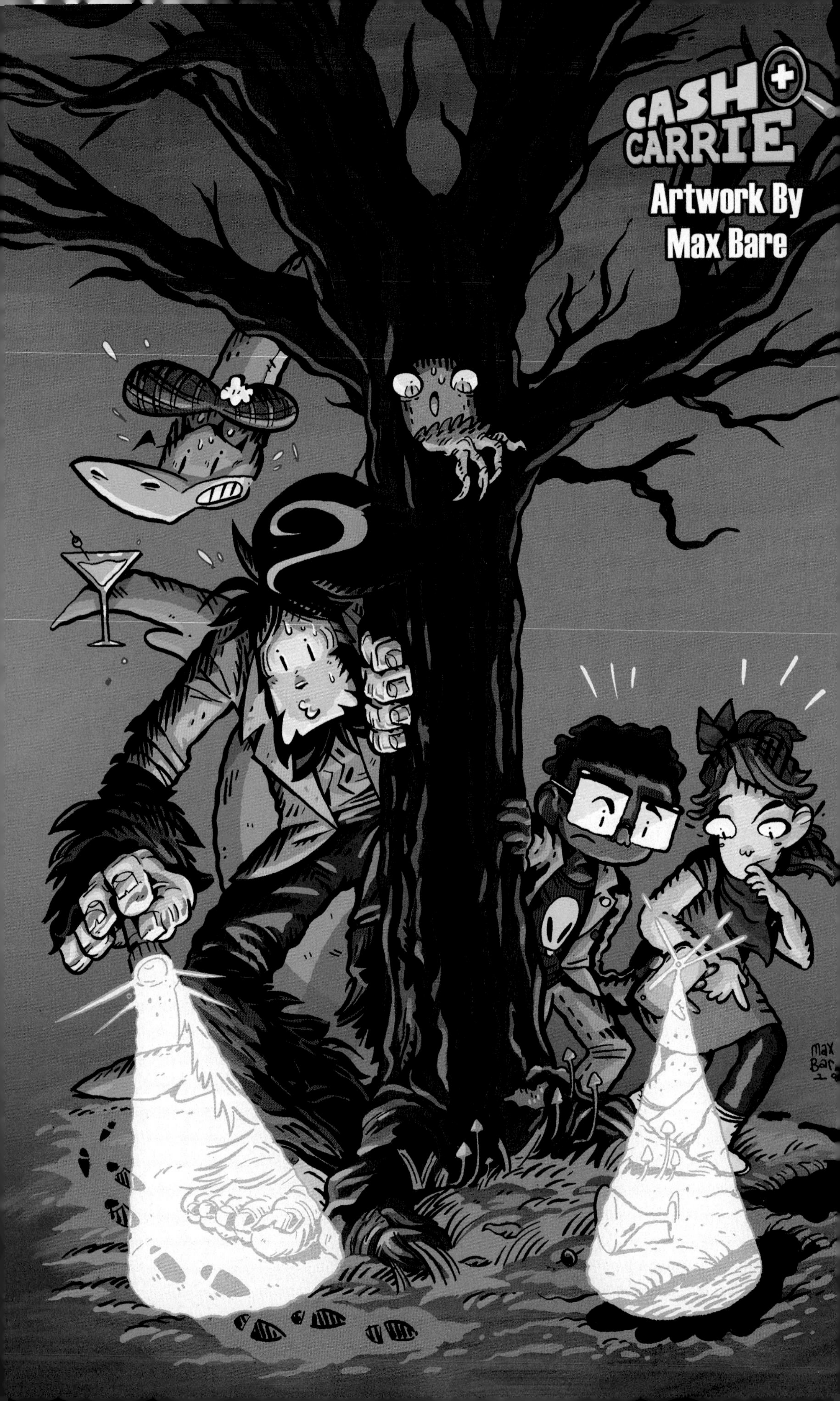
CASH + CARRIE
Artwork By
Max Bare

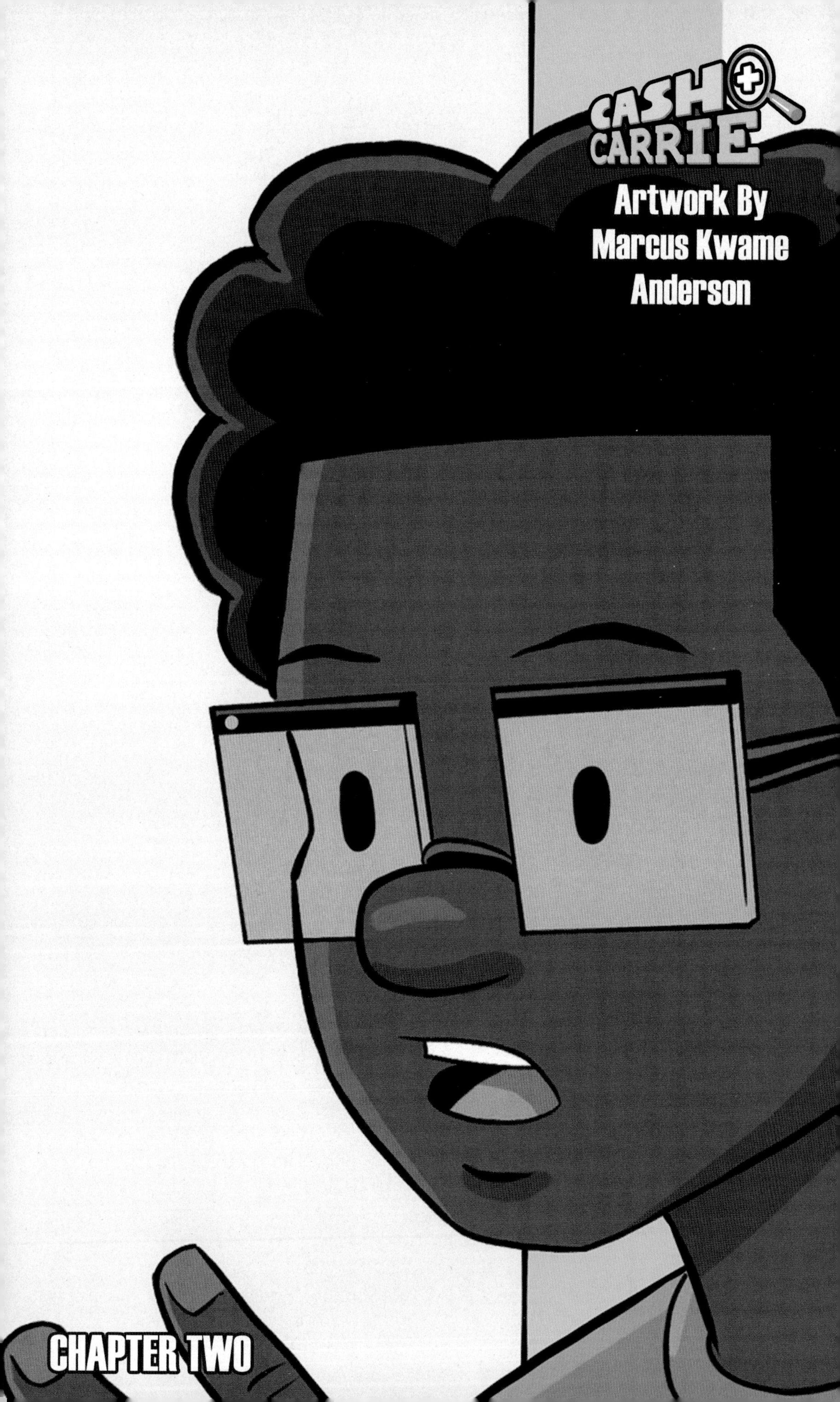
CASH CARRIE
Artwork By
Marcus Kwame
Anderson
CHAPTER TWO

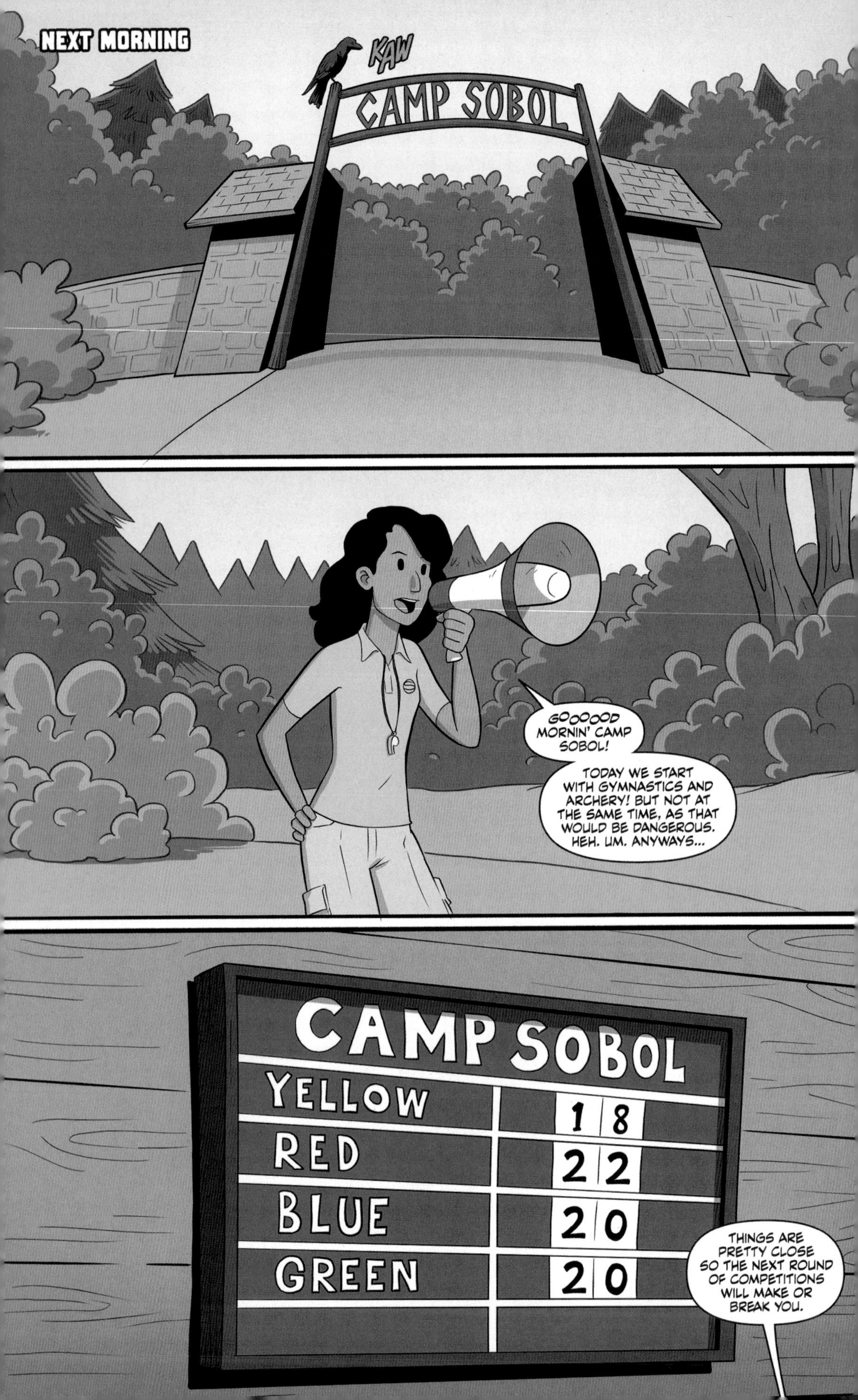
NEXT MORNING
KAW
CAMP SOBOL
GOOOOOD MORNIN' CAMP SOBOL!
TODAY WE START WITH GYMNASTICS AND ARCHERY! BUT NOT AT THE SAME TIME, AS THAT WOULD BE DANGEROUS. HEH. UM. ANYWAYS...
CAMP SOBOL
YELLOW 18
RED 22
BLUE 20
GREEN 20
THINGS ARE PRETTY CLOSE SO THE NEXT ROUND OF COMPETITIONS WILL MAKE OR BREAK YOU.

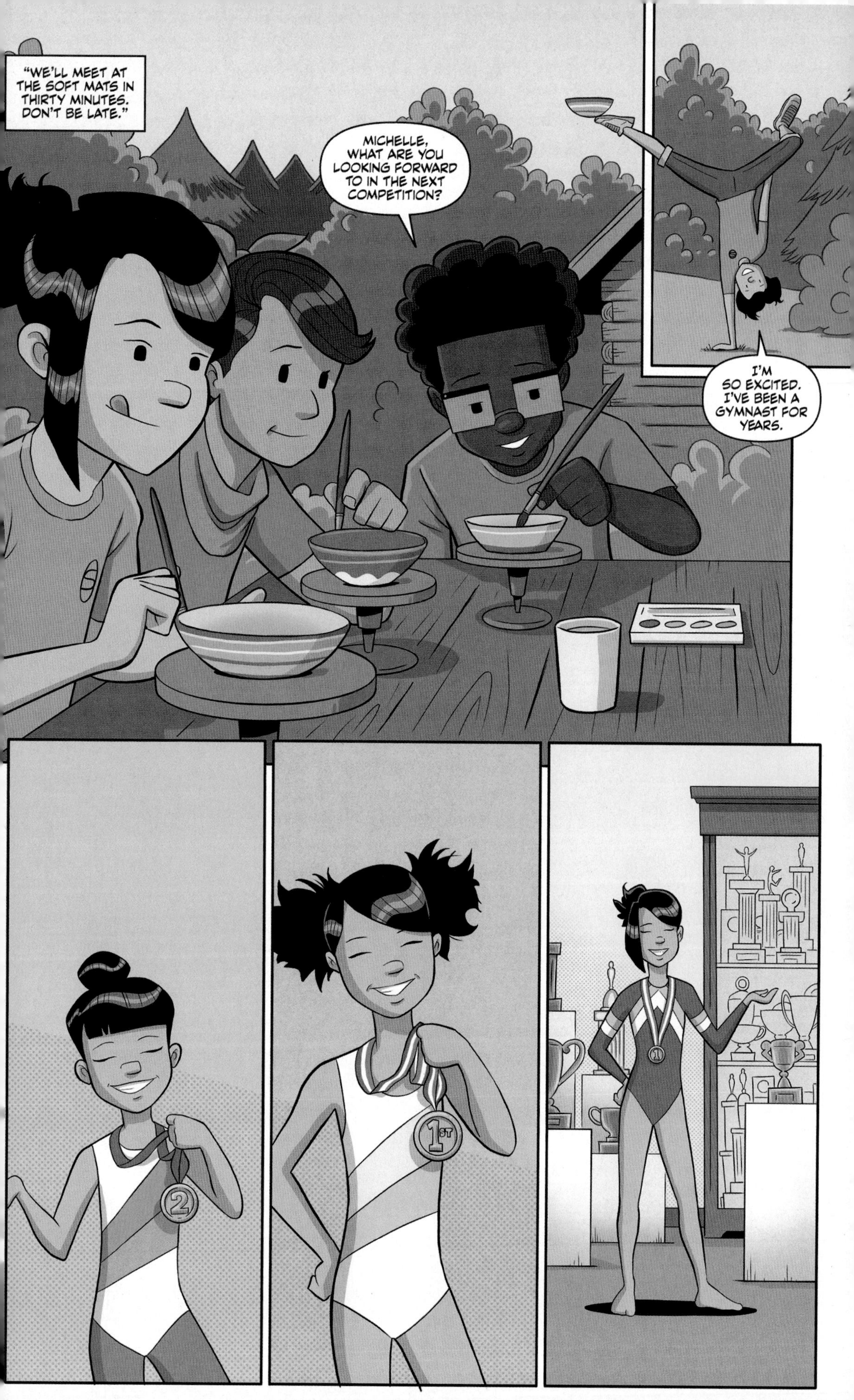
"WE'LL MEET AT THE SOFT MATS IN THIRTY MINUTES. DON'T BE LATE."
MICHELLE, WHAT ARE YOU LOOKING FORWARD TO IN THE NEXT COMPETITION?
I'M SO EXCITED. I'VE BEEN A GYMNAST FOR YEARS.

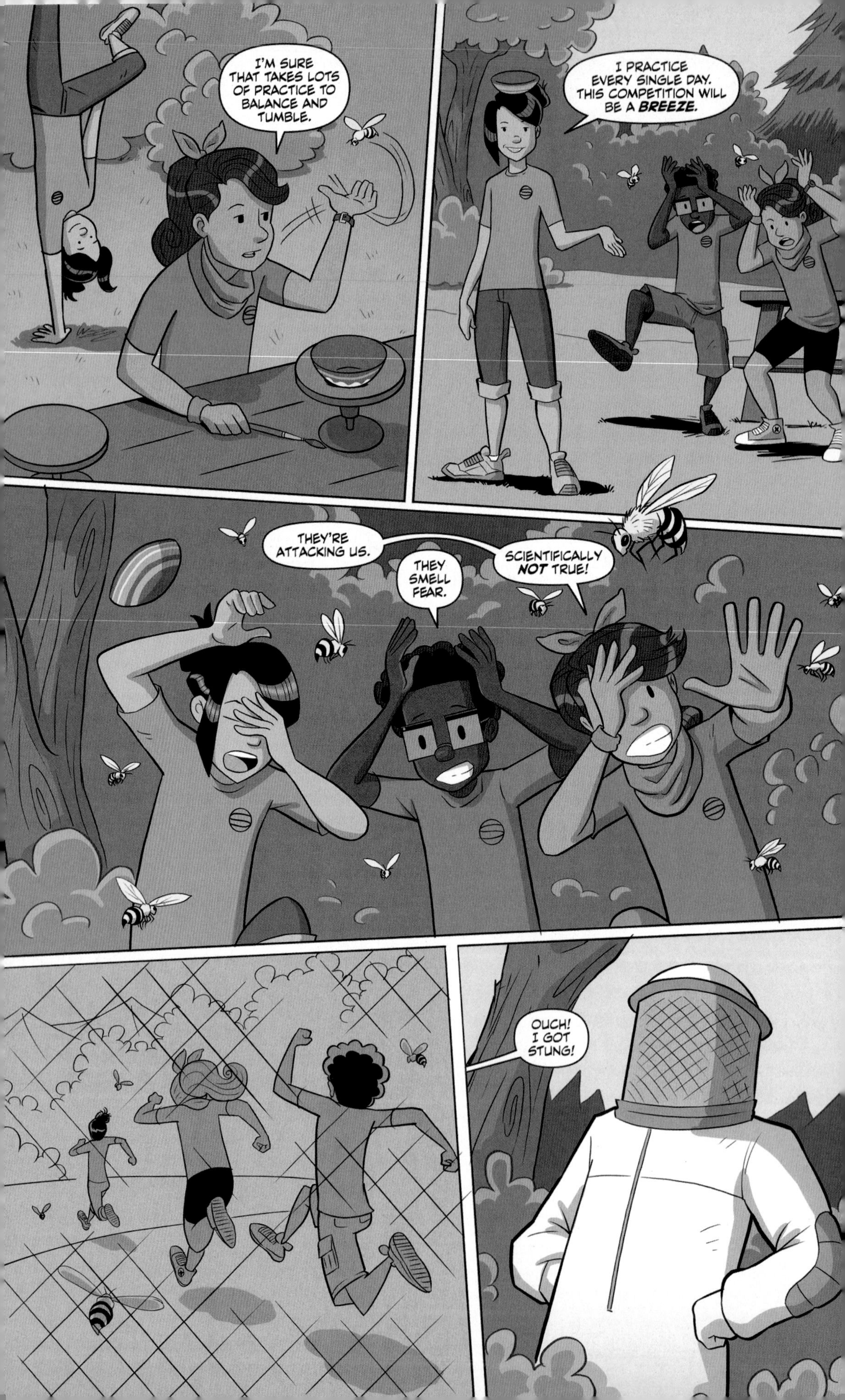
I'M SURE THAT TAKES LOTS OF PRACTICE TO BALANCE AND TUMBLE.
I PRACTICE EVERY SINGLE DAY. THIS COMPETITION WILL BE A **BREEZE.**
THEY'RE ATTACKING US.
SCIENTIFICALLY **NOT** TRUE!
THEY SMELL FEAR.
OUCH! I GOT STUNG!

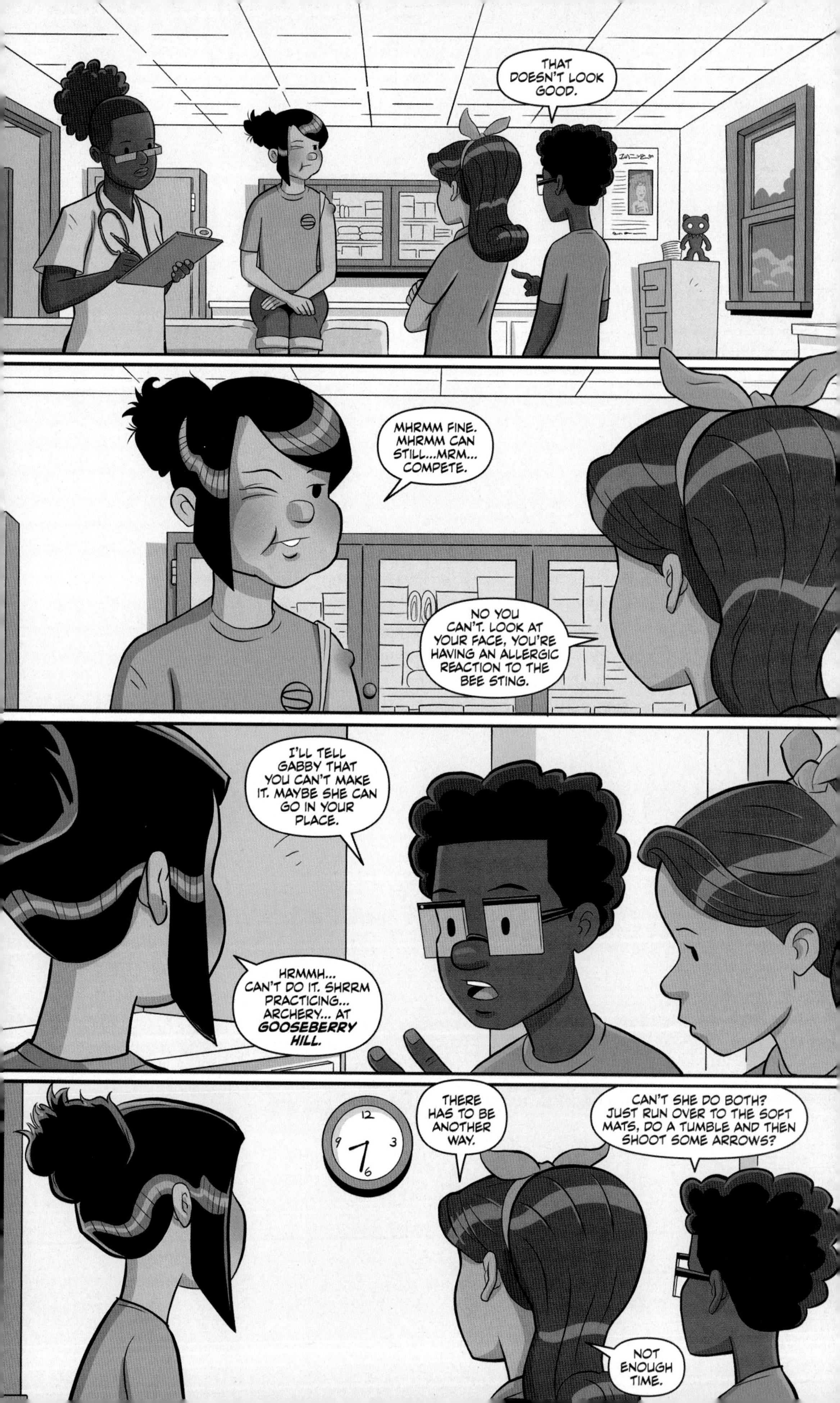

THAT DOESN'T LOOK GOOD.
MHRMM FINE. MHRMM CAN STILL...MRM... COMPETE.
NO YOU CAN'T. LOOK AT YOUR FACE, YOU'RE HAVING AN ALLERGIC REACTION TO THE BEE STING.
I'LL TELL GABBY THAT YOU CAN'T MAKE IT. MAYBE SHE CAN GO IN YOUR PLACE.
HRMMH... CAN'T DO IT. SHRRM PRACTICING... ARCHERY... AT *GOOSEBERRY HILL.*
THERE HAS TO BE ANOTHER WAY.
CAN'T SHE DO BOTH? JUST RUN OVER TO THE SOFT MATS, DO A TUMBLE AND THEN SHOOT SOME ARROWS?
NOT ENOUGH TIME.

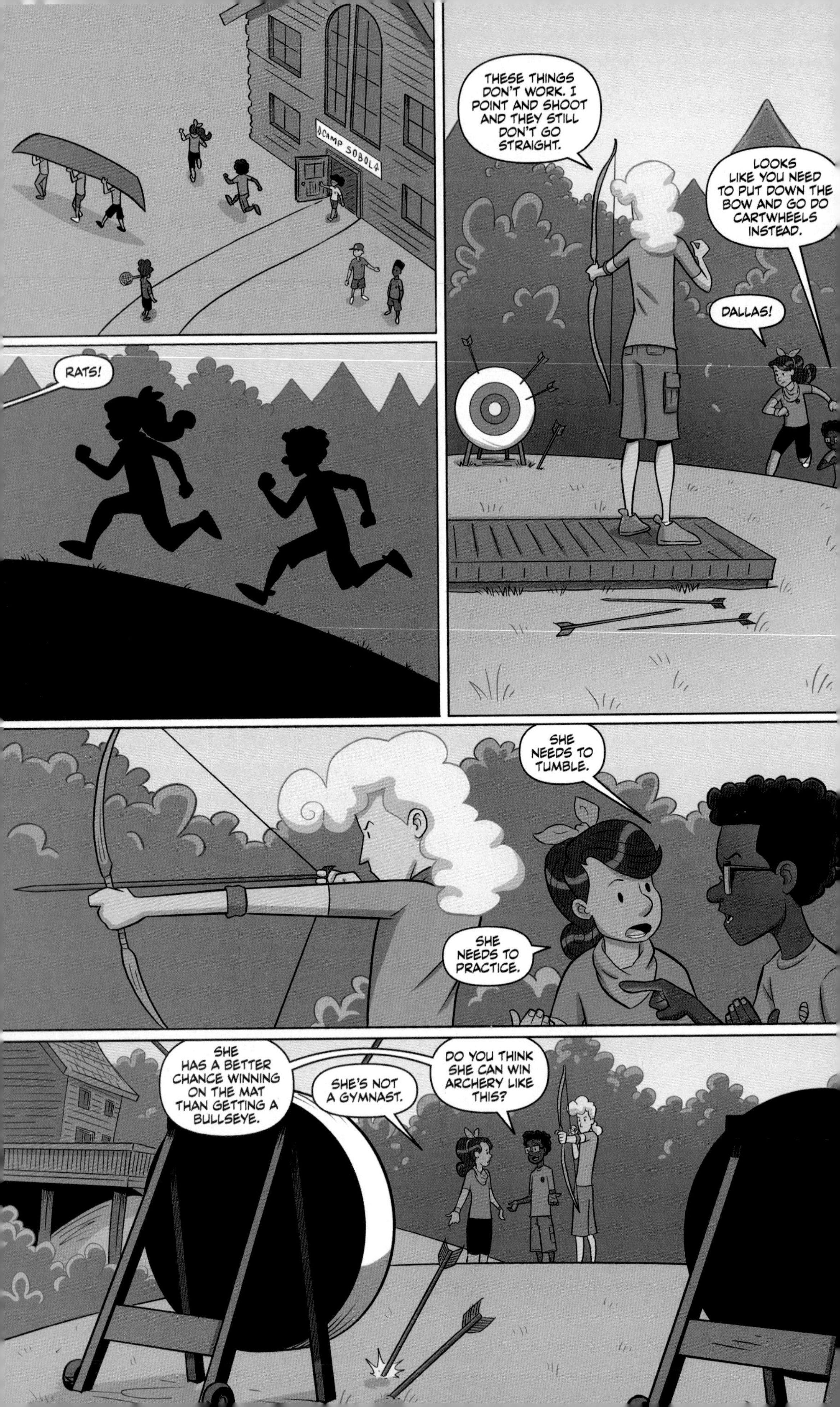

A CAMP SOBOLA
RATS!
THESE THINGS DON'T WORK. I POINT AND SHOOT AND THEY STILL DON'T GO STRAIGHT.
LOOKS LIKE YOU NEED TO PUT DOWN THE BOW AND GO DO CARTWHEELS INSTEAD.
DALLAS!
SHE NEEDS TO TUMBLE.
SHE NEEDS TO PRACTICE.
DO YOU THINK SHE CAN WIN ARCHERY LIKE THIS?
SHE'S NOT A GYMNAST.
SHE HAS A BETTER CHANCE WINNING ON THE MAT THAN GETTING A BULLSEYE.

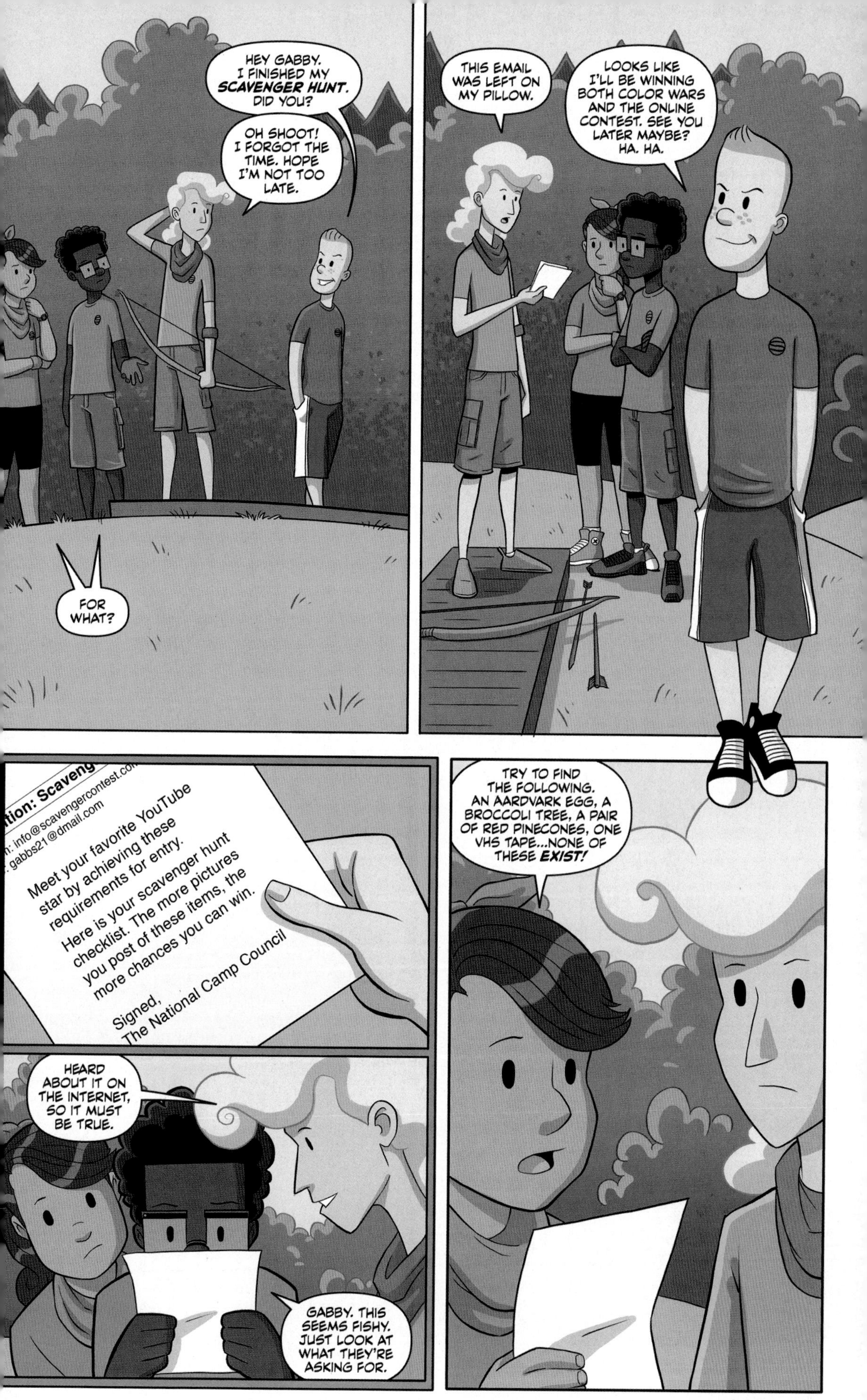
HEY GABBY. I FINISHED MY SCAVENGER HUNT. DID YOU?
OH SHOOT! I FORGOT THE TIME. HOPE I'M NOT TOO LATE.
FOR WHAT?
THIS EMAIL WAS LEFT ON MY PILLOW.
LOOKS LIKE I'LL BE WINNING BOTH COLOR WARS AND THE ONLINE CONTEST. SEE YOU LATER MAYBE? HA. HA.
tion: Scaveng
n: info@scavengercontest.co
gabbs21@dmail.com
Meet your favorite YouTube star by achieving these requirements for entry.
Here is your scavenger hunt checklist. The more pictures you post of these items, the more chances you can win.
Signed,
The National Camp Council
HEARD ABOUT IT ON THE INTERNET, SO IT MUST BE TRUE.
GABBY. THIS SEEMS FISHY. JUST LOOK AT WHAT THEY'RE ASKING FOR.
TRY TO FIND THE FOLLOWING. AN AARDVARK EGG, A BROCCOLI TREE, A PAIR OF RED PINECONES, ONE VHS TAPE...NONE OF THESE EXIST!

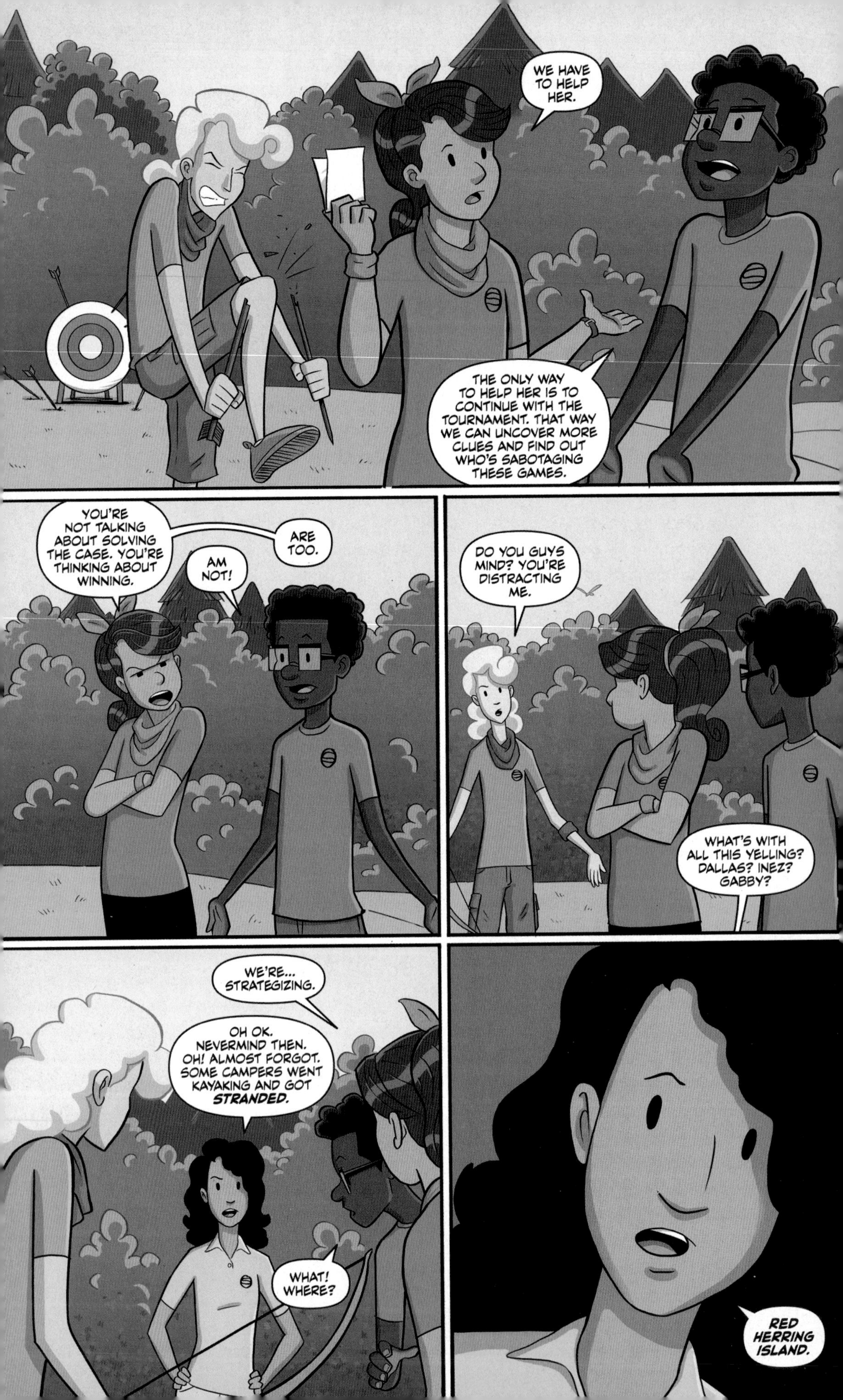
WE HAVE TO HELP HER.
THE ONLY WAY TO HELP HER IS TO CONTINUE WITH THE TOURNAMENT. THAT WAY WE CAN UNCOVER MORE CLUES AND FIND OUT WHO'S SABOTAGING THESE GAMES.
YOU'RE NOT TALKING ABOUT SOLVING THE CASE. YOU'RE THINKING ABOUT WINNING.
AM NOT!
ARE TOO.
DO YOU GUYS MIND? YOU'RE DISTRACTING ME.
WHAT'S WITH ALL THIS YELLING? DALLAS? INEZ? GABBY?
WE'RE... STRATEGIZING.
OH OK. NEVERMIND THEN. OH! ALMOST FORGOT. SOME CAMPERS WENT KAYAKING AND GOT ***STRANDED.***
WHAT! WHERE?
RED HERRING ISLAND.

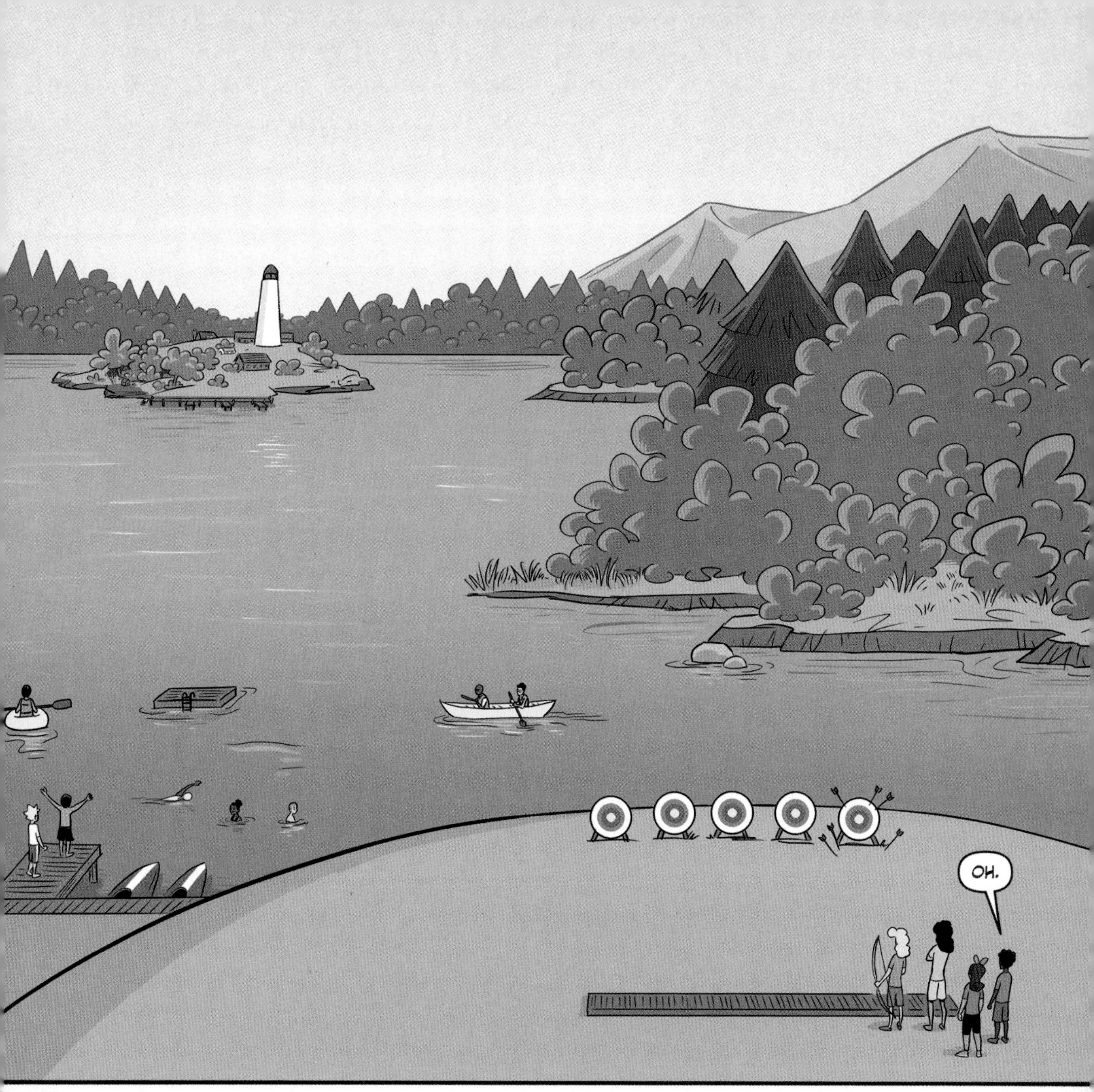
OH.

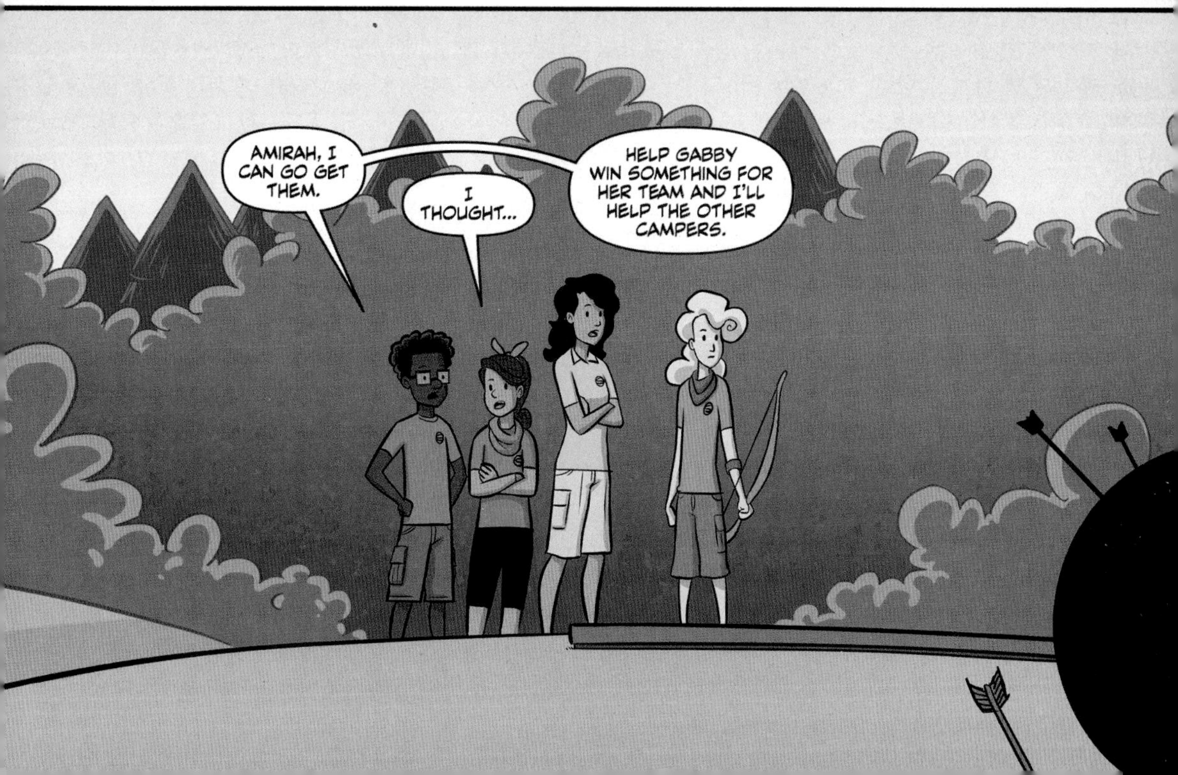
AMIRAH, I CAN GO GET THEM.
I THOUGHT...
HELP GABBY WIN SOMETHING FOR HER TEAM AND I'LL HELP THE OTHER CAMPERS.

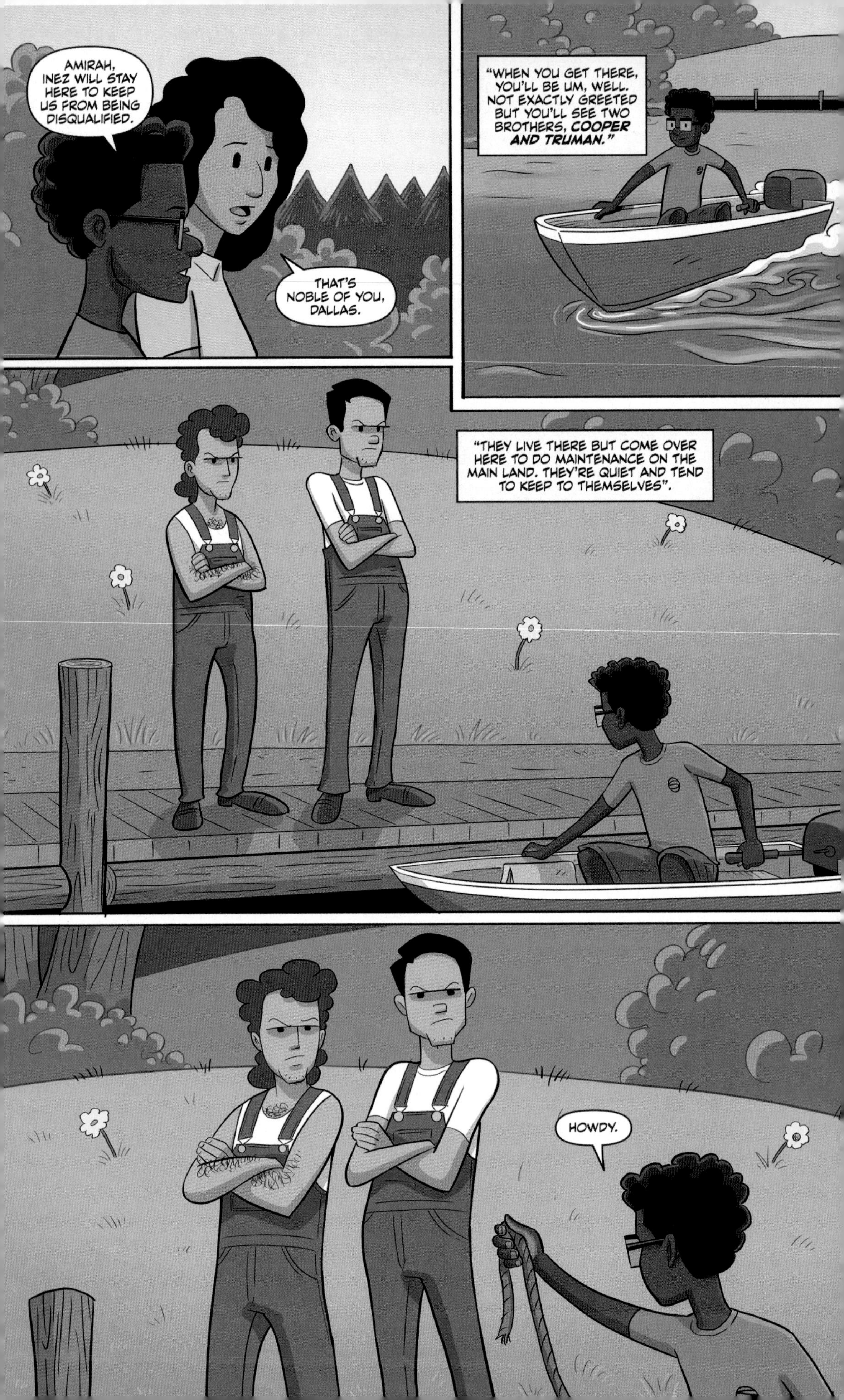
AMIRAH, INEZ WILL STAY HERE TO KEEP US FROM BEING DISQUALIFIED.
THAT'S NOBLE OF YOU, DALLAS.
"WHEN YOU GET THERE, YOU'LL BE UM, WELL. NOT EXACTLY GREETED BUT YOU'LL SEE TWO BROTHERS, ***COOPER AND TRUMAN.***"
"THEY LIVE THERE BUT COME OVER HERE TO DO MAINTENANCE ON THE MAIN LAND. THEY'RE QUIET AND TEND TO KEEP TO THEMSELVES".
HOWDY.

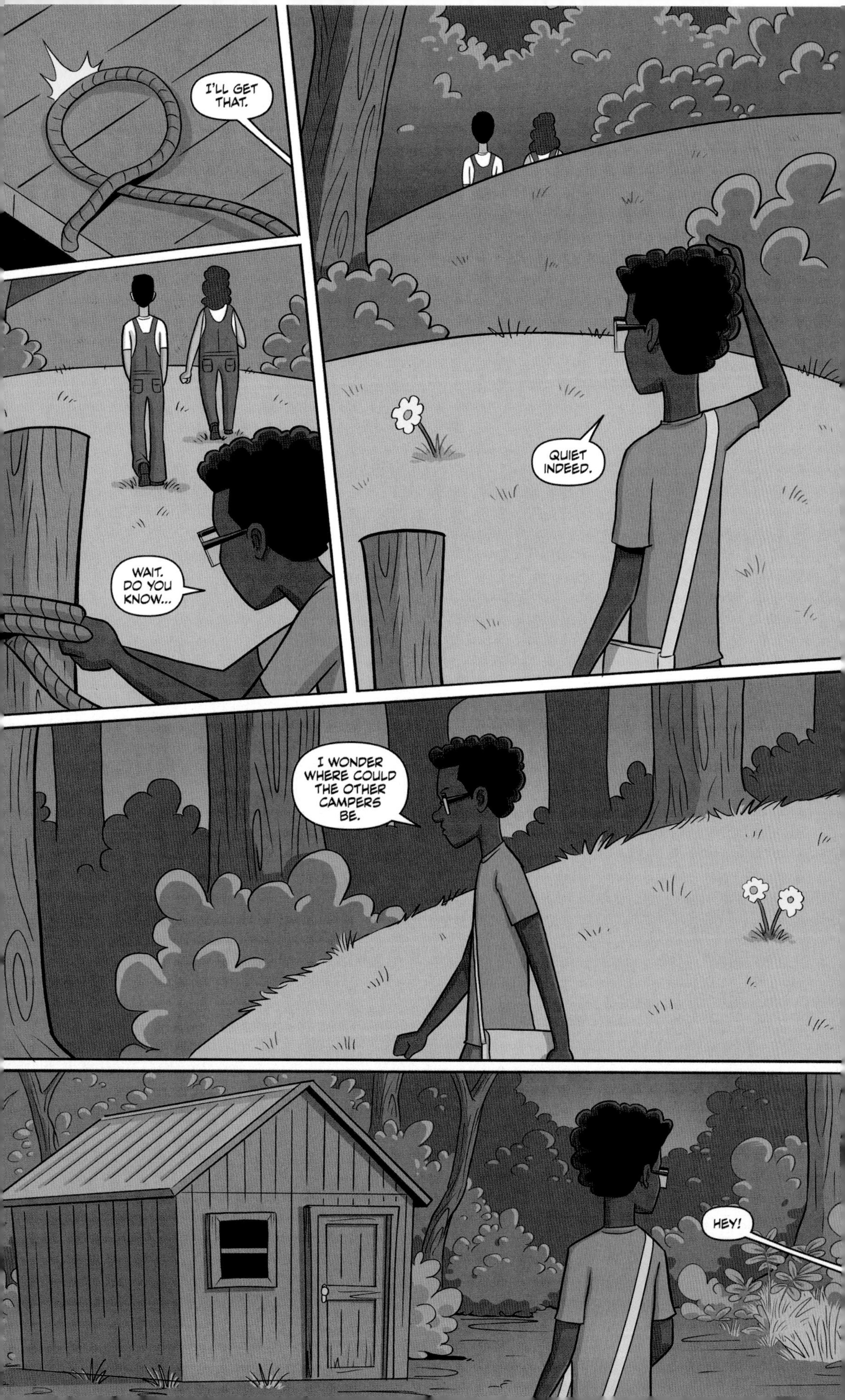
I'LL GET THAT.
WAIT. DO YOU KNOW...
QUIET INDEED.
I WONDER WHERE COULD THE OTHER CAMPERS BE.
HEY!

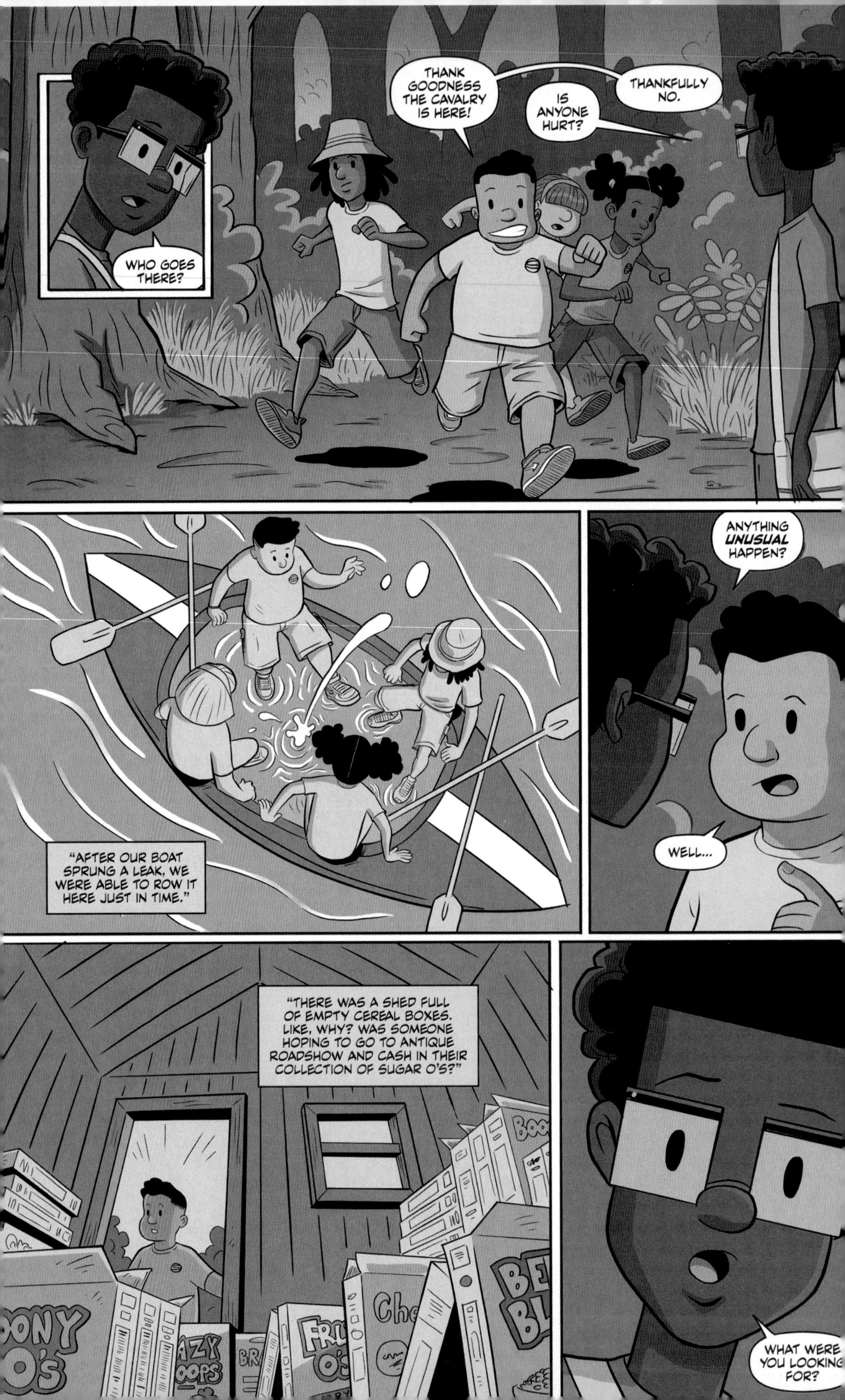
WHO GOES THERE?
THANK GOODNESS THE CAVALRY IS HERE!
IS ANYONE HURT?
THANKFULLY NO.
"AFTER OUR BOAT SPRUNG A LEAK, WE WERE ABLE TO ROW IT HERE JUST IN TIME."
ANYTHING *UNUSUAL* HAPPEN?
WELL...
"THERE WAS A SHED FULL OF EMPTY CEREAL BOXES. LIKE, WHY? WAS SOMEONE HOPING TO GO TO ANTIQUE ROADSHOW AND CASH IN THEIR COLLECTION OF SUGAR O'S?"
WHAT WERE YOU LOOKING FOR?

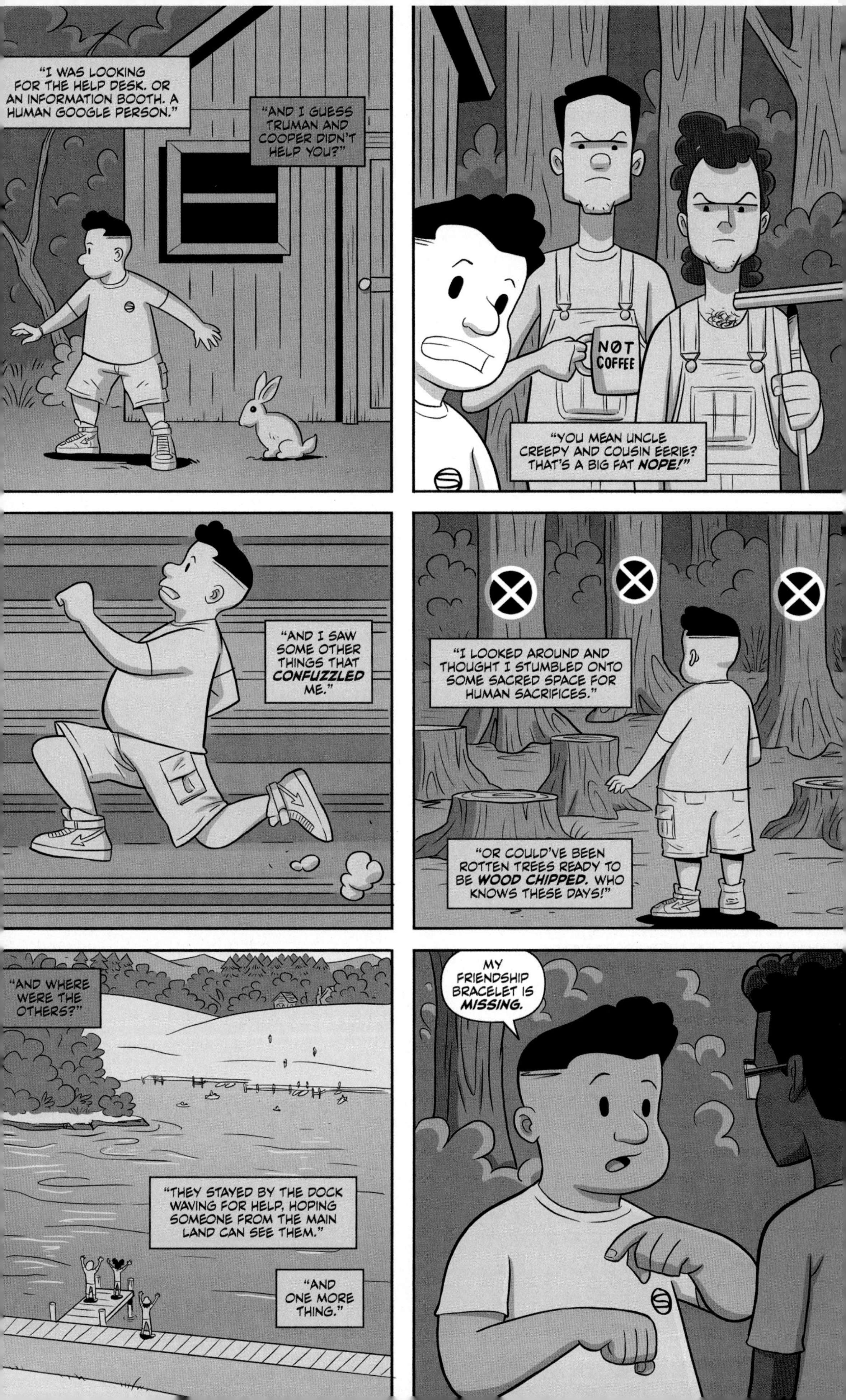
"I WAS LOOKING FOR THE HELP DESK. OR AN INFORMATION BOOTH. A HUMAN GOOGLE PERSON."
"AND I GUESS TRUMAN AND COOPER DIDN'T HELP YOU?"
NØT COFFEE
"YOU MEAN UNCLE CREEPY AND COUSIN EERIE? THAT'S A BIG FAT NOPE!"
"AND I SAW SOME OTHER THINGS THAT CONFUZZLED ME."
"I LOOKED AROUND AND THOUGHT I STUMBLED ONTO SOME SACRED SPACE FOR HUMAN SACRIFICES."
"OR COULD'VE BEEN ROTTEN TREES READY TO BE WOOD CHIPPED. WHO KNOWS THESE DAYS!"
"AND WHERE WERE THE OTHERS?"
"THEY STAYED BY THE DOCK WAVING FOR HELP, HOPING SOMEONE FROM THE MAIN LAND CAN SEE THEM."
"AND ONE MORE THING."
MY FRIENDSHIP BRACELET IS MISSING.

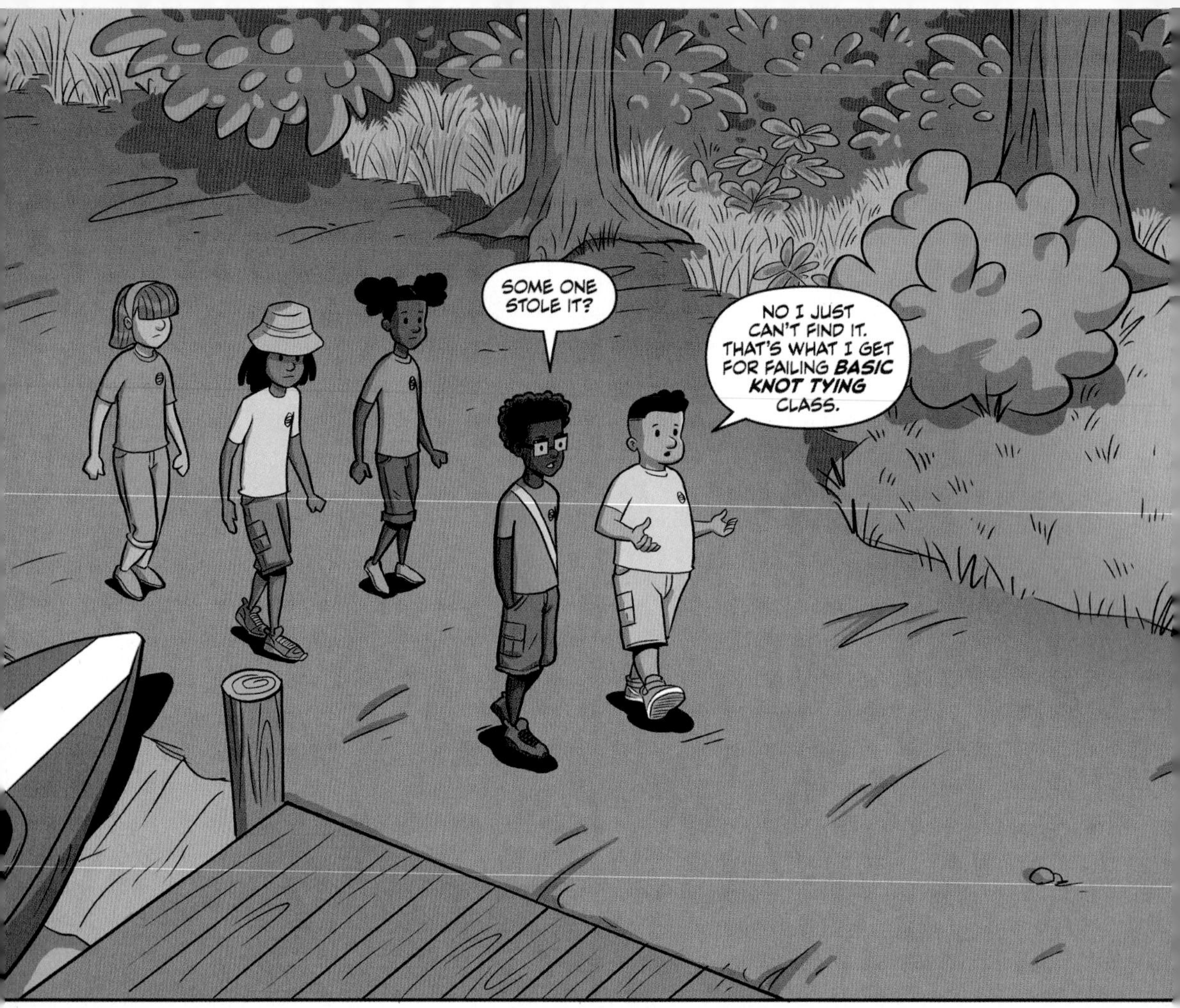
SOME ONE STOLE IT?
NO I JUST CAN'T FIND IT. THAT'S WHAT I GET FOR FAILING **BASIC KNOT TYING** CLASS.

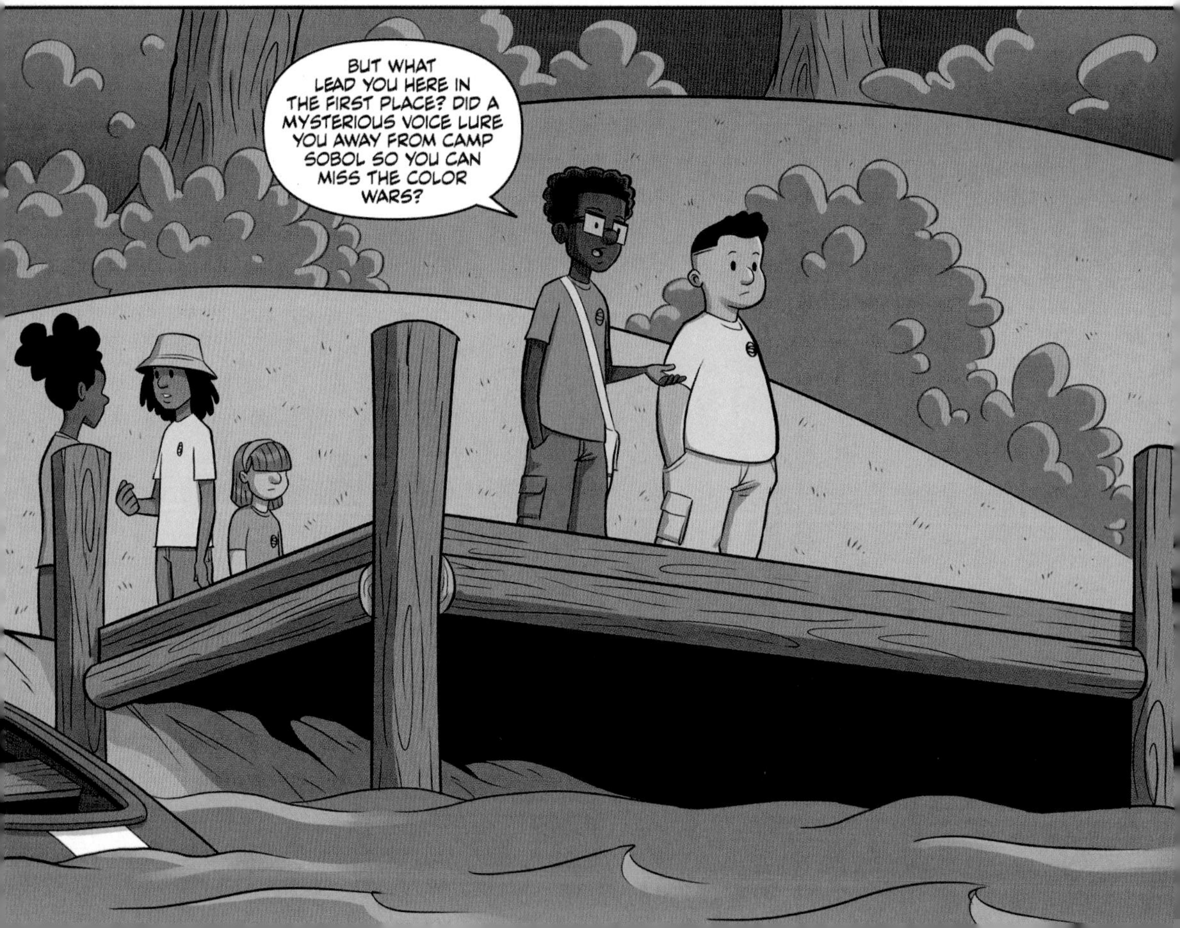
BUT WHAT LEAD YOU HERE IN THE FIRST PLACE? DID A MYSTERIOUS VOICE LURE YOU AWAY FROM CAMP SOBOL SO YOU CAN MISS THE COLOR WARS?

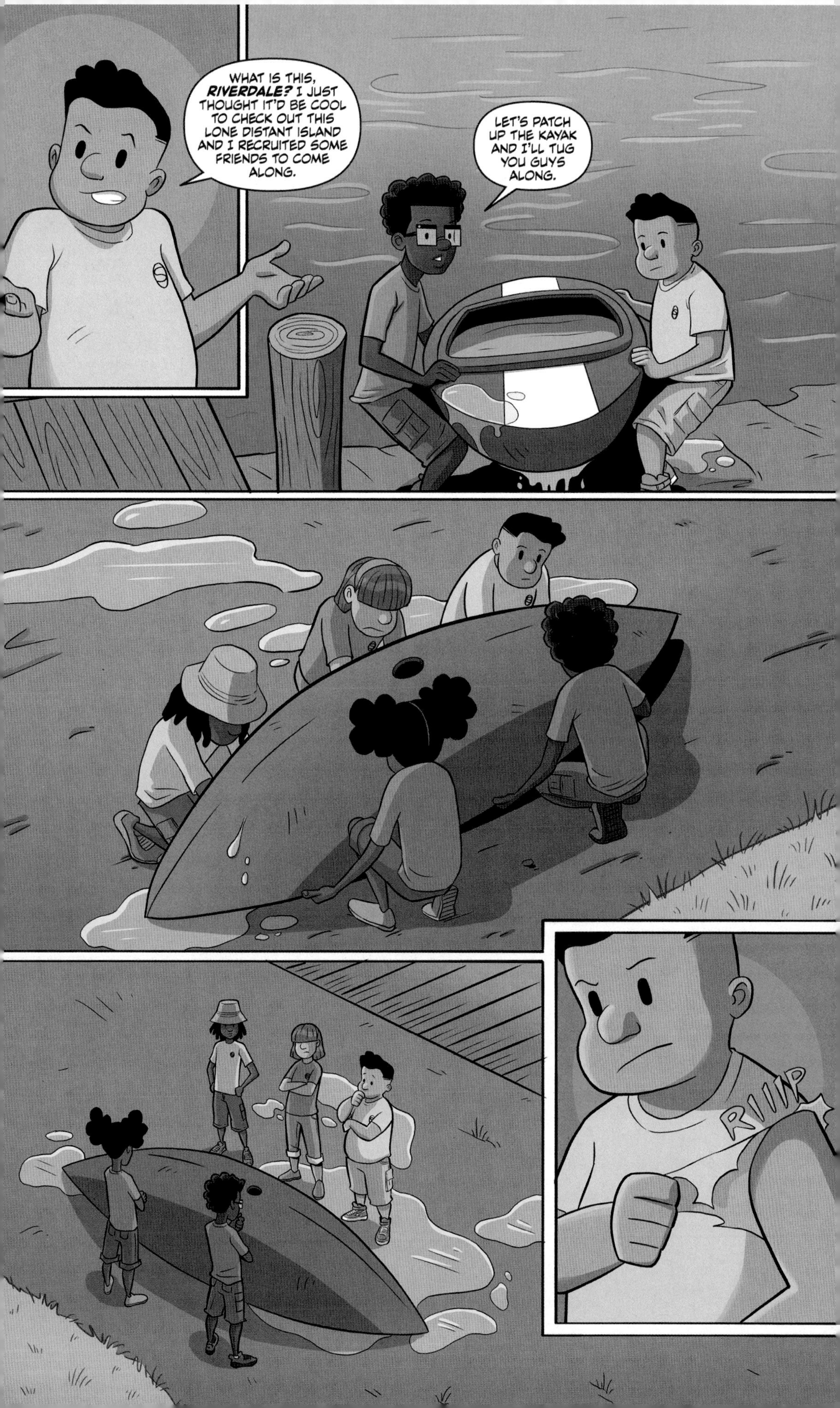
WHAT IS THIS, RIVERDALE? I JUST THOUGHT IT'D BE COOL TO CHECK OUT THIS LONE DISTANT ISLAND AND I RECRUITED SOME FRIENDS TO COME ALONG.
LET'S PATCH UP THE KAYAK AND I'LL TUG YOU GUYS ALONG.
RIIIP

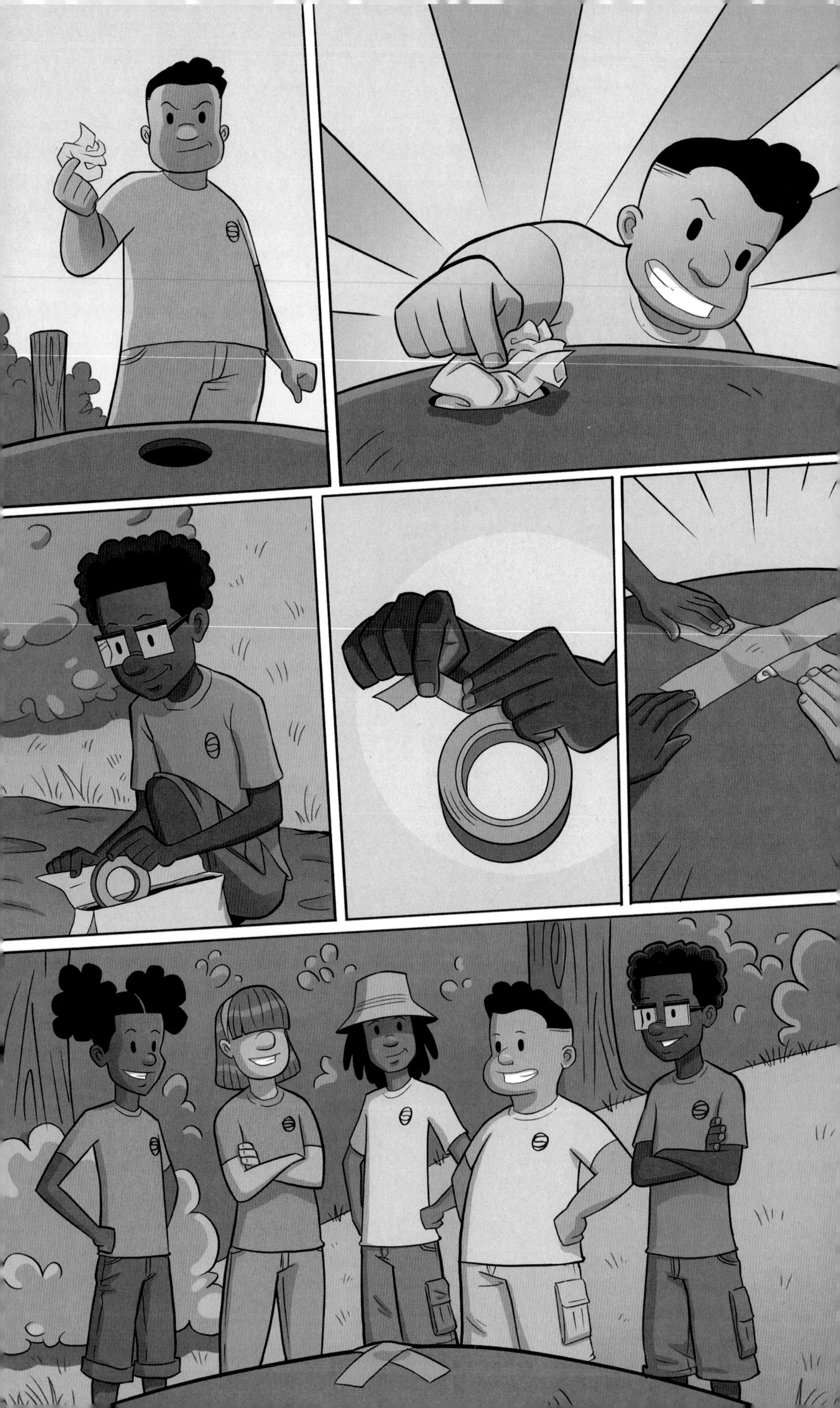

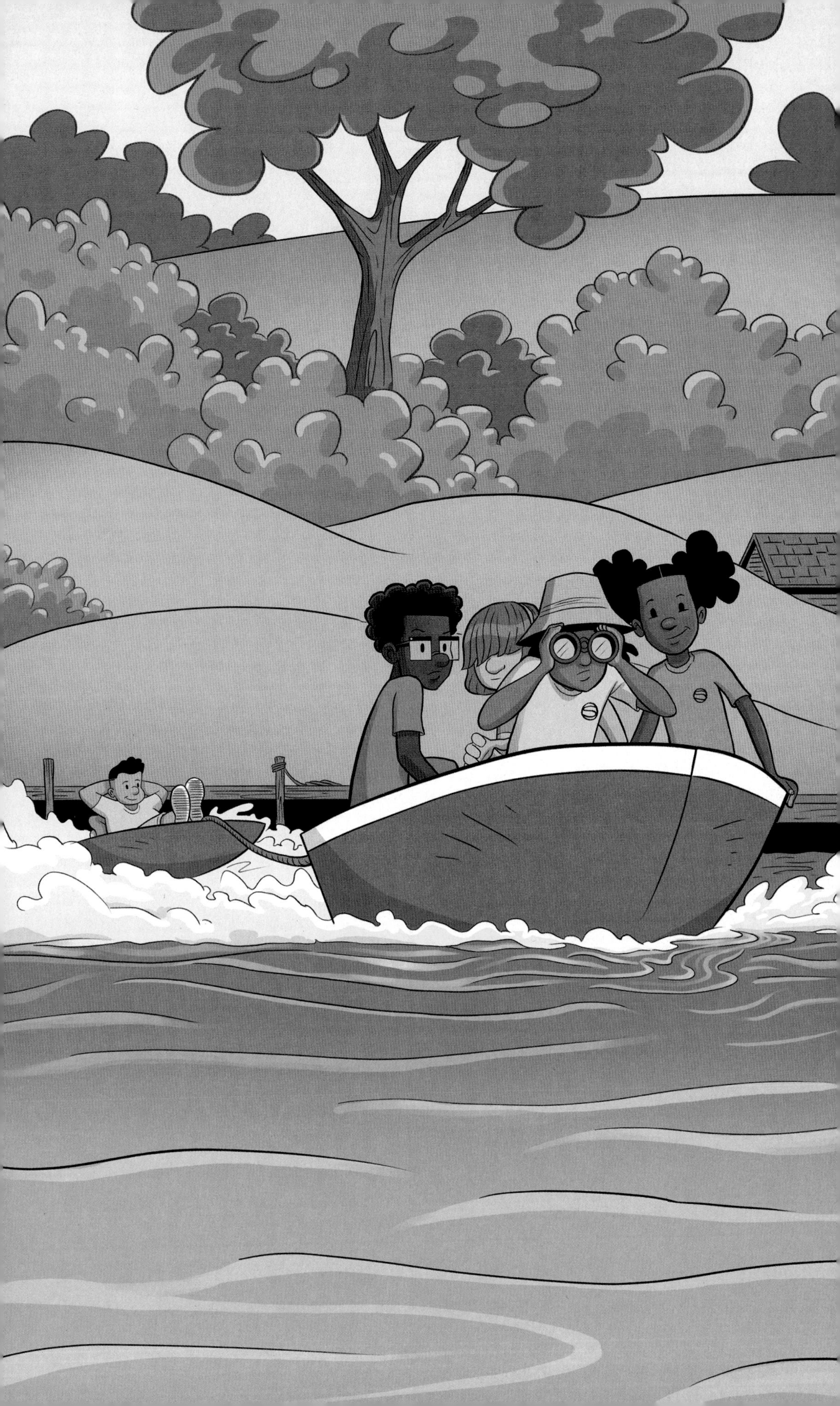

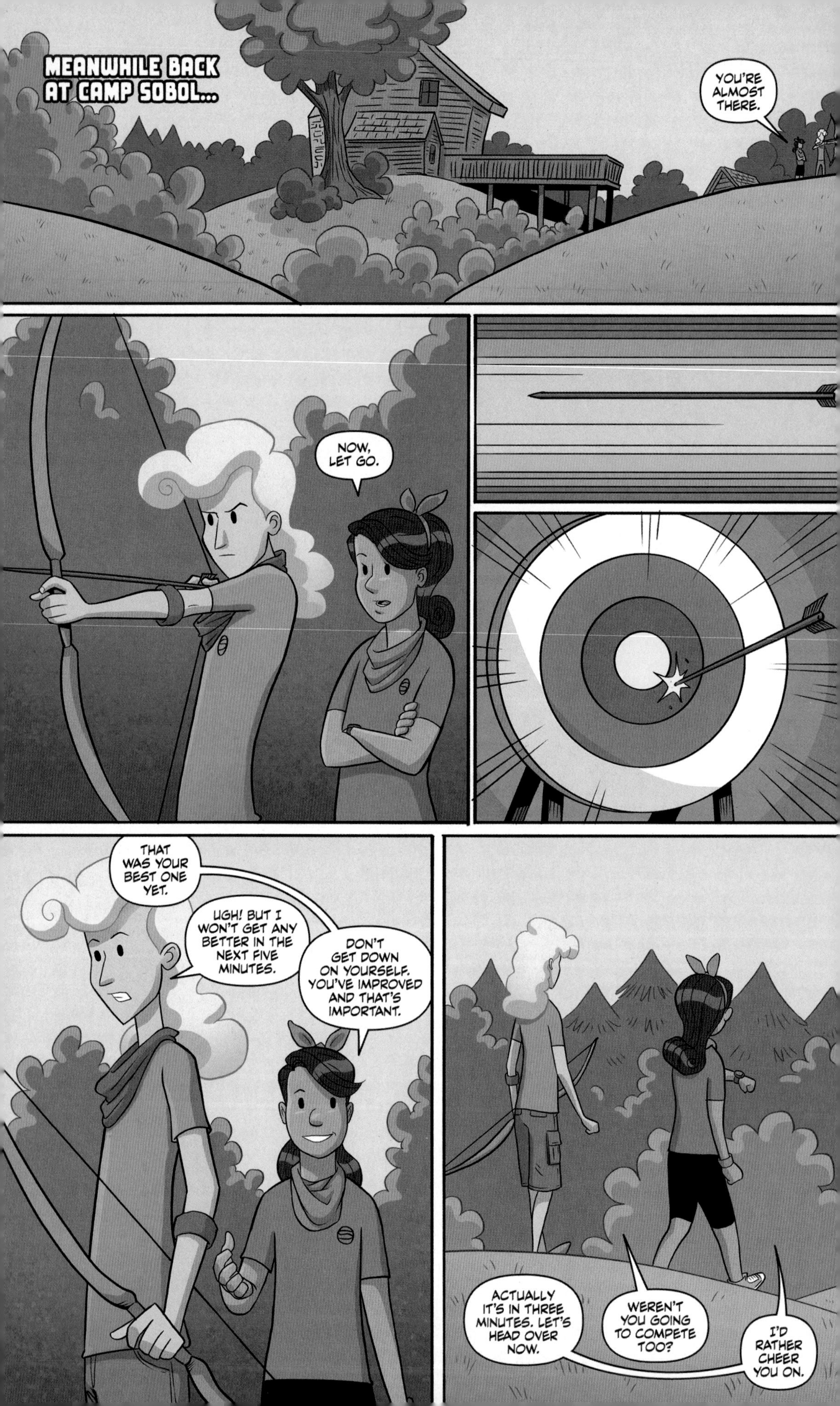
MEANWHILE BACK AT CAMP SOBOL...
YOU'RE ALMOST THERE.
NOW, LET GO.
THAT WAS YOUR BEST ONE YET.
UGH! BUT I WON'T GET ANY BETTER IN THE NEXT FIVE MINUTES.
DON'T GET DOWN ON YOURSELF. YOU'VE IMPROVED AND THAT'S IMPORTANT.
ACTUALLY IT'S IN THREE MINUTES. LET'S HEAD OVER NOW.
WEREN'T YOU GOING TO COMPETE TOO?
I'D RATHER CHEER YOU ON.

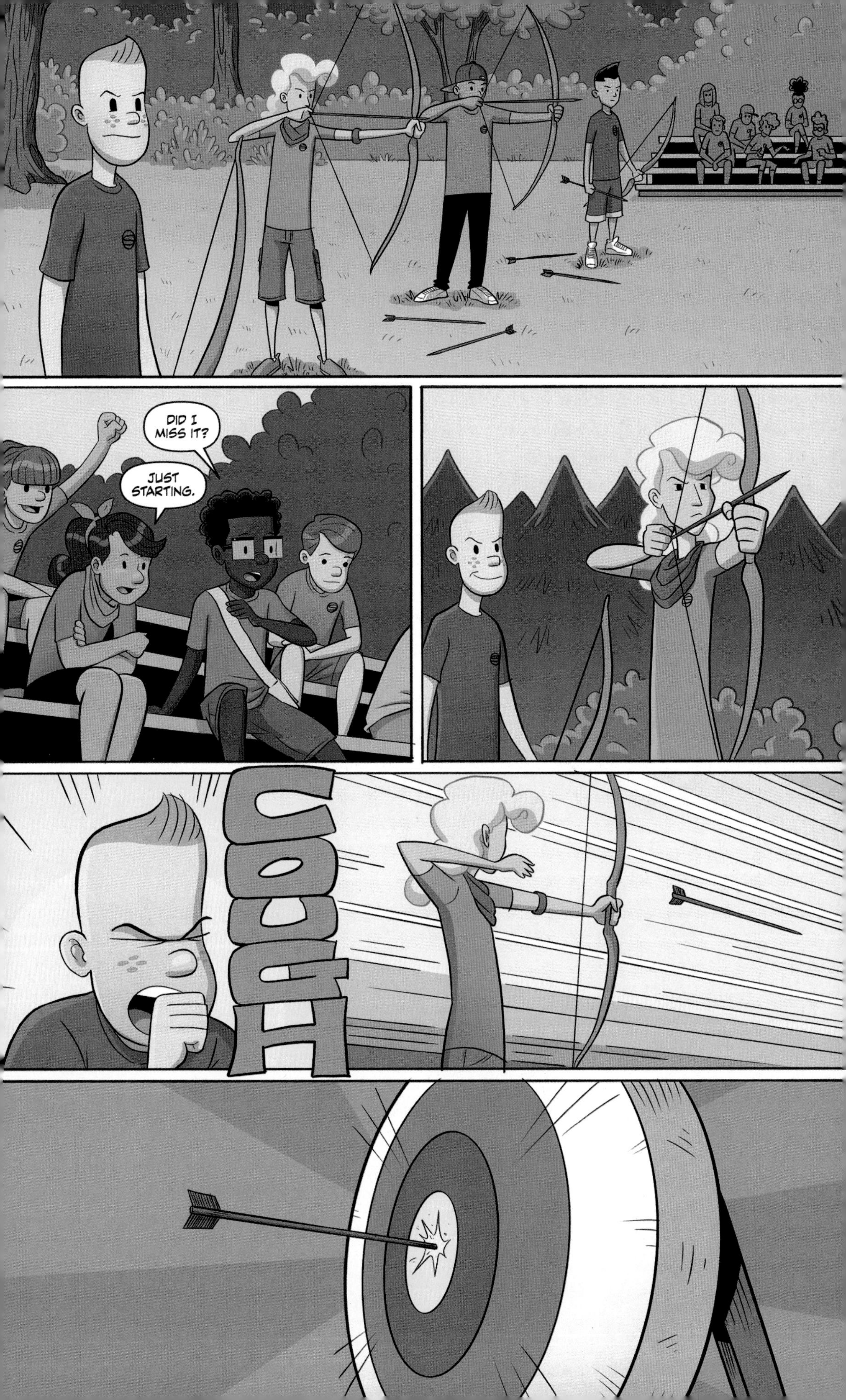
DID I MISS IT?
JUST STARTING.
COUGH

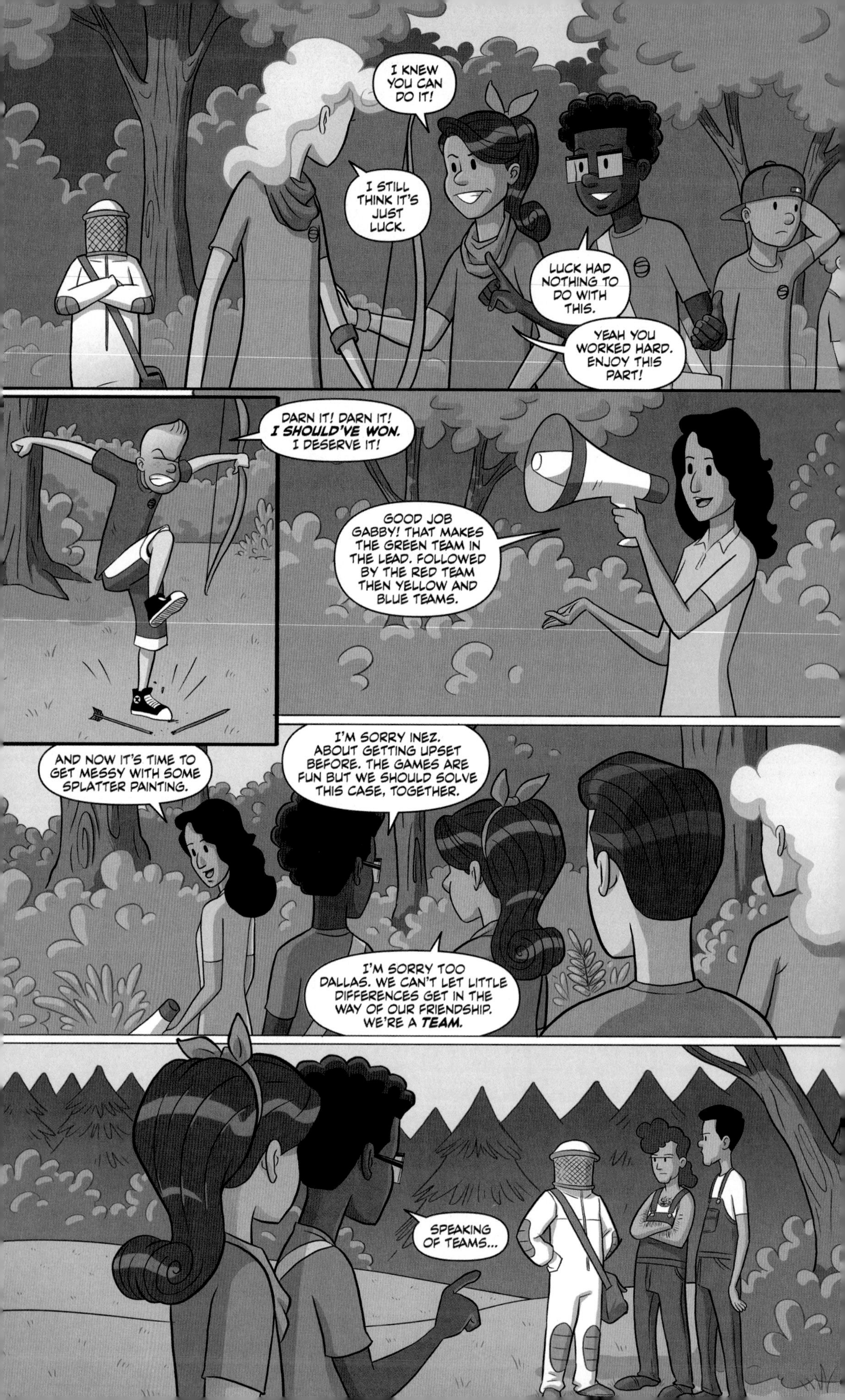
I KNEW YOU CAN DO IT!
I STILL THINK IT'S JUST LUCK.
LUCK HAD NOTHING TO DO WITH THIS.
YEAH YOU WORKED HARD. ENJOY THIS PART!
DARN IT! DARN IT! **I SHOULD'VE WON.** I DESERVE IT!
GOOD JOB GABBY! THAT MAKES THE GREEN TEAM IN THE LEAD. FOLLOWED BY THE RED TEAM THEN YELLOW AND BLUE TEAMS.
AND NOW IT'S TIME TO GET MESSY WITH SOME SPLATTER PAINTING.
I'M SORRY INEZ. ABOUT GETTING UPSET BEFORE. THE GAMES ARE FUN BUT WE SHOULD SOLVE THIS CASE, TOGETHER.
I'M SORRY TOO DALLAS. WE CAN'T LET LITTLE DIFFERENCES GET IN THE WAY OF OUR FRIENDSHIP. WE'RE A **TEAM.**
SPEAKING OF TEAMS...

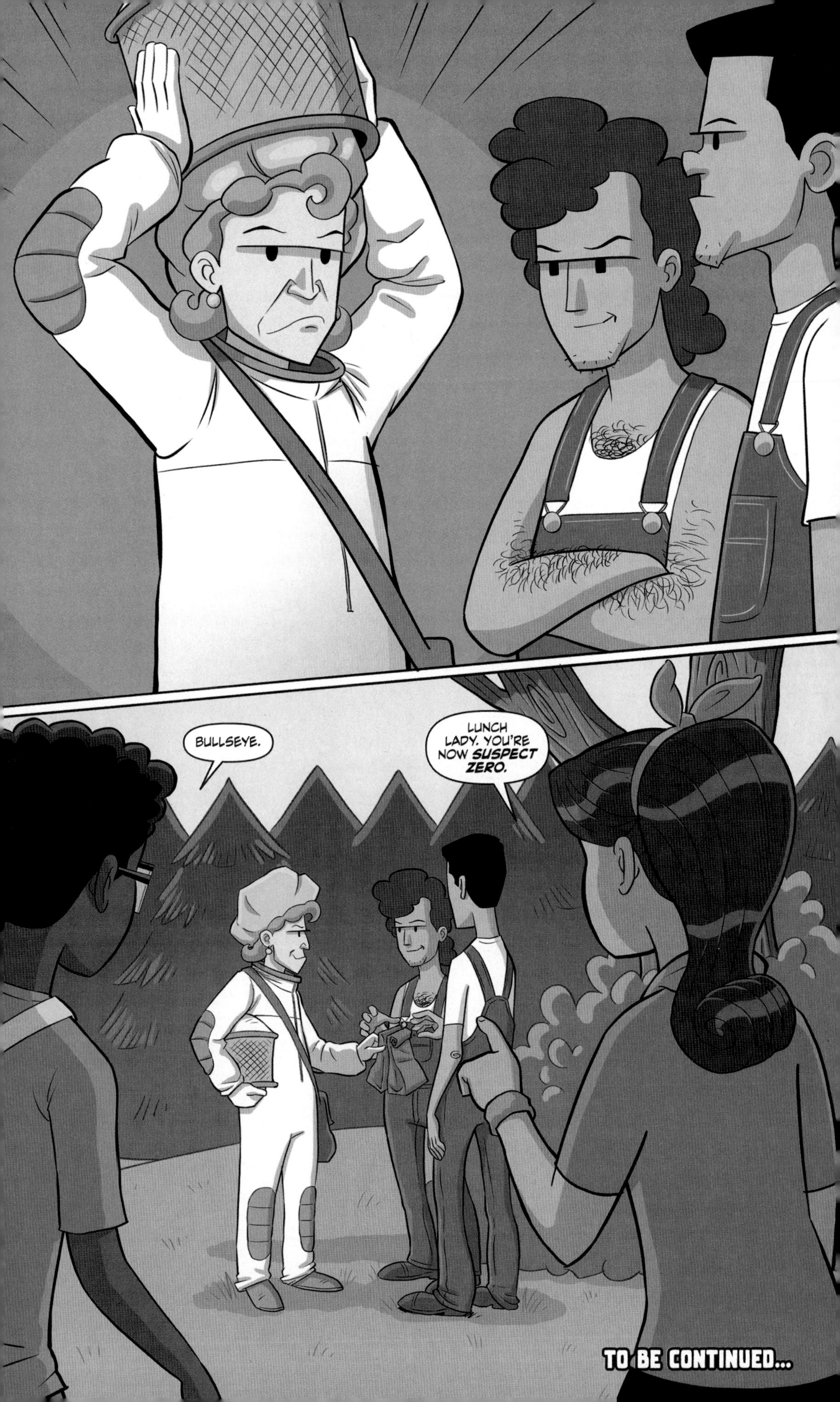
BULLSEYE.
LUNCH LADY. YOU'RE NOW *SUSPECT ZERO.*
TO BE CONTINUED...

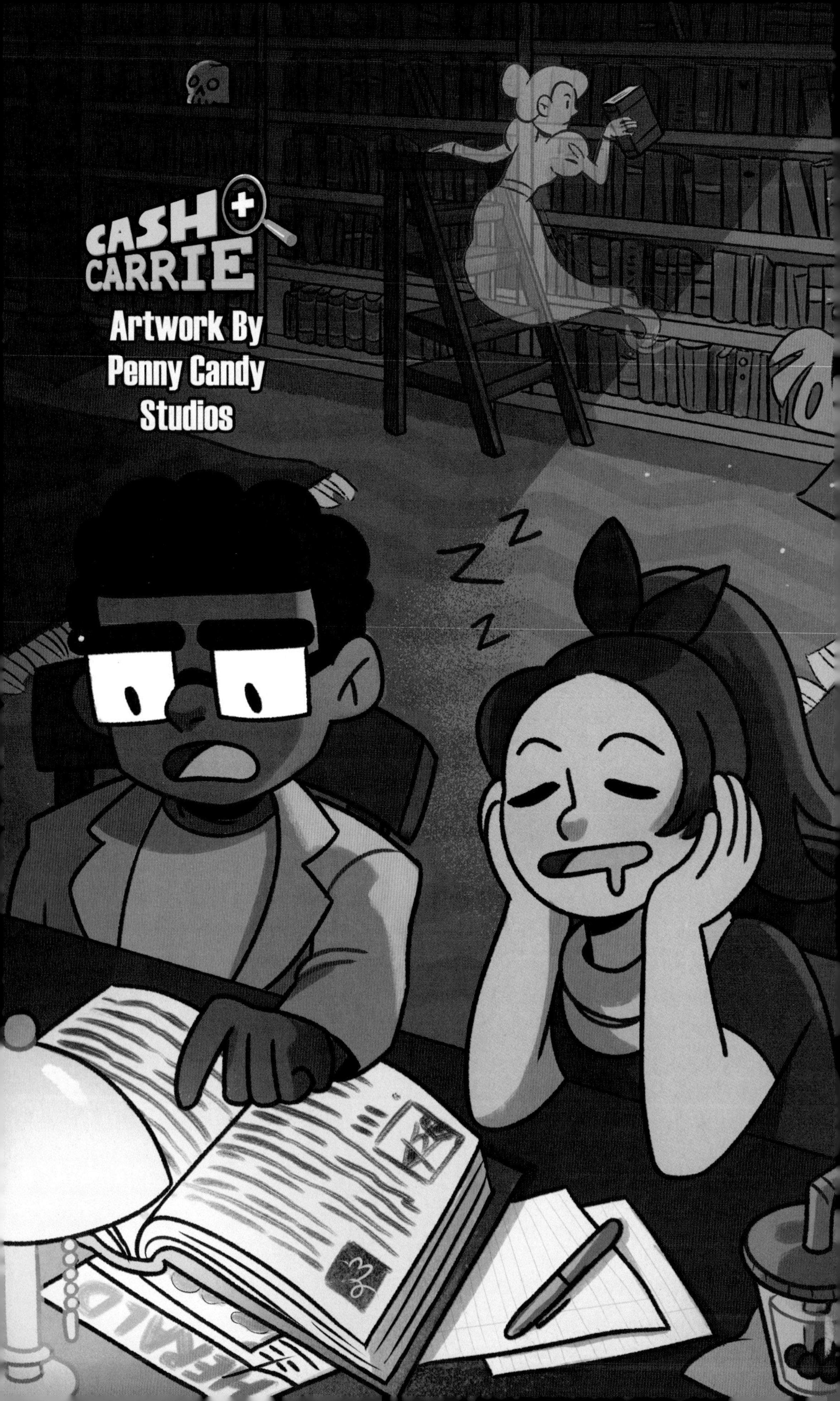

CASH + CARRIE
Artwork By
Penny Candy
Studios
Z Z Z

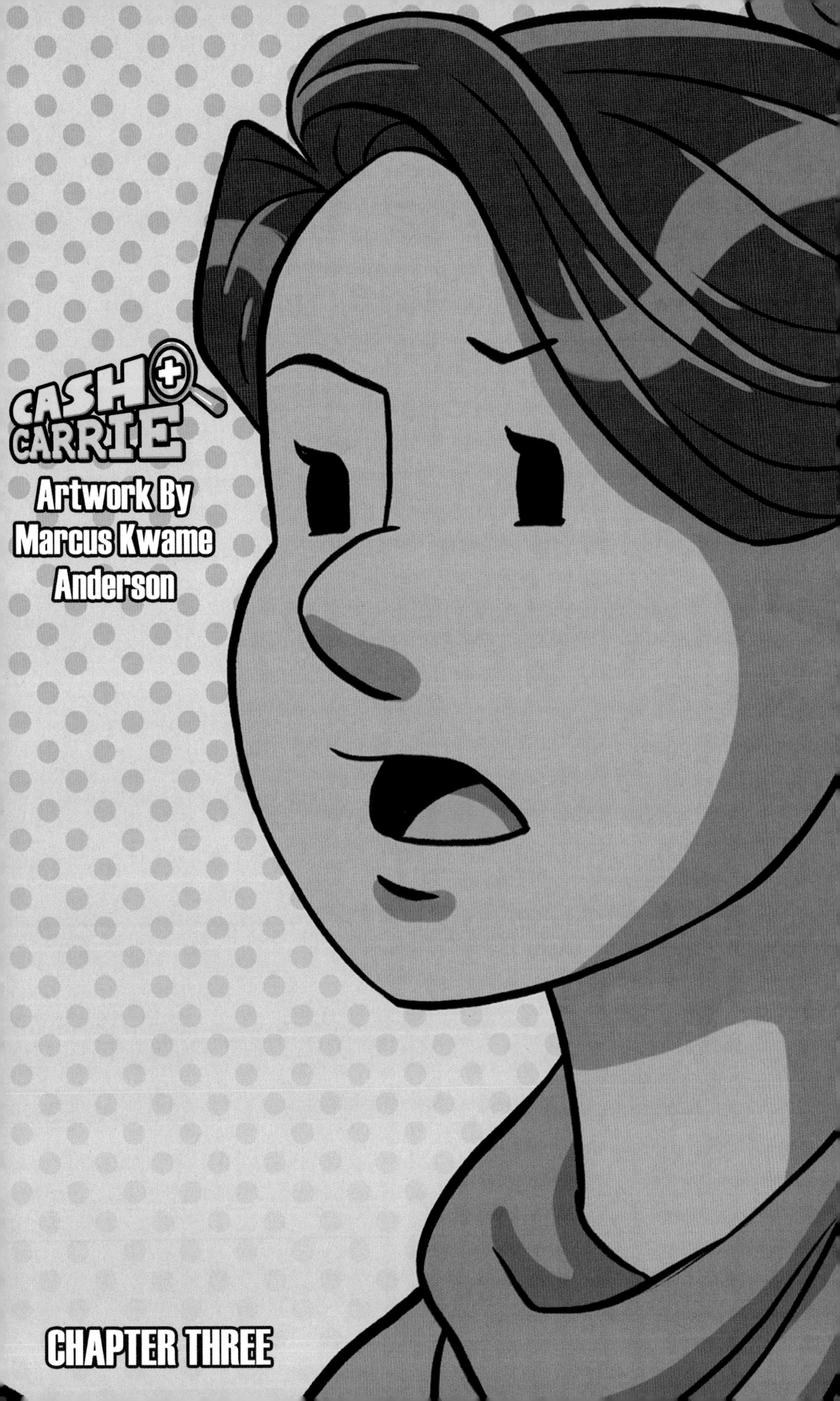
CASH + CARRIE
Artwork By
Marcus Kwame
Anderson
CHAPTER THREE

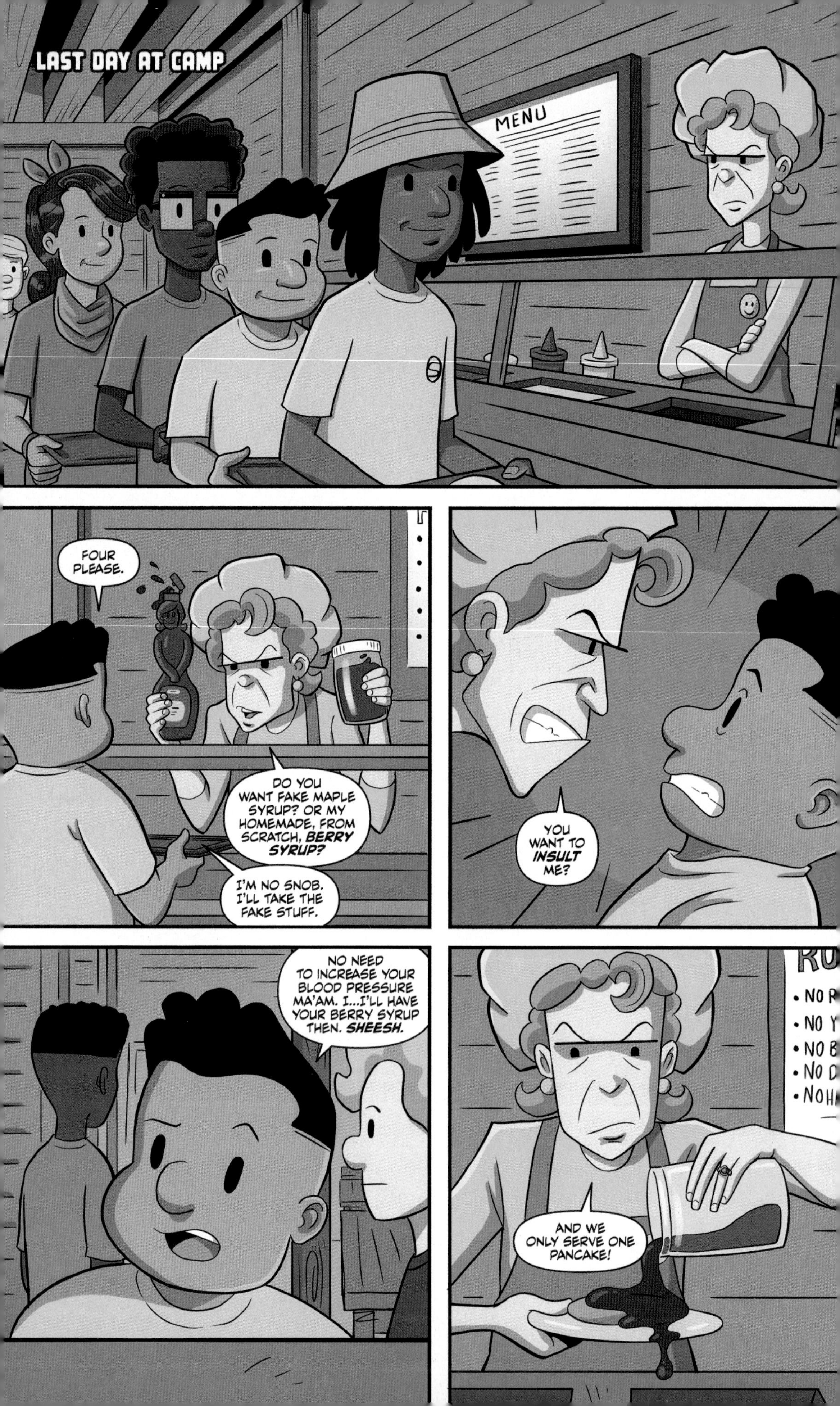
LAST DAY AT CAMP
MENU
FOUR PLEASE.
DO YOU WANT FAKE MAPLE SYRUP? OR MY HOMEMADE, FROM SCRATCH, BERRY SYRUP?
I'M NO SNOB. I'LL TAKE THE FAKE STUFF.
YOU WANT TO INSULT ME?
NO NEED TO INCREASE YOUR BLOOD PRESSURE MA'AM. I...I'LL HAVE YOUR BERRY SYRUP THEN. SHEESH.
AND WE ONLY SERVE ONE PANCAKE!

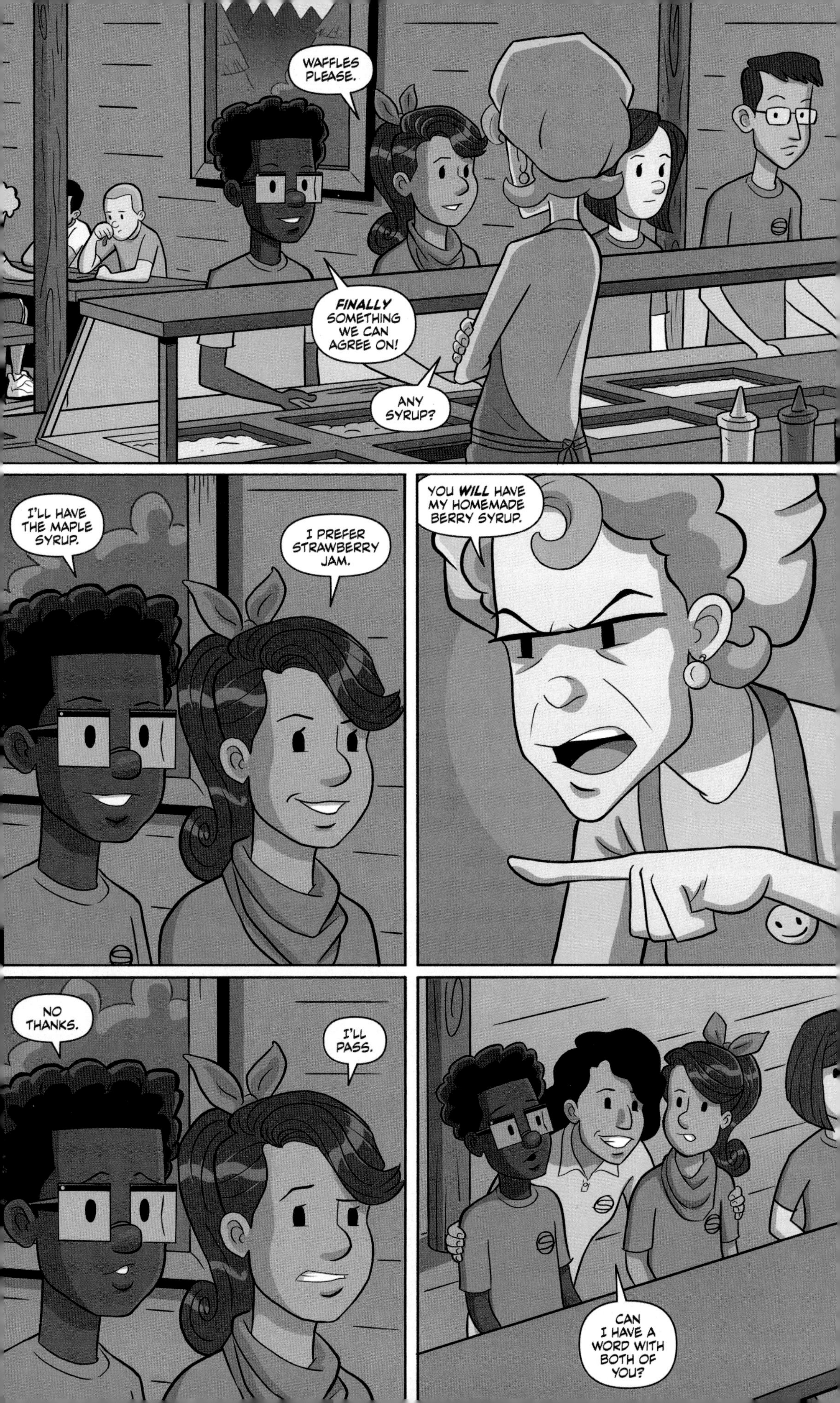
WAFFLES PLEASE.
FINALLY SOMETHING WE CAN AGREE ON!
ANY SYRUP?
I'LL HAVE THE MAPLE SYRUP.
I PREFER STRAWBERRY JAM.
YOU WILL HAVE MY HOMEMADE BERRY SYRUP.
NO THANKS.
I'LL PASS.
CAN I HAVE A WORD WITH BOTH OF YOU?

KWAN YOU HAVE TO TRUST ME. I KNOW WE CAN WIN THIS. THE GREEN TEAM WILL DO BLAND VEGGIE DISHES WHICH NONE OF THE JUDGES WILL LIKE. THEY'RE NO THREAT TO US.
BUT RAMSAY, OSCAR'S GOT COOKING SKILLS AND DOC JONES CAN DEFINITELY KEEP UP. I DON'T FEEL TOO CONFIDENT IN OUR RECIPES.
DON'T WORRY ABOUT OSCAR. HE'S TAKEN CARE OF.
BELIEVE ME.

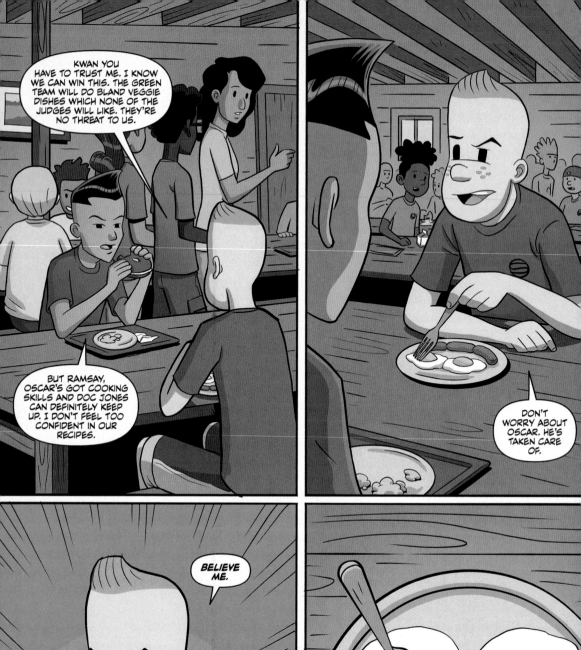

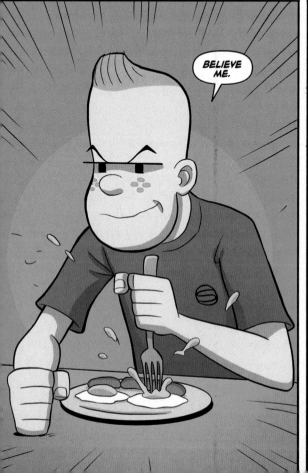

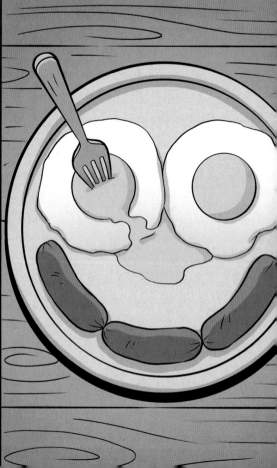

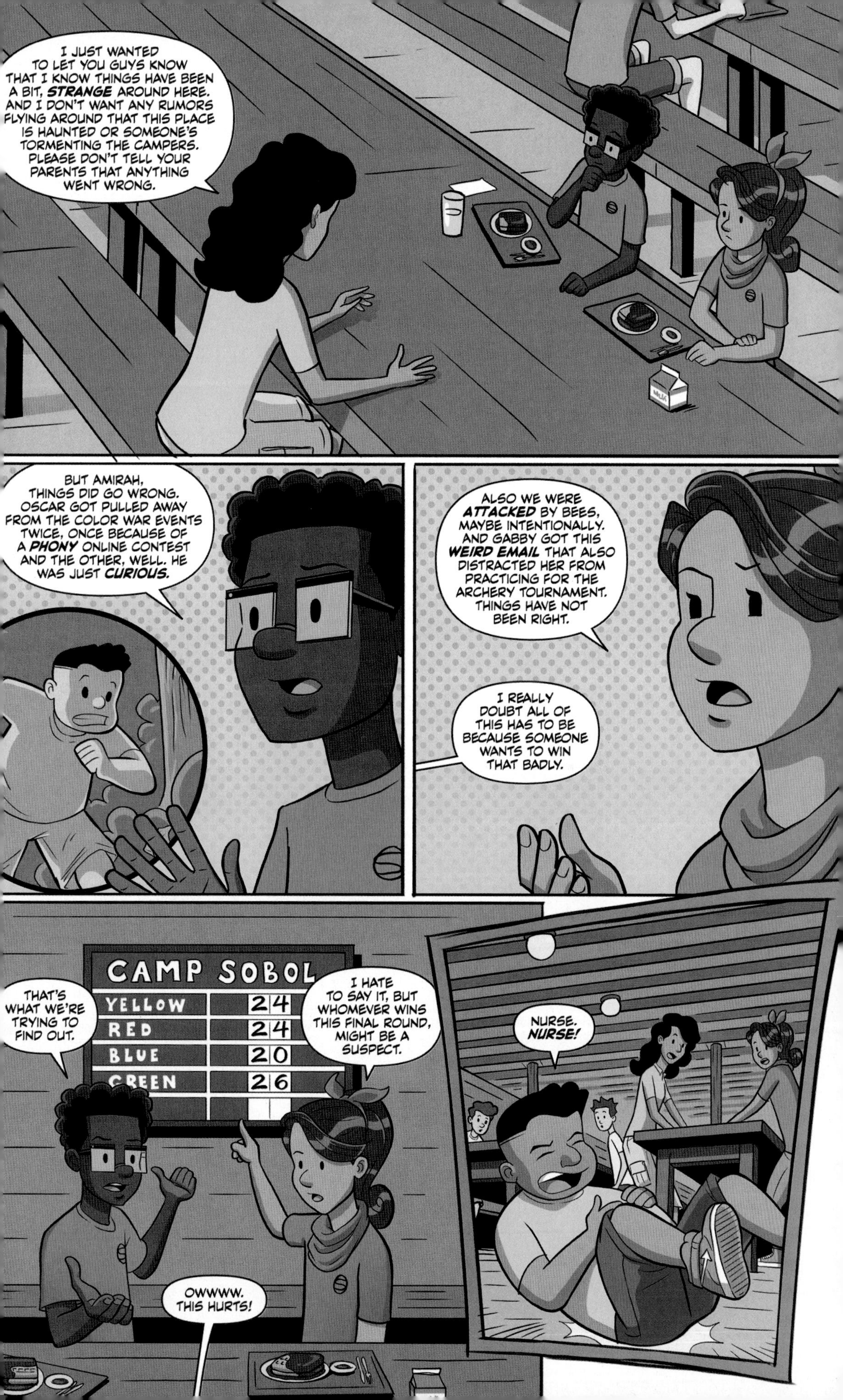
I JUST WANTED TO LET YOU GUYS KNOW THAT I KNOW THINGS HAVE BEEN A BIT, STRANGE AROUND HERE. AND I DON'T WANT ANY RUMORS FLYING AROUND THAT THIS PLACE IS HAUNTED OR SOMEONE'S TORMENTING THE CAMPERS. PLEASE DON'T TELL YOUR PARENTS THAT ANYTHING WENT WRONG.
BUT AMIRAH, THINGS DID GO WRONG. OSCAR GOT PULLED AWAY FROM THE COLOR WAR EVENTS TWICE, ONCE BECAUSE OF A PHONY ONLINE CONTEST AND THE OTHER, WELL. HE WAS JUST CURIOUS.
ALSO WE WERE ATTACKED BY BEES, MAYBE INTENTIONALLY. AND GABBY GOT THIS WEIRD EMAIL THAT ALSO DISTRACTED HER FROM PRACTICING FOR THE ARCHERY TOURNAMENT. THINGS HAVE NOT BEEN RIGHT.
I REALLY DOUBT ALL OF THIS HAS TO BE BECAUSE SOMEONE WANTS TO WIN THAT BADLY.
CAMP SOBOL
YELLOW 24
RED 24
BLUE 20
GREEN 26
THAT'S WHAT WE'RE TRYING TO FIND OUT.
I HATE TO SAY IT, BUT WHOMEVER WINS THIS FINAL ROUND, MIGHT BE A SUSPECT.
NURSE. NURSE!
OWWWW. THIS HURTS!

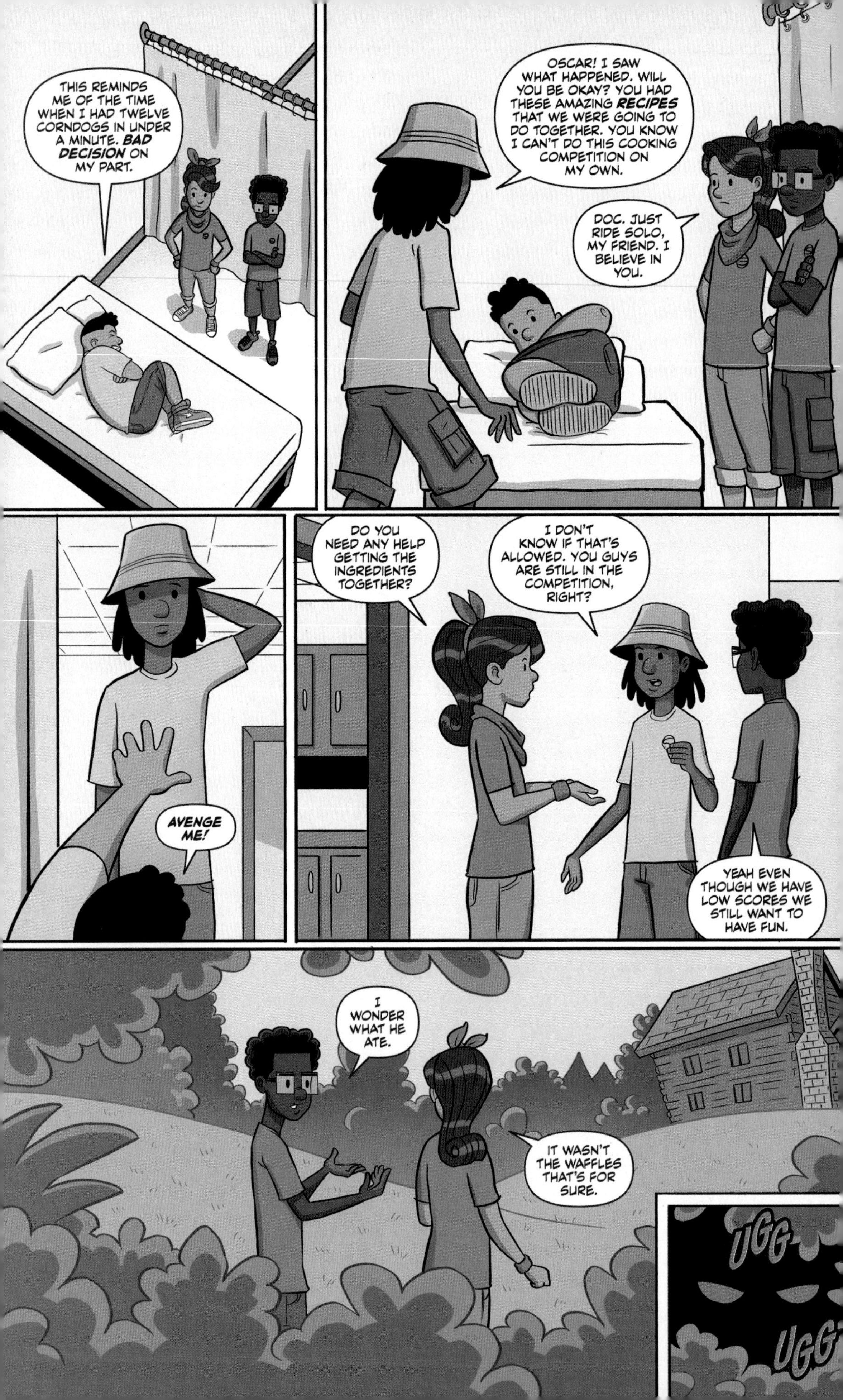
THIS REMINDS ME OF THE TIME WHEN I HAD TWELVE CORNDOGS IN UNDER A MINUTE. BAD DECISION ON MY PART.
OSCAR! I SAW WHAT HAPPENED. WILL YOU BE OKAY? YOU HAD THESE AMAZING RECIPES THAT WE WERE GOING TO DO TOGETHER. YOU KNOW I CAN'T DO THIS COOKING COMPETITION ON MY OWN.
DOC. JUST RIDE SOLO, MY FRIEND. I BELIEVE IN YOU.
AVENGE ME!
DO YOU NEED ANY HELP GETTING THE INGREDIENTS TOGETHER?
I DON'T KNOW IF THAT'S ALLOWED. YOU GUYS ARE STILL IN THE COMPETITION, RIGHT?
YEAH EVEN THOUGH WE HAVE LOW SCORES WE STILL WANT TO HAVE FUN.
I WONDER WHAT HE ATE.
IT WASN'T THE WAFFLES THAT'S FOR SURE.
UGG
UGG

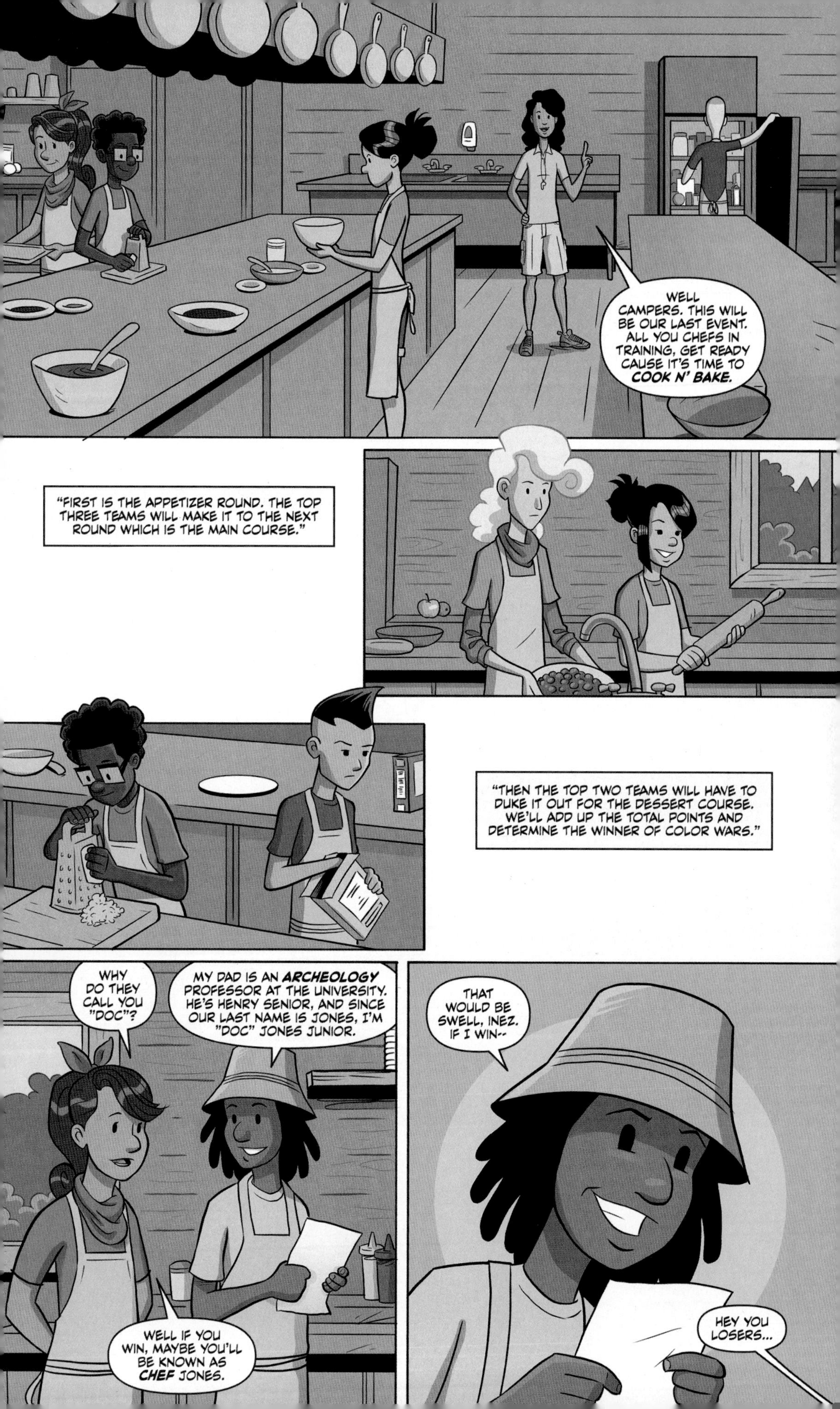
WELL CAMPERS. THIS WILL BE OUR LAST EVENT. ALL YOU CHEFS IN TRAINING, GET READY CAUSE IT'S TIME TO COOK N' BAKE.
"FIRST IS THE APPETIZER ROUND. THE TOP THREE TEAMS WILL MAKE IT TO THE NEXT ROUND WHICH IS THE MAIN COURSE."
"THEN THE TOP TWO TEAMS WILL HAVE TO DUKE IT OUT FOR THE DESSERT COURSE. WE'LL ADD UP THE TOTAL POINTS AND DETERMINE THE WINNER OF COLOR WARS."
WHY DO THEY CALL YOU "DOC"?
MY DAD IS AN ARCHEOLOGY PROFESSOR AT THE UNIVERSITY. HE'S HENRY SENIOR, AND SINCE OUR LAST NAME IS JONES, I'M "DOC" JONES JUNIOR.
WELL IF YOU WIN, MAYBE YOU'LL BE KNOWN AS CHEF JONES.
THAT WOULD BE SWELL, INEZ. IF I WIN--
HEY YOU LOSERS...

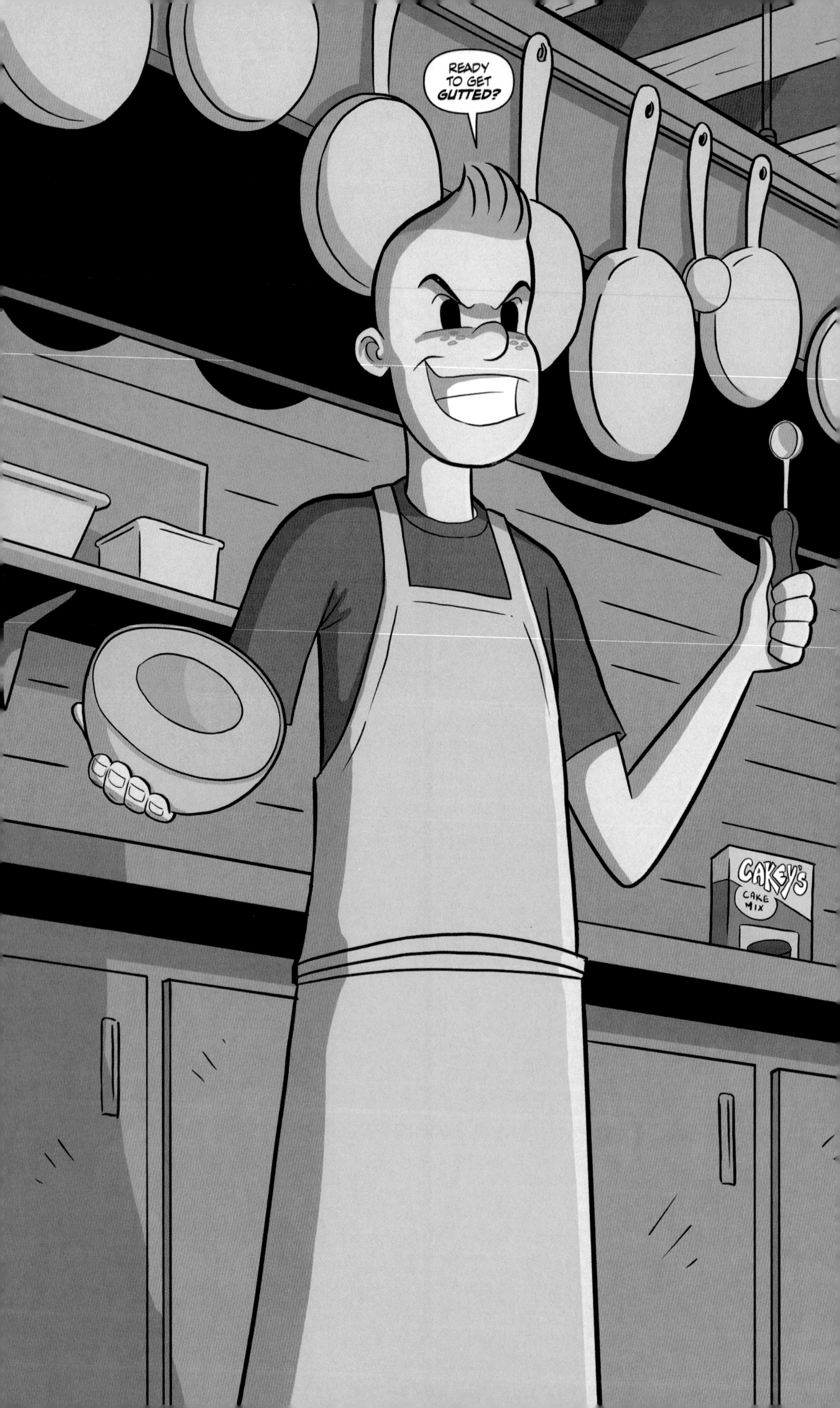
READY TO GET GUTTED?
CAKEY'S
CAKE MIX

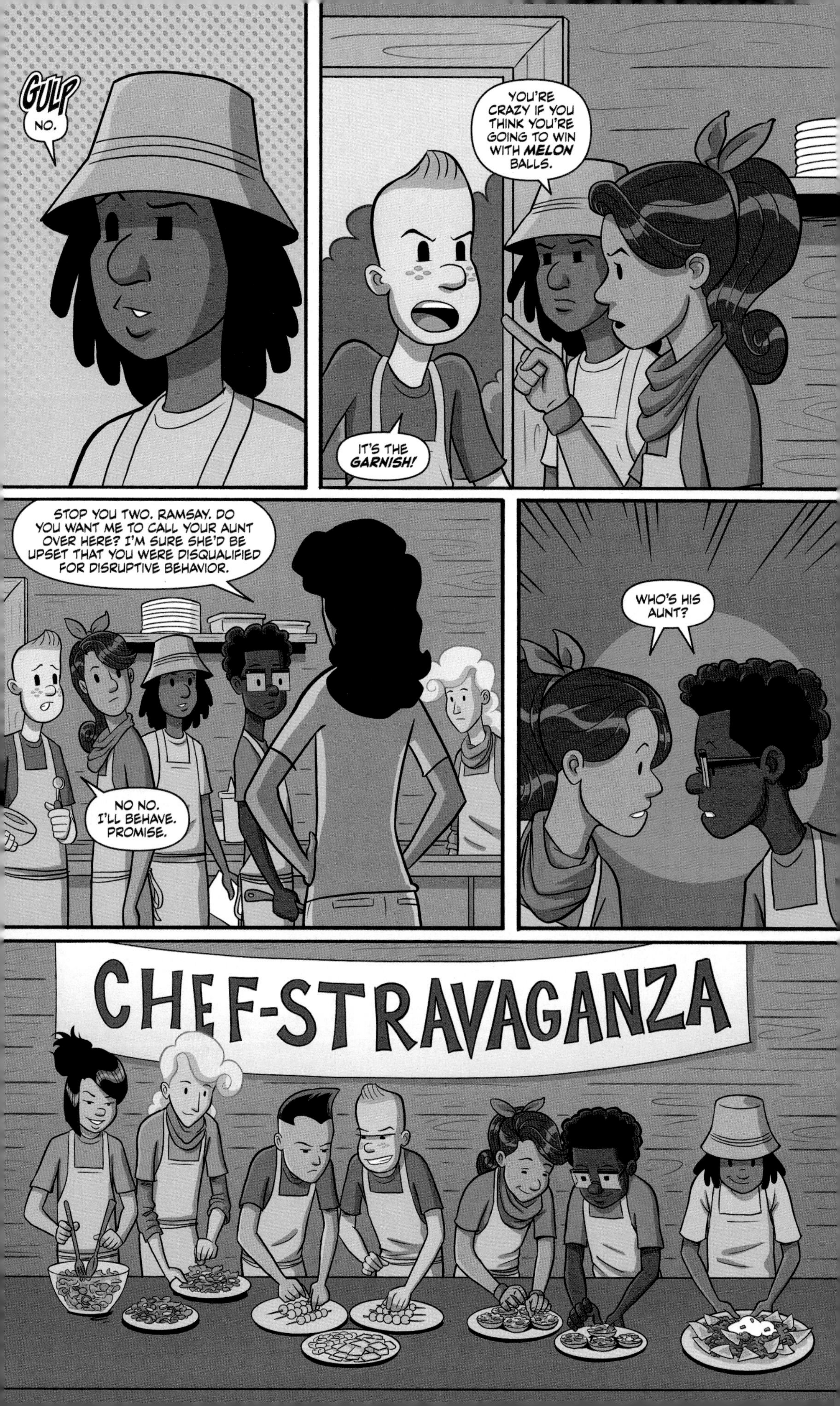

GULP
NO.
YOU'RE CRAZY IF YOU THINK YOU'RE GOING TO WIN WITH MELON BALLS.
IT'S THE GARNISH!
STOP YOU TWO. RAMSAY. DO YOU WANT ME TO CALL YOUR AUNT OVER HERE? I'M SURE SHE'D BE UPSET THAT YOU WERE DISQUALIFIED FOR DISRUPTIVE BEHAVIOR.
NO NO. I'LL BEHAVE. PROMISE.
WHO'S HIS AUNT?
CHEF-STRAVAGANZA

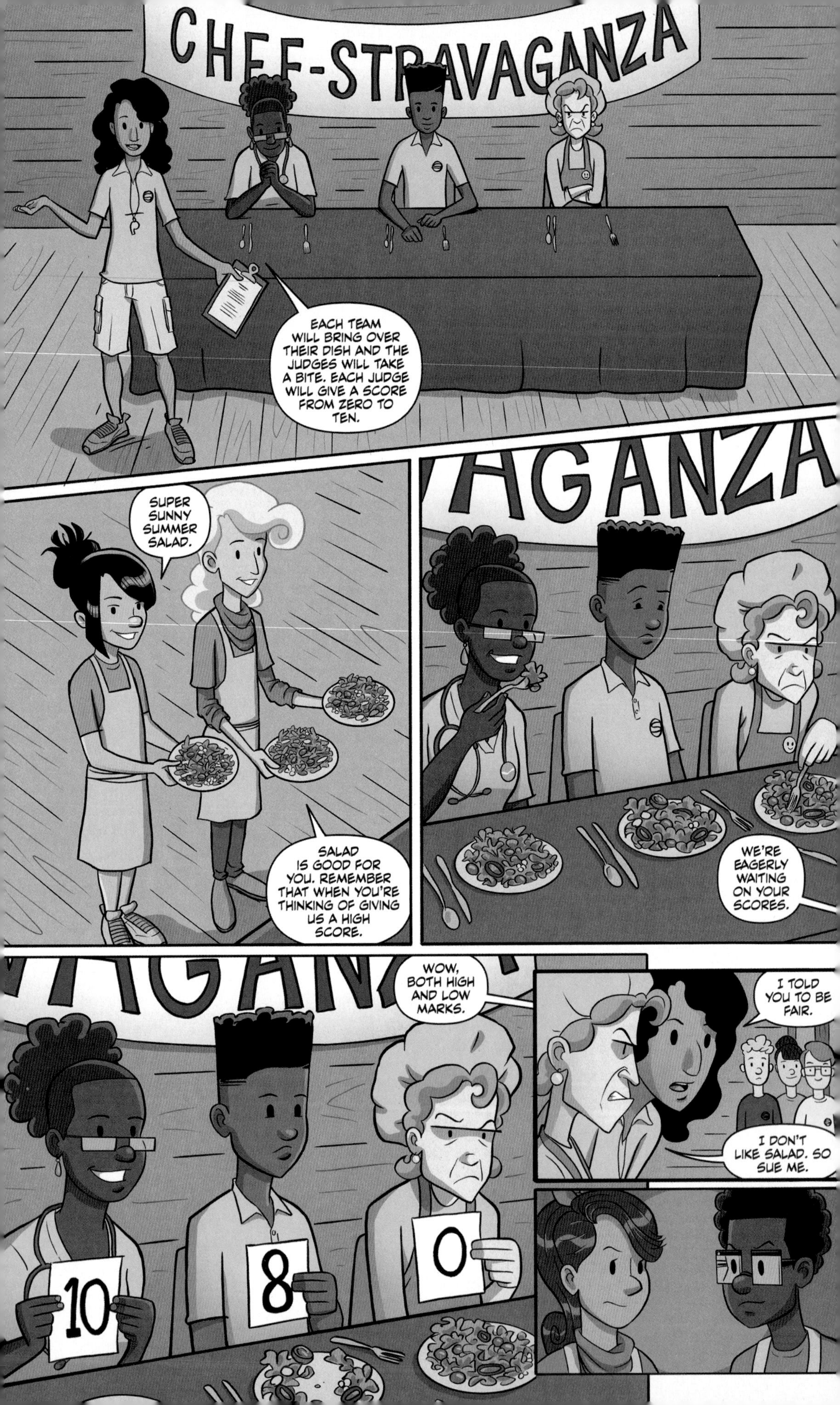
CHEF-STRAVAGANZA
EACH TEAM WILL BRING OVER THEIR DISH AND THE JUDGES WILL TAKE A BITE. EACH JUDGE WILL GIVE A SCORE FROM ZERO TO TEN.
SUPER SUNNY SUMMER SALAD.
SALAD IS GOOD FOR YOU. REMEMBER THAT WHEN YOU'RE THINKING OF GIVING US A HIGH SCORE.
AGANZA
WE'RE EAGERLY WAITING ON YOUR SCORES.
WOW, BOTH HIGH AND LOW MARKS.
10
8
0
I TOLD YOU TO BE FAIR.
I DON'T LIKE SALAD. SO SUE ME.

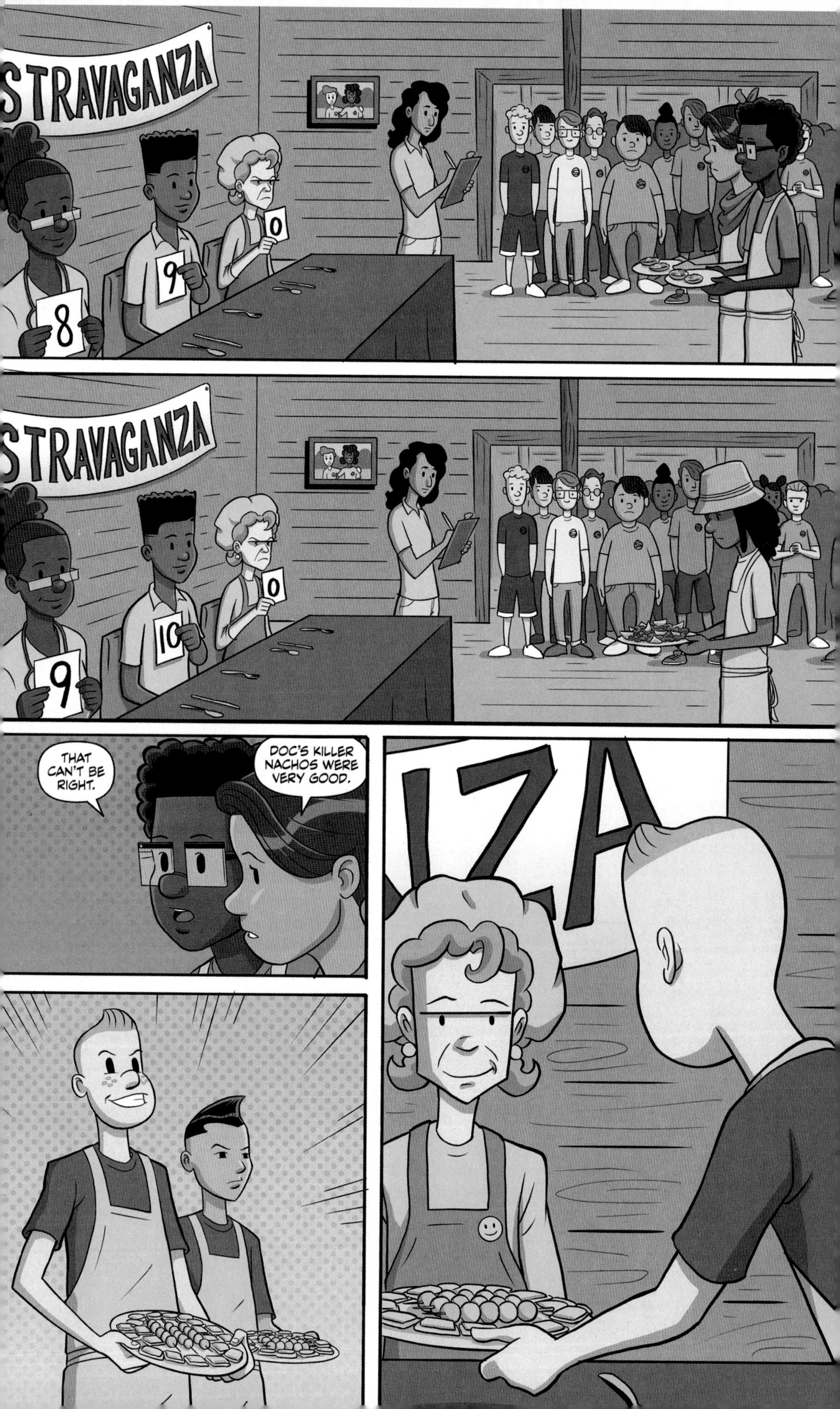
STRAVAGANZA
8
9
0
STRAVAGANZA
9
10
0
THAT CAN'T BE RIGHT.
DOC'S KILLER NACHOS WERE VERY GOOD.
ZA

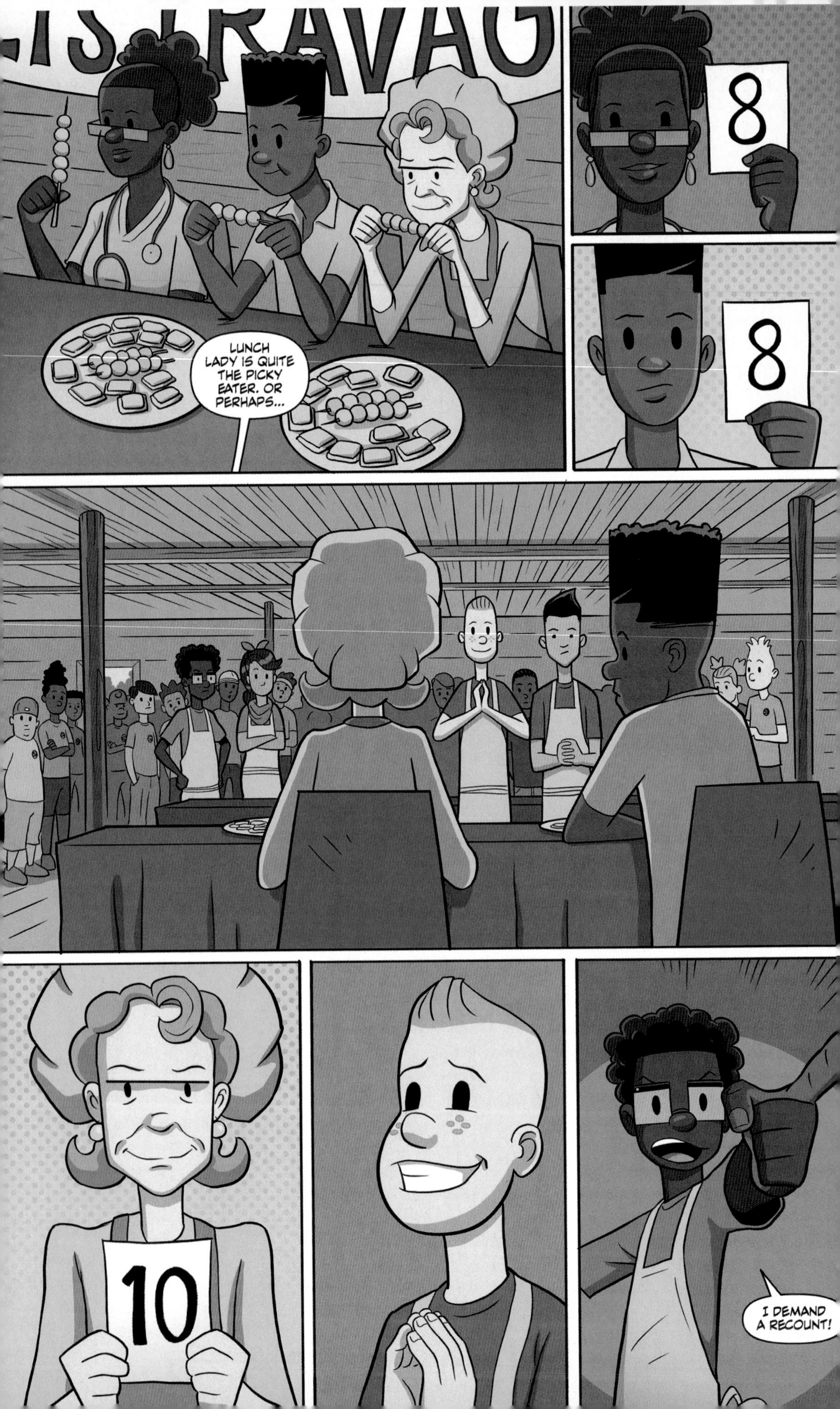

LUNCH LADY IS QUITE THE PICKY EATER. OR PERHAPS...
8
8
10
I DEMAND A RECOUNT!

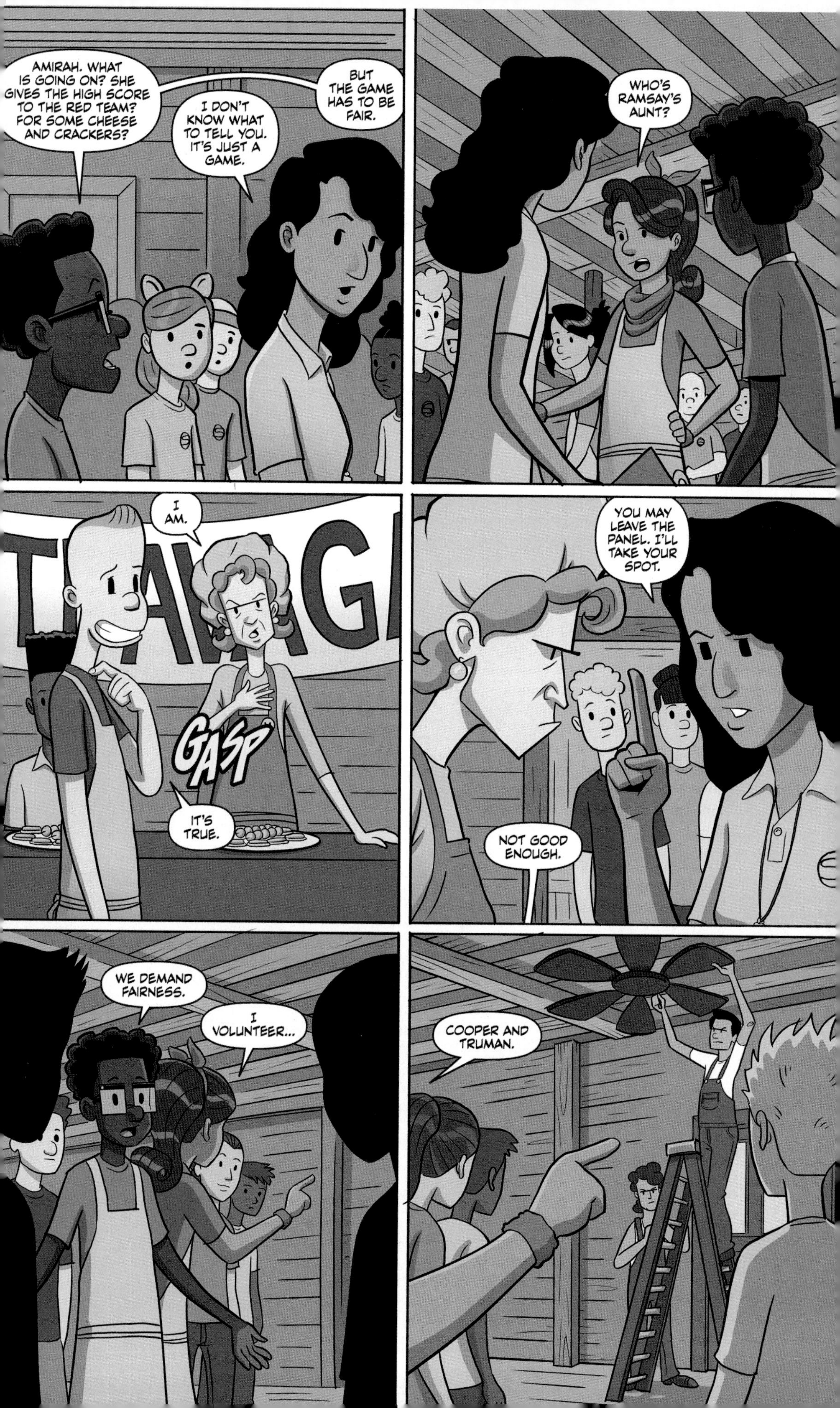

AMIRAH. WHAT IS GOING ON? SHE GIVES THE HIGH SCORE TO THE RED TEAM? FOR SOME CHEESE AND CRACKERS?
I DON'T KNOW WHAT TO TELL YOU. IT'S JUST A GAME.
BUT THE GAME HAS TO BE FAIR.
WHO'S RAMSAY'S AUNT?
I AM.
GASP
IT'S TRUE.
YOU MAY LEAVE THE PANEL. I'LL TAKE YOUR SPOT.
NOT GOOD ENOUGH.
WE DEMAND FAIRNESS.
I VOLUNTEER...
COOPER AND TRUMAN.

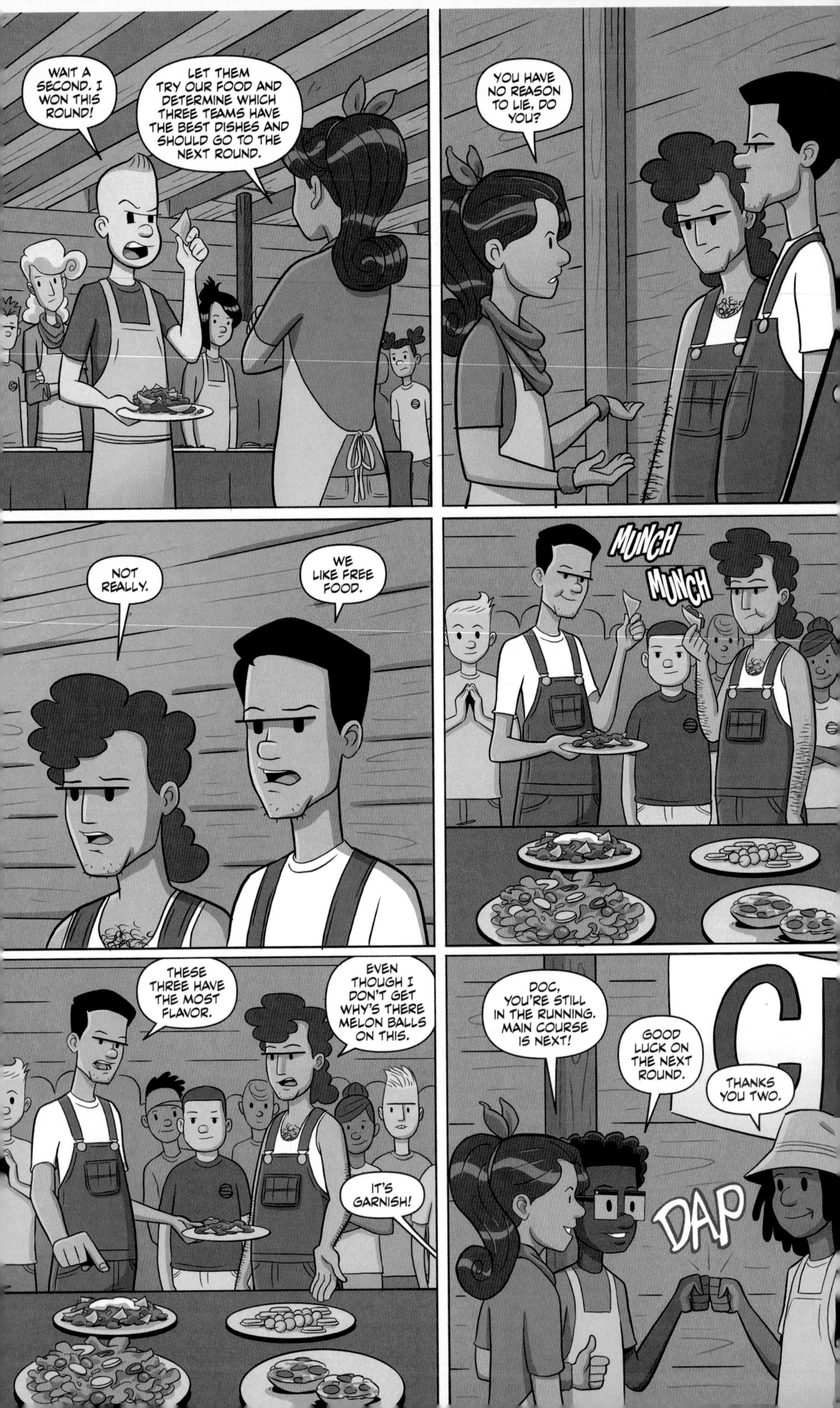
WAIT A SECOND. I WON THIS ROUND!
LET THEM TRY OUR FOOD AND DETERMINE WHICH THREE TEAMS HAVE THE BEST DISHES AND SHOULD GO TO THE NEXT ROUND.
YOU HAVE NO REASON TO LIE, DO YOU?
NOT REALLY.
WE LIKE FREE FOOD.
MUNCH
MUNCH
THESE THREE HAVE THE MOST FLAVOR.
EVEN THOUGH I DON'T GET WHY'S THERE MELON BALLS ON THIS.
IT'S GARNISH!
DOC, YOU'RE STILL IN THE RUNNING. MAIN COURSE IS NEXT!
GOOD LUCK ON THE NEXT ROUND.
THANKS YOU TWO.
DAP

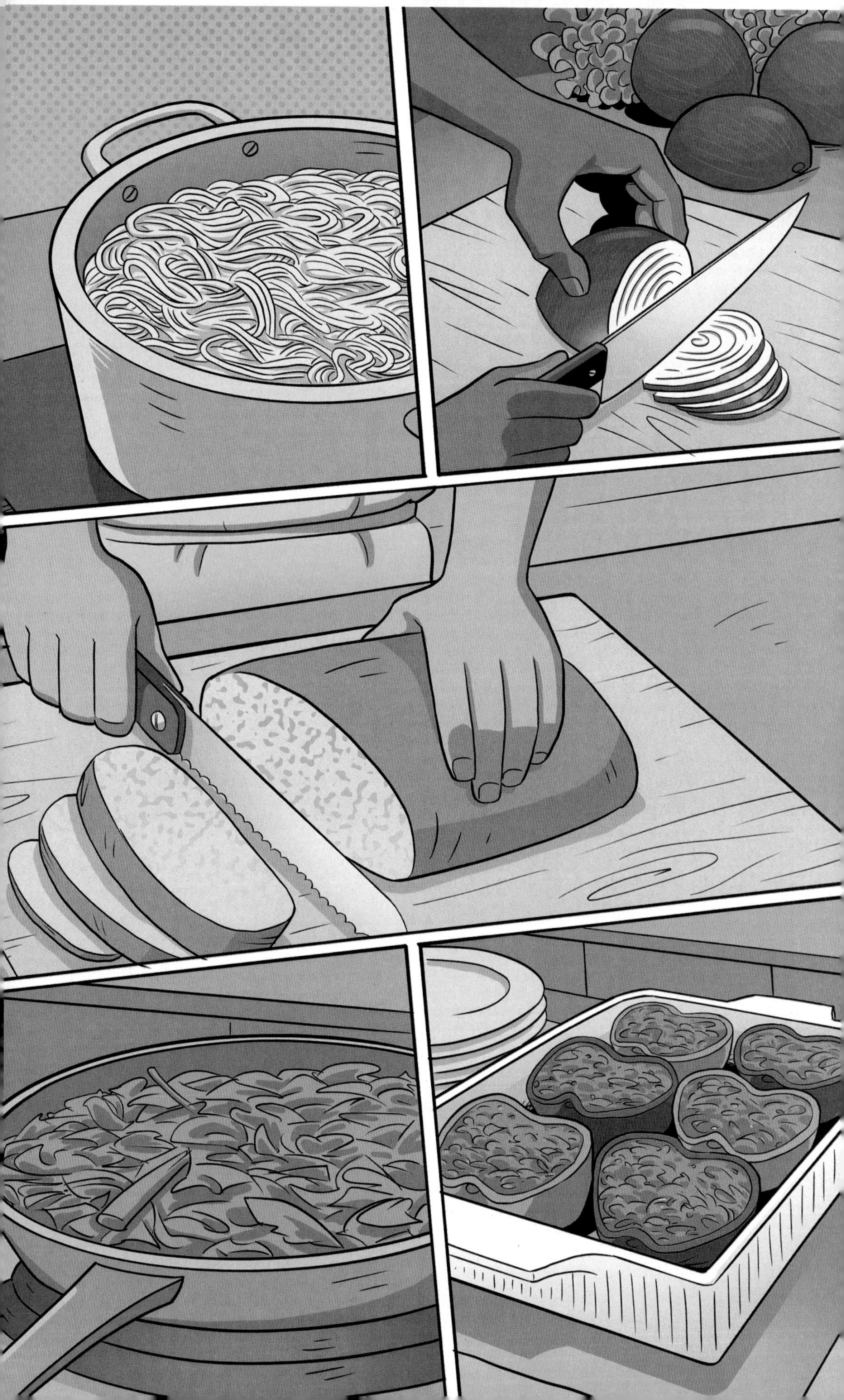

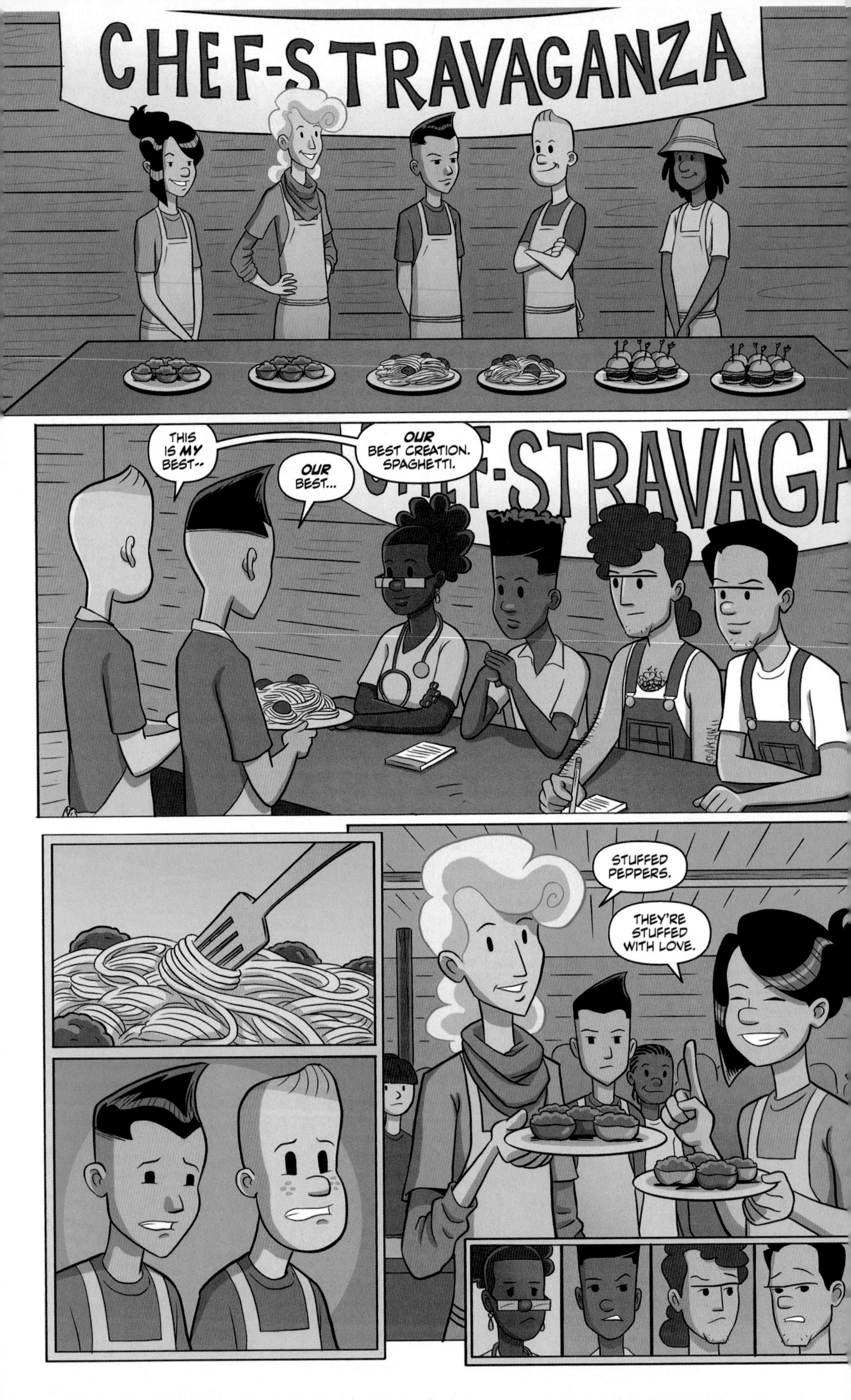
CHEF-STRAVAGANZA
THIS IS MY BEST--
OUR BEST...
OUR BEST CREATION. SPAGHETTI.
CHEF-STRAVAGA
STUFFED PEPPERS.
THEY'RE STUFFED WITH LOVE.

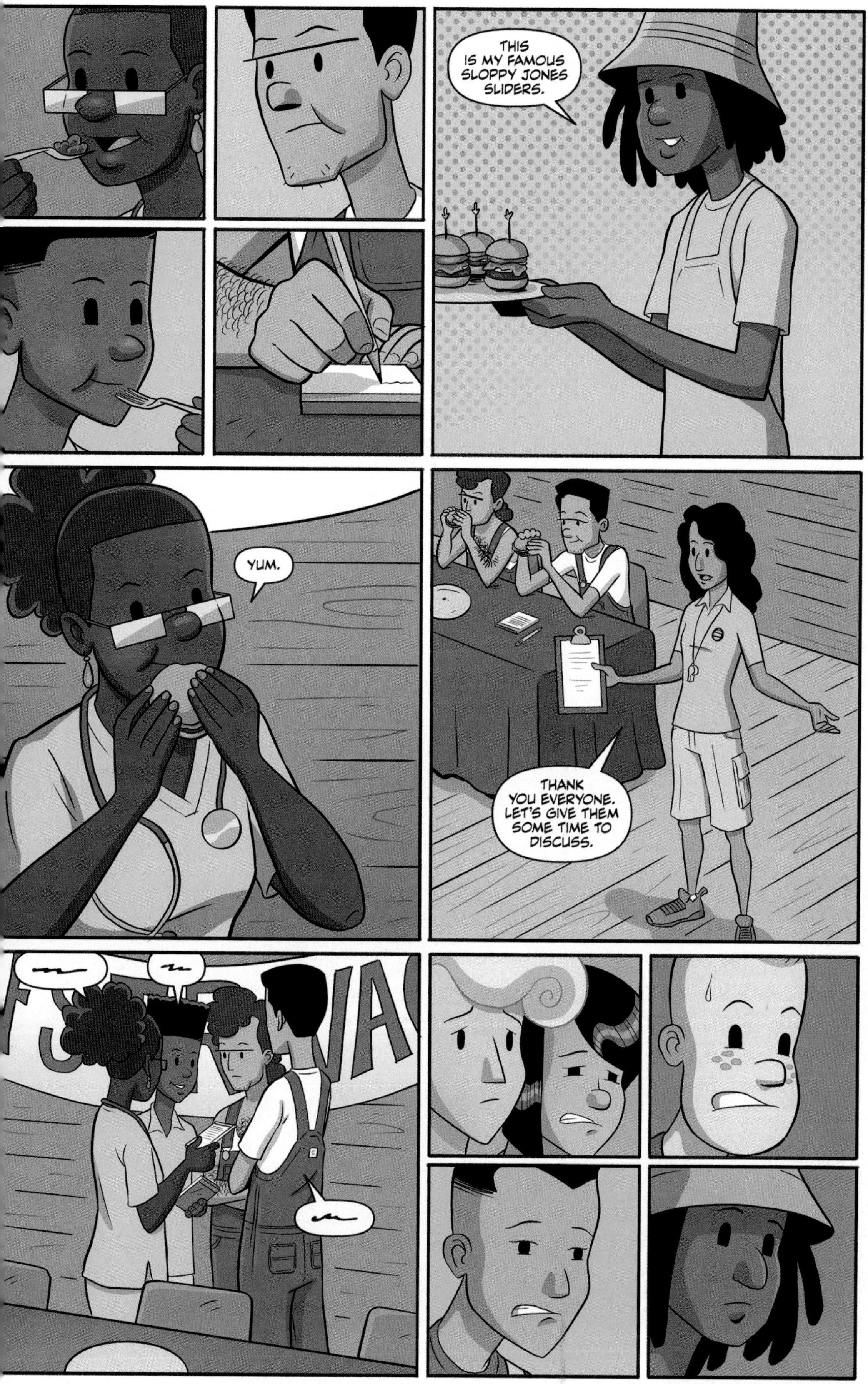
THIS IS MY FAMOUS SLOPPY JONES SLIDERS.
YUM.
THANK YOU EVERYONE. LET'S GIVE THEM SOME TIME TO DISCUSS.

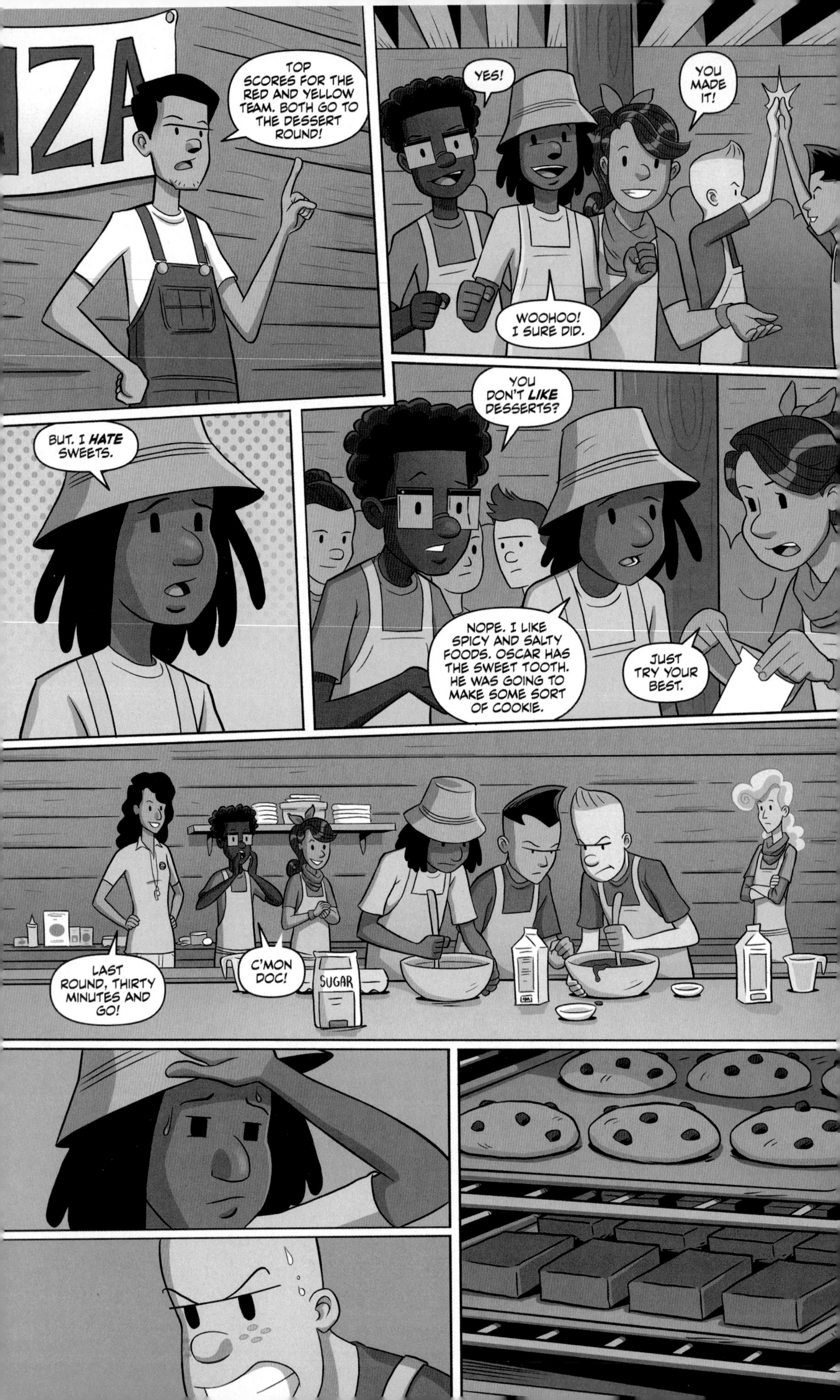

IZA
TOP SCORES FOR THE RED AND YELLOW TEAM. BOTH GO TO THE DESSERT ROUND!
YES!
YOU MADE IT!
WOOHOO! I SURE DID.
BUT. I HATE SWEETS.
YOU DON'T LIKE DESSERTS?
NOPE. I LIKE SPICY AND SALTY FOODS. OSCAR HAS THE SWEET TOOTH. HE WAS GOING TO MAKE SOME SORT OF COOKIE.
JUST TRY YOUR BEST.
LAST ROUND, THIRTY MINUTES AND GO!
C'MON DOC!
SUGAR

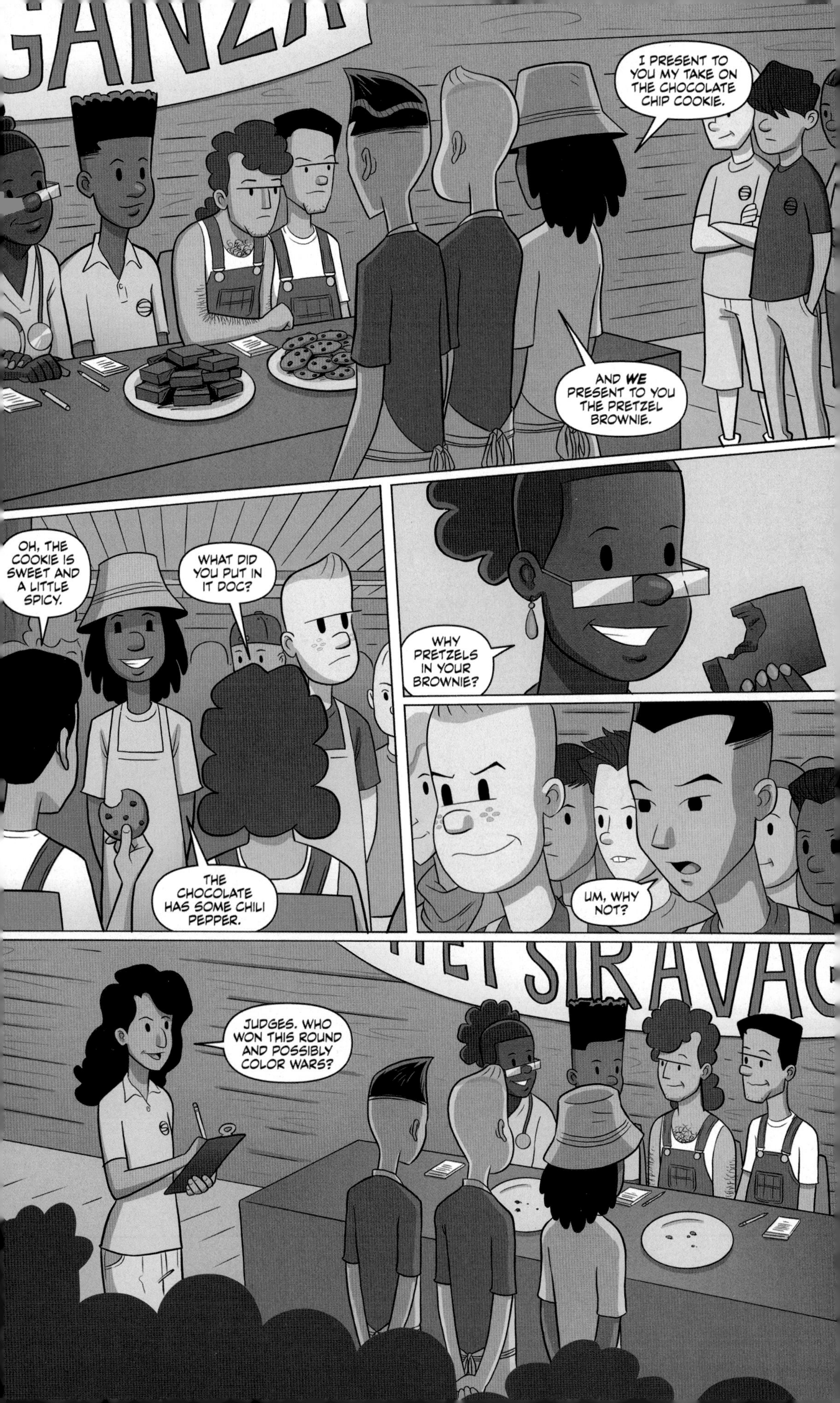
GANZA
I PRESENT TO YOU MY TAKE ON THE CHOCOLATE CHIP COOKIE.
AND WE PRESENT TO YOU THE PRETZEL BROWNIE.
OH, THE COOKIE IS SWEET AND A LITTLE SPICY.
WHAT DID YOU PUT IN IT DOC?
THE CHOCOLATE HAS SOME CHILI PEPPER.
WHY PRETZELS IN YOUR BROWNIE?
UM, WHY NOT?
JUDGES. WHO WON THIS ROUND AND POSSIBLY COLOR WARS?

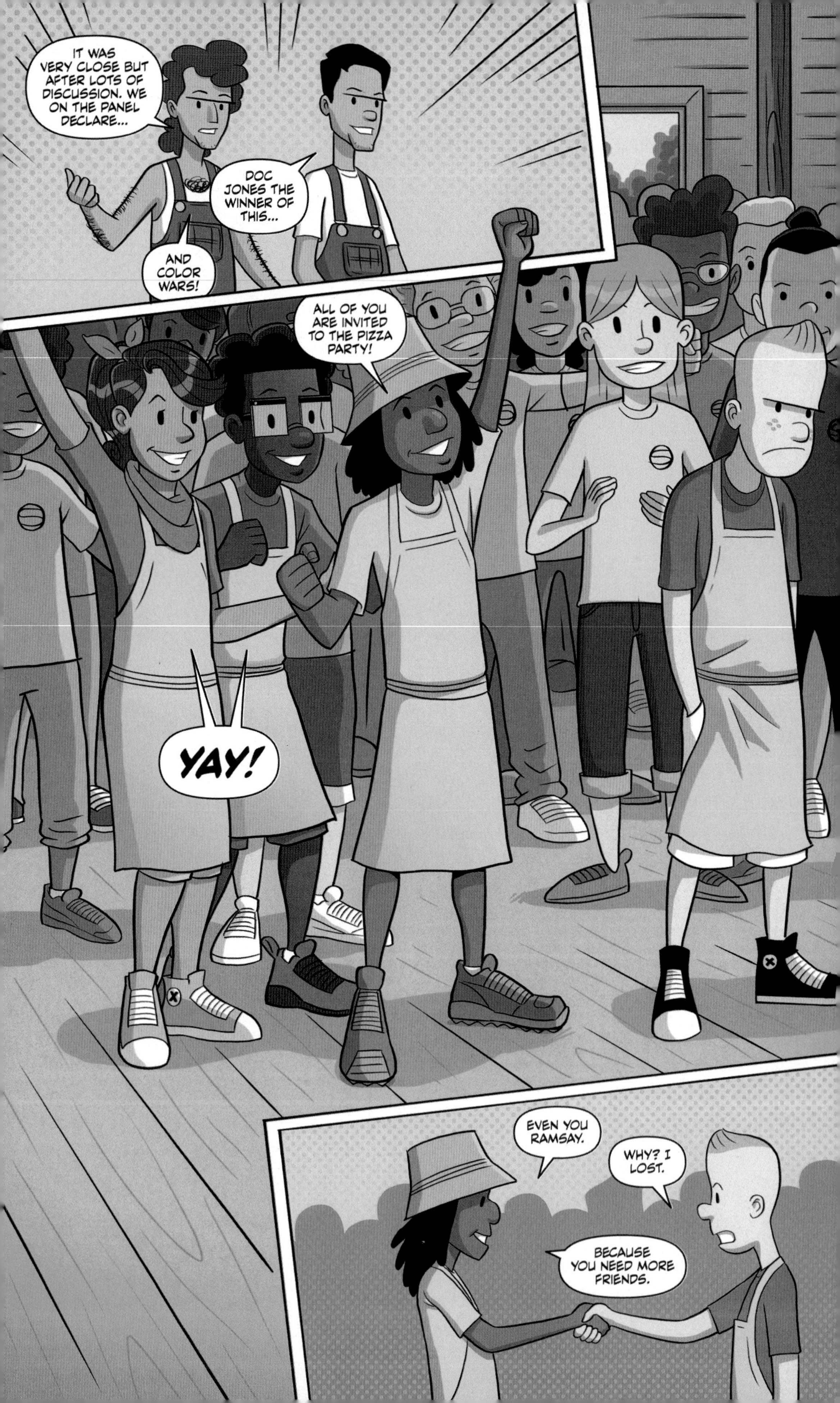
IT WAS VERY CLOSE BUT AFTER LOTS OF DISCUSSION. WE ON THE PANEL DECLARE...
DOC JONES THE WINNER OF THIS...
AND COLOR WARS!
ALL OF YOU ARE INVITED TO THE PIZZA PARTY!
YAY!
EVEN YOU RAMSAY.
WHY? I LOST.
BECAUSE YOU NEED MORE FRIENDS.

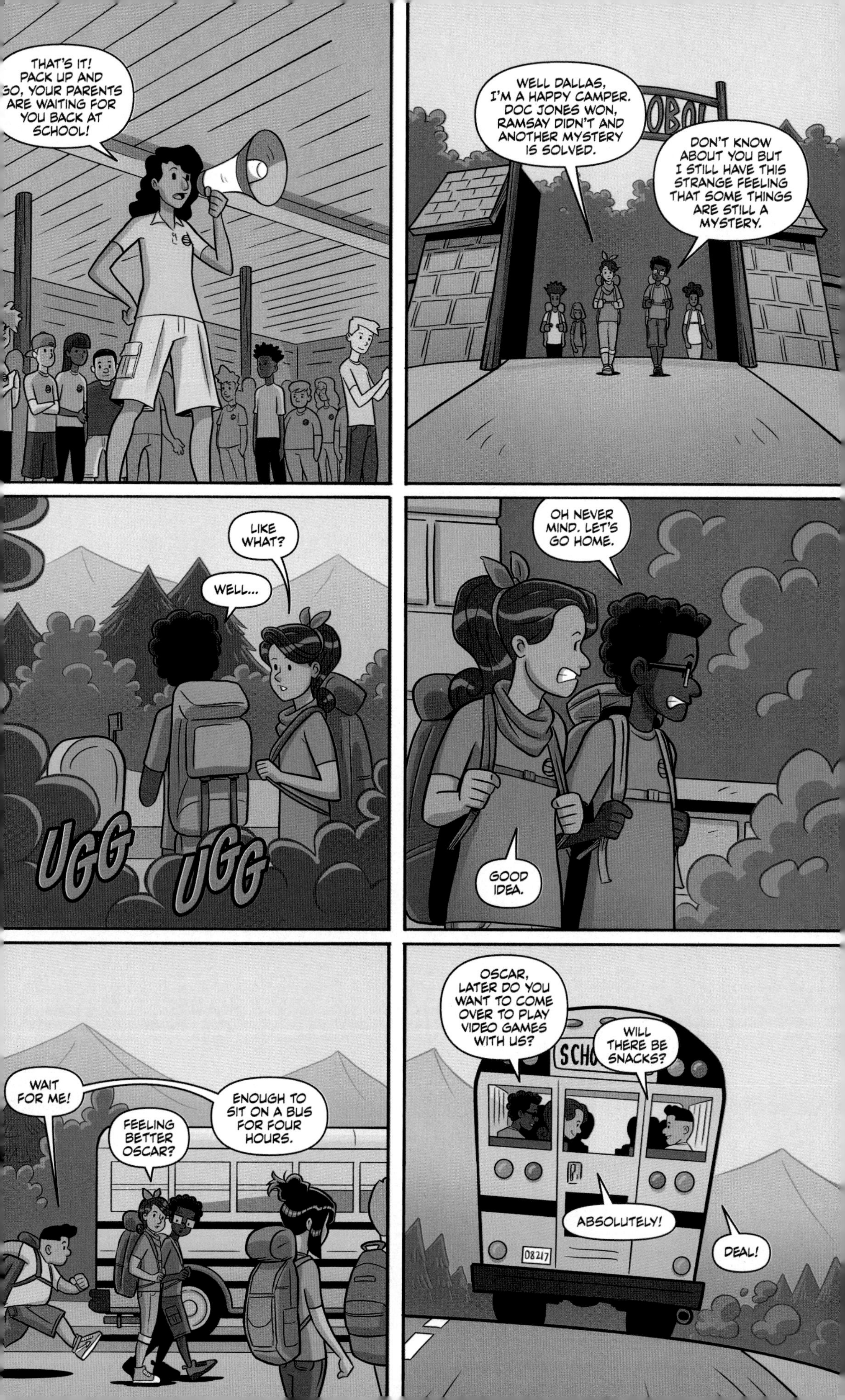

THAT'S IT! PACK UP AND GO, YOUR PARENTS ARE WAITING FOR YOU BACK AT SCHOOL!
WELL DALLAS, I'M A HAPPY CAMPER. DOC JONES WON, RAMSAY DIDN'T AND ANOTHER MYSTERY IS SOLVED.
DON'T KNOW ABOUT YOU BUT I STILL HAVE THIS STRANGE FEELING THAT SOME THINGS ARE STILL A MYSTERY.
LIKE WHAT?
WELL...
UGG
UGG
OH NEVER MIND. LET'S GO HOME.
GOOD IDEA.
WAIT FOR ME!
FEELING BETTER OSCAR?
ENOUGH TO SIT ON A BUS FOR FOUR HOURS.
OSCAR, LATER DO YOU WANT TO COME OVER TO PLAY VIDEO GAMES WITH US?
WILL THERE BE SNACKS?
ABSOLUTELY!
DEAL!

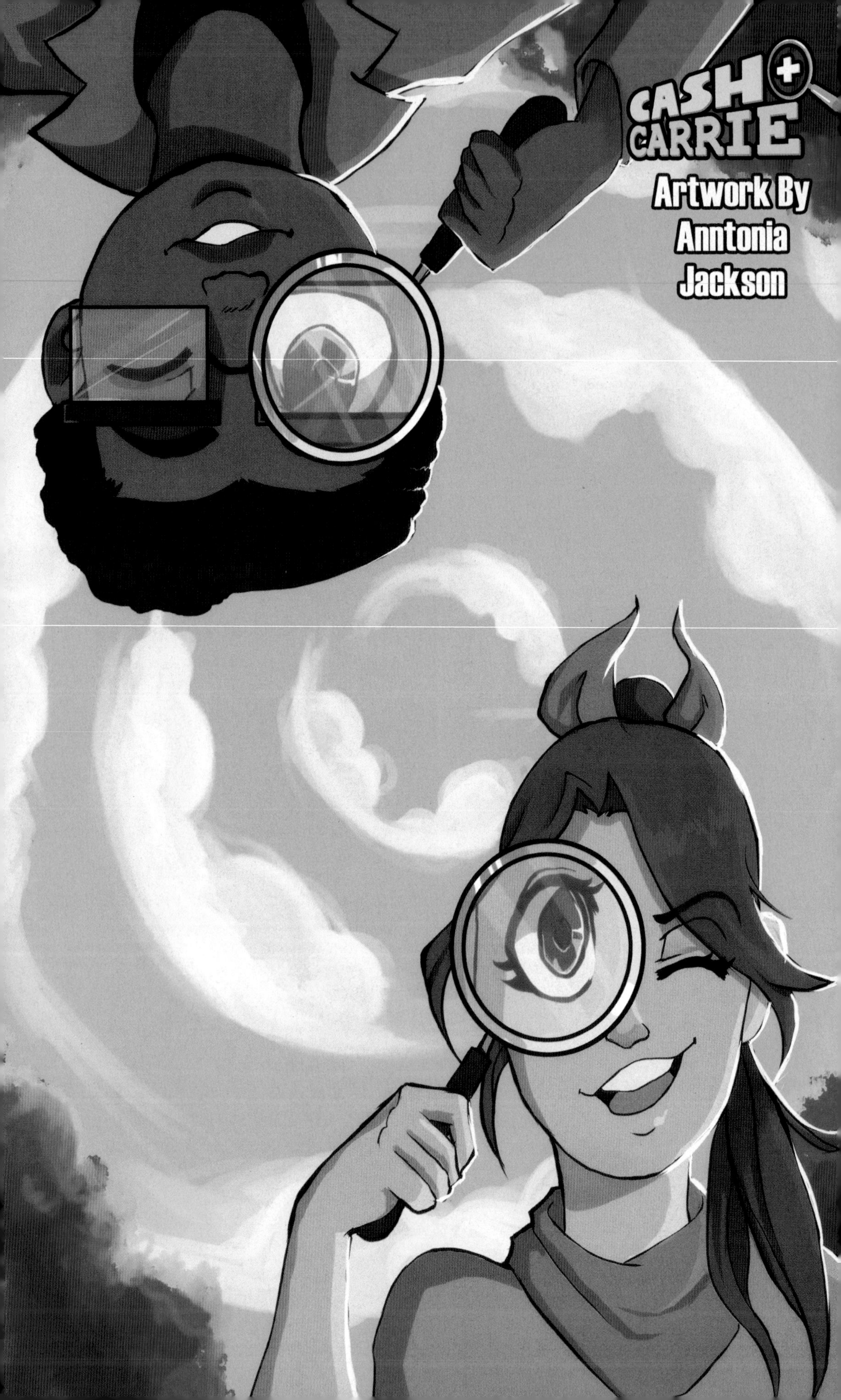
CASH + CARRIE
Artwork By
Anntonia
Jackson

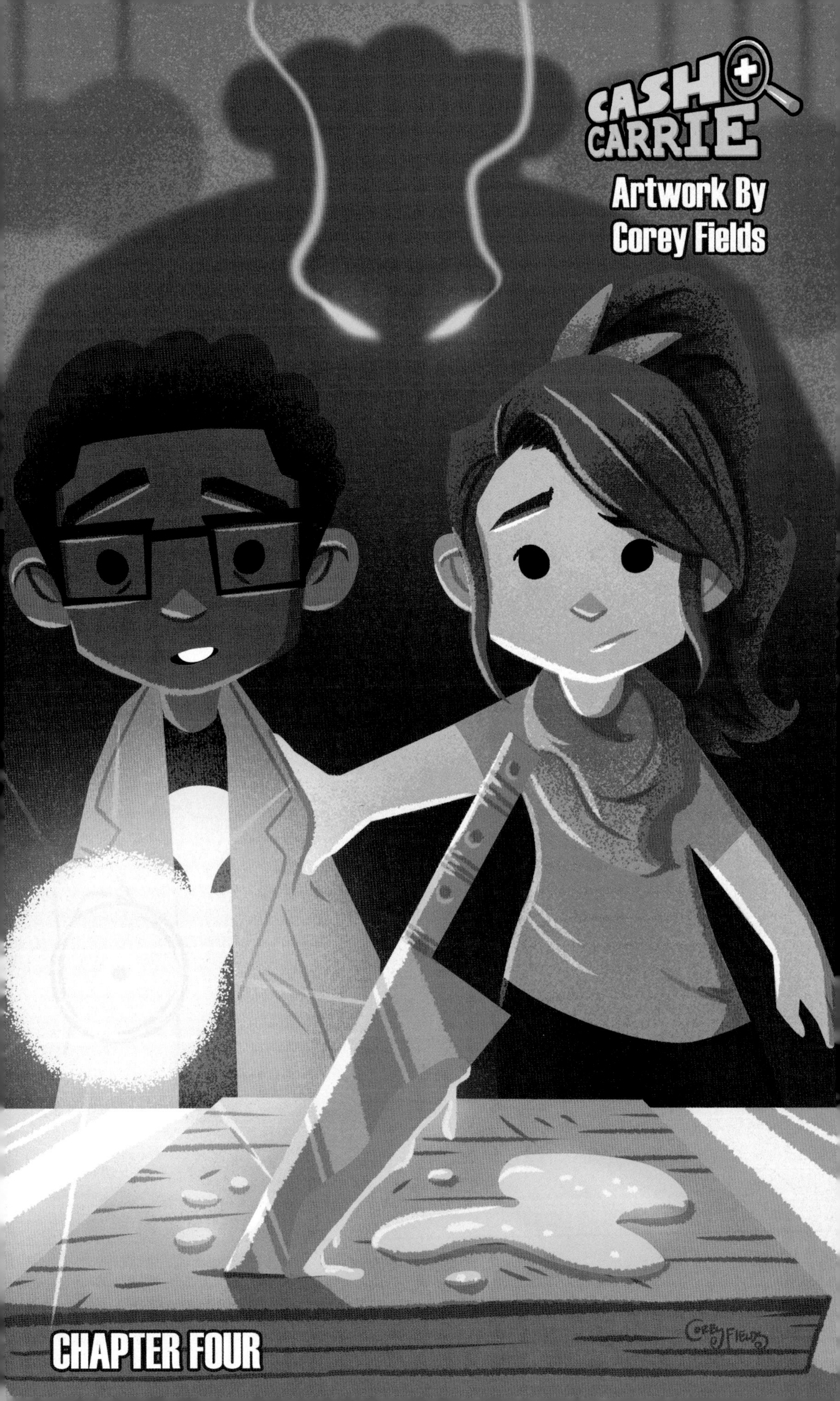
CASH + CARRIE
Artwork By
Corey Fields
COREY FIELDS
CHAPTER FOUR

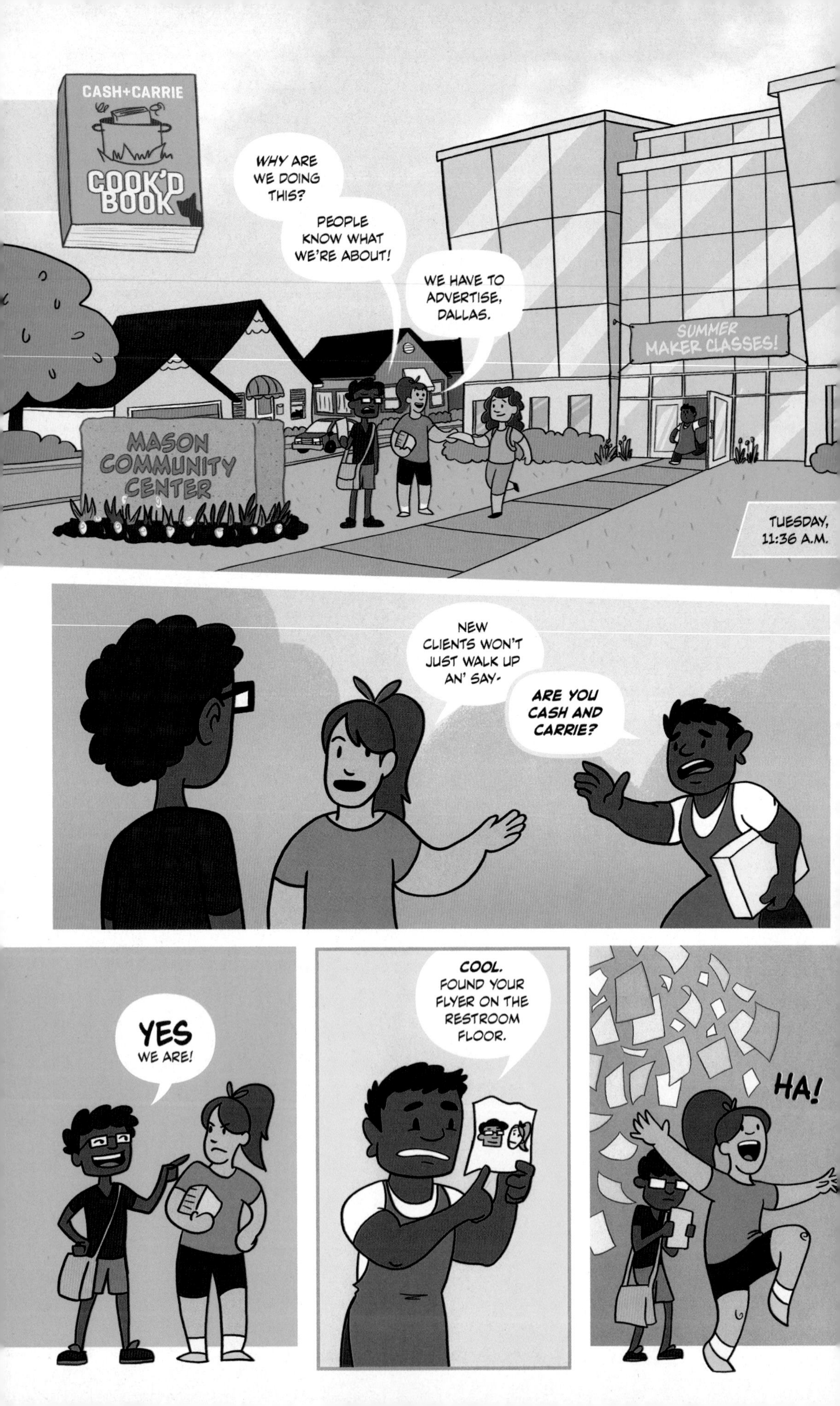

CASH+CARRIE
COOK'D BOOK
WHY ARE WE DOING THIS?
PEOPLE KNOW WHAT WE'RE ABOUT!
WE HAVE TO ADVERTISE, DALLAS.
SUMMER MAKER CLASSES!
MASON COMMUNITY CENTER
TUESDAY, 11:36 A.M.
NEW CLIENTS WON'T JUST WALK UP AN' SAY-
ARE YOU CASH AND CARRIE?
YES WE ARE!
COOL. FOUND YOUR FLYER ON THE RESTROOM FLOOR.
HA!

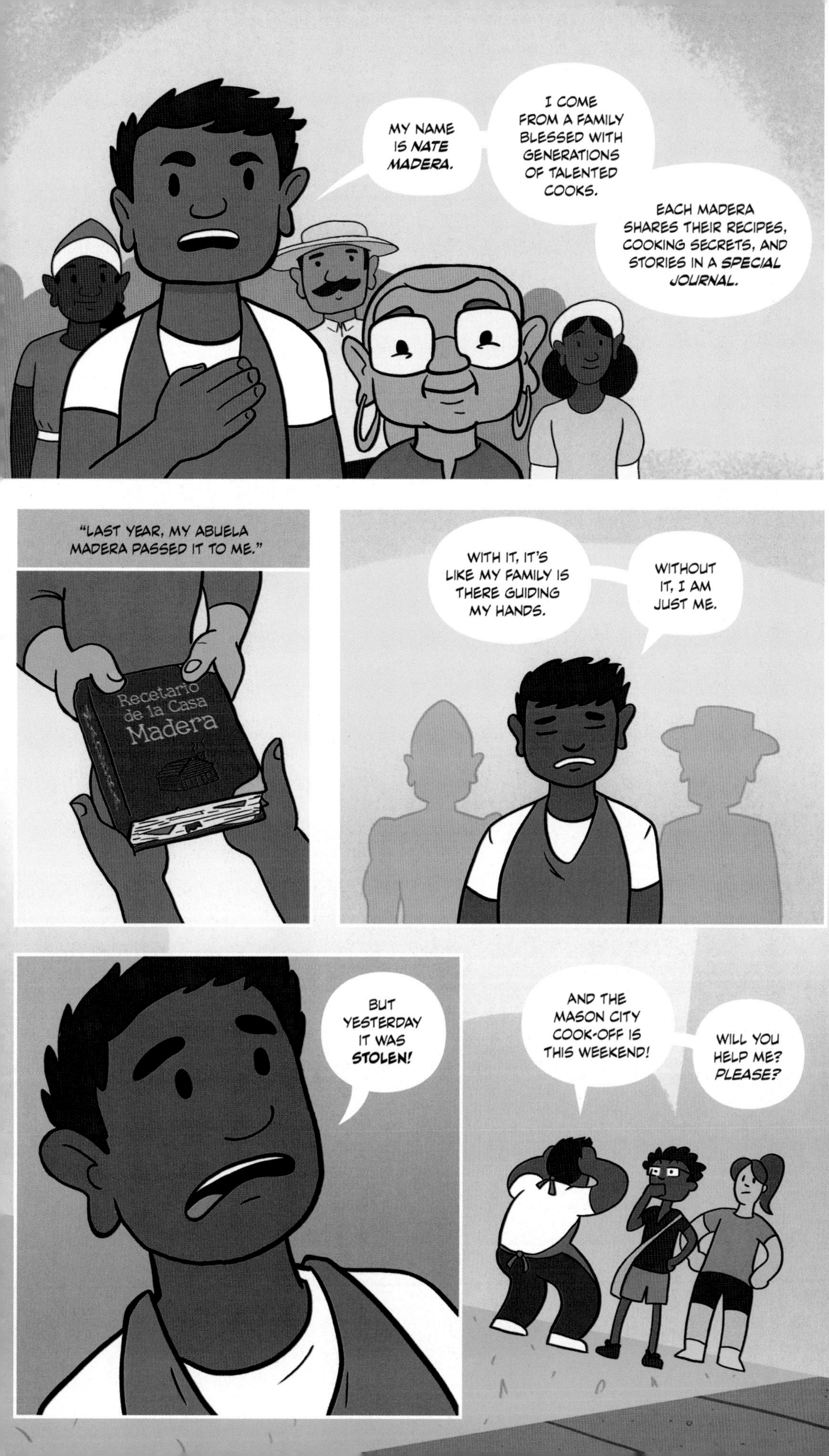
MY NAME IS *NATE MADERA.*
I COME FROM A FAMILY BLESSED WITH GENERATIONS OF TALENTED COOKS.
EACH MADERA SHARES THEIR RECIPES, COOKING SECRETS, AND STORIES IN A *SPECIAL JOURNAL.*
"LAST YEAR, MY ABUELA MADERA PASSED IT TO ME."
Recetario de la Casa Madera
WITH IT, IT'S LIKE MY FAMILY IS THERE GUIDING MY HANDS.
WITHOUT IT, I AM JUST ME.
BUT YESTERDAY IT WAS **STOLEN!**
AND THE MASON CITY COOK-OFF IS THIS WEEKEND!
WILL YOU HELP ME? *PLEASE?*

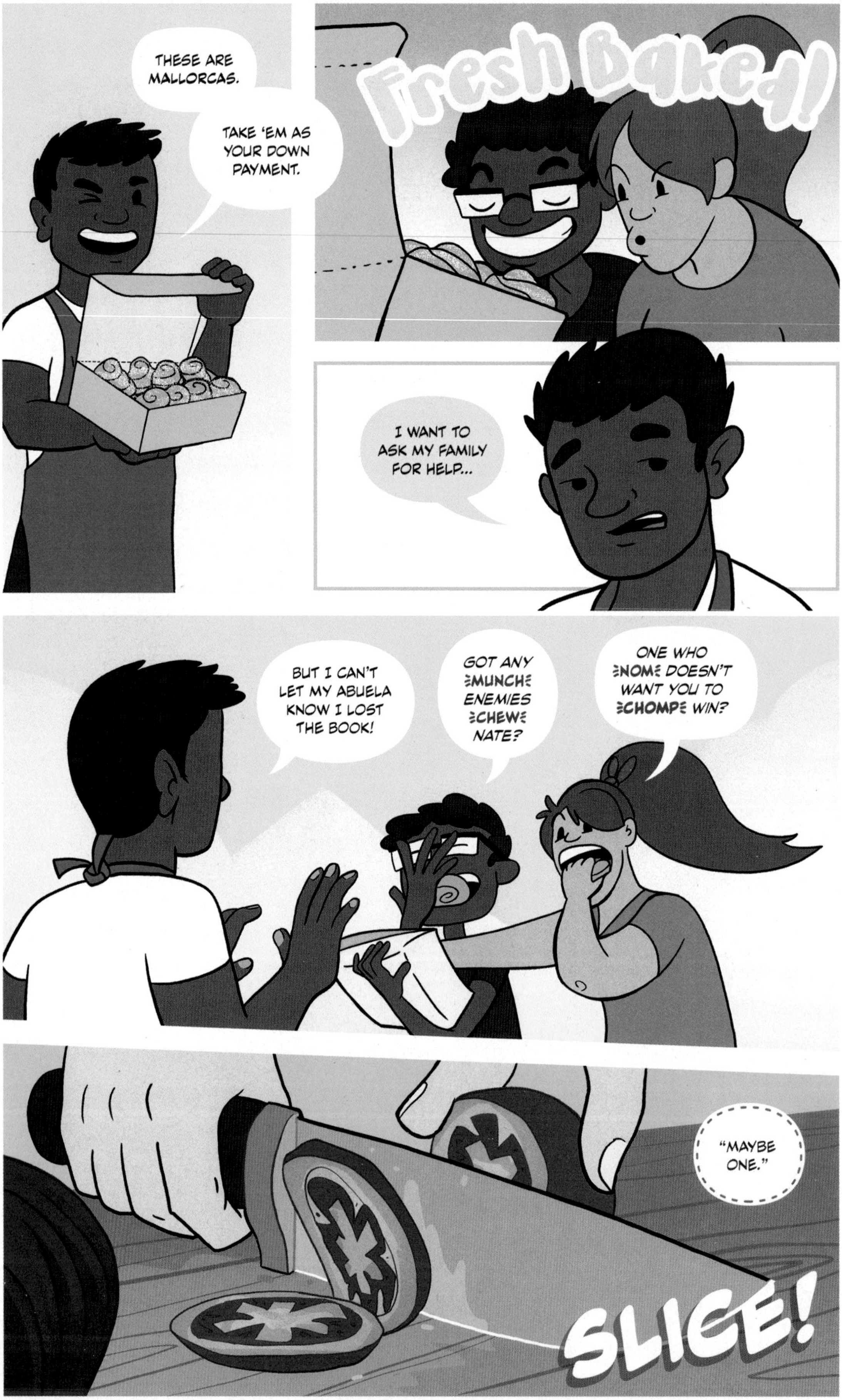
THESE ARE MALLORCAS.
TAKE 'EM AS YOUR DOWN PAYMENT.
Fresh Baked!
I WANT TO ASK MY FAMILY FOR HELP...
BUT I CAN'T LET MY ABUELA KNOW I LOST THE BOOK!
GOT ANY MUNCH ENEMIES CHEW NATE?
ONE WHO NOM DOESN'T WANT YOU TO CHOMP WIN?
"MAYBE ONE."
SLICE!

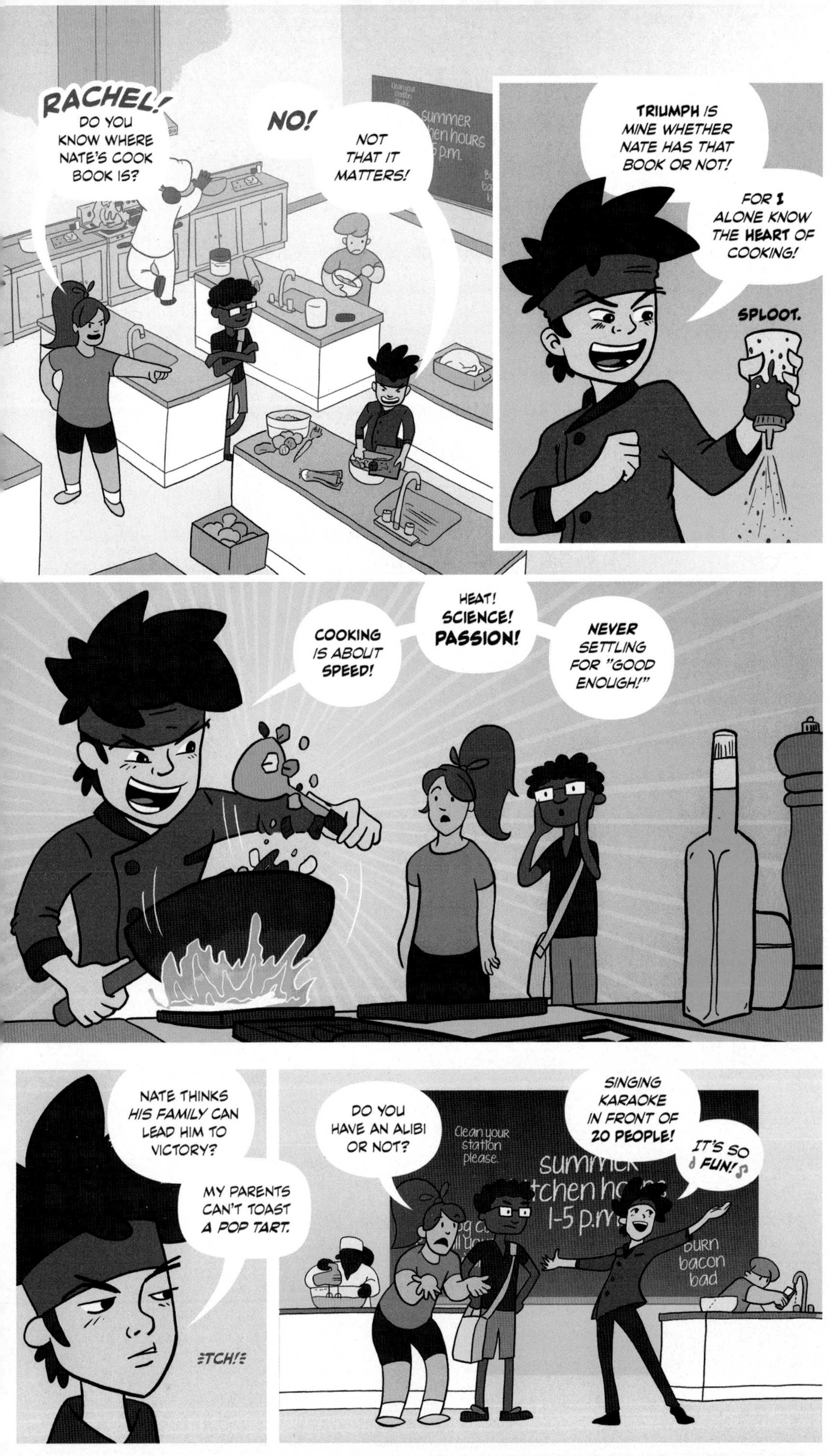
RACHEL!
DO YOU KNOW WHERE NATE'S COOK BOOK IS?
NO!
NOT THAT IT MATTERS!
Clean your station please.
summer kitchen hours 1-5 p.m.
TRIUMPH IS MINE WHETHER NATE HAS THAT BOOK OR NOT!
FOR I ALONE KNOW THE HEART OF COOKING!
SPLOOT.
COOKING IS ABOUT SPEED!
HEAT! SCIENCE! PASSION!
NEVER SETTLING FOR "GOOD ENOUGH!"
NATE THINKS HIS FAMILY CAN LEAD HIM TO VICTORY?
MY PARENTS CAN'T TOAST A POP TART.
TCH!
DO YOU HAVE AN ALIBI OR NOT?
Clean your station please.
SINGING KARAOKE IN FRONT OF 20 PEOPLE!
IT'S SO FUN!
burn bacon bad

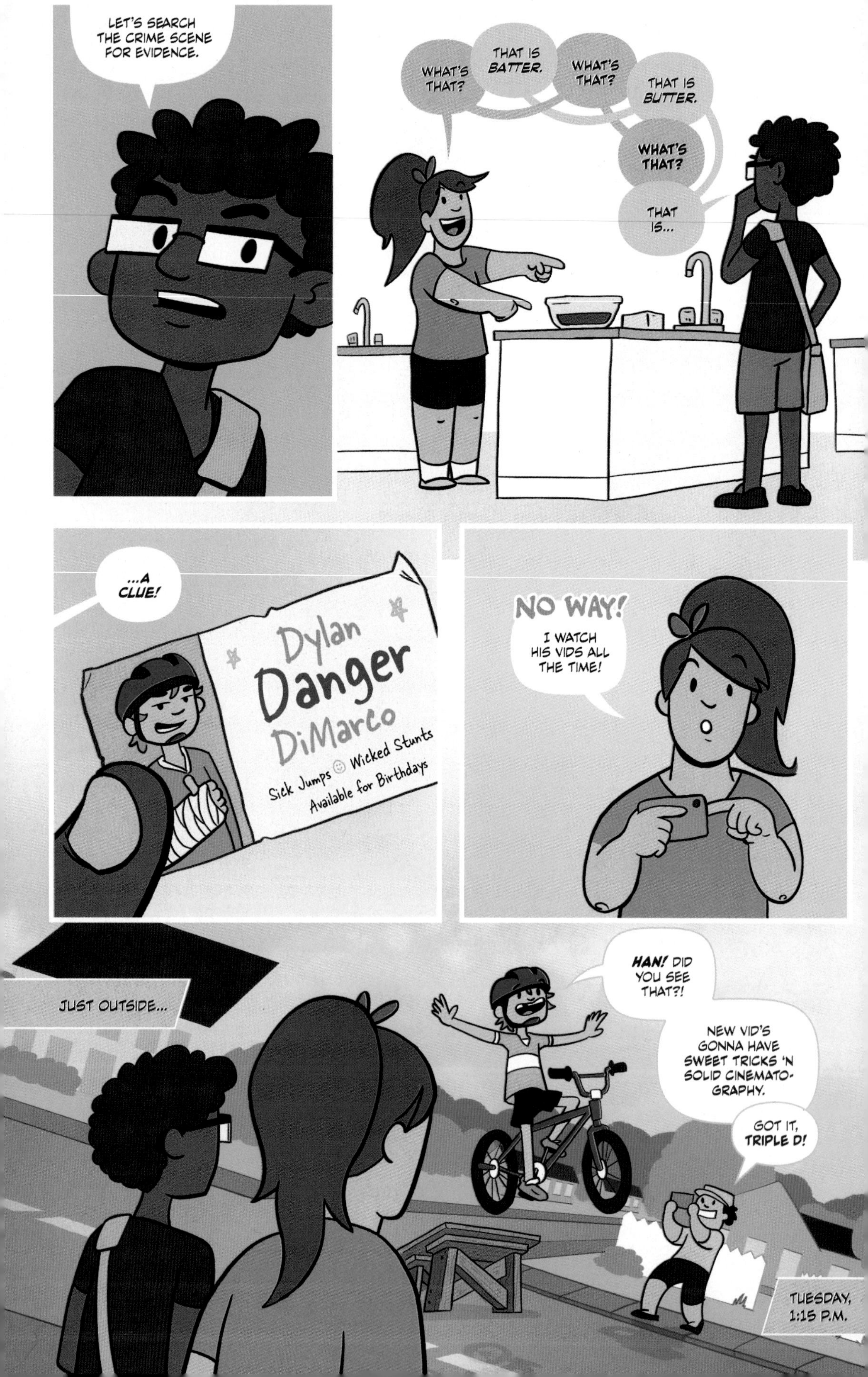

LET'S SEARCH THE CRIME SCENE FOR EVIDENCE.
WHAT'S THAT?
THAT IS BATTER.
WHAT'S THAT?
THAT IS BUTTER.
WHAT'S THAT?
THAT IS...
...A CLUE!
Dylan Danger DiMarco
Sick Jumps ☺ Wicked Stunts
Available for Birthdays
NO WAY!
I WATCH HIS VIDS ALL THE TIME!
JUST OUTSIDE...
HAN! DID YOU SEE THAT?!
NEW VID'S GONNA HAVE SWEET TRICKS 'N SOLID CINEMATO-GRAPHY.
GOT IT, TRIPLE D!
TUESDAY, 1:15 P.M.

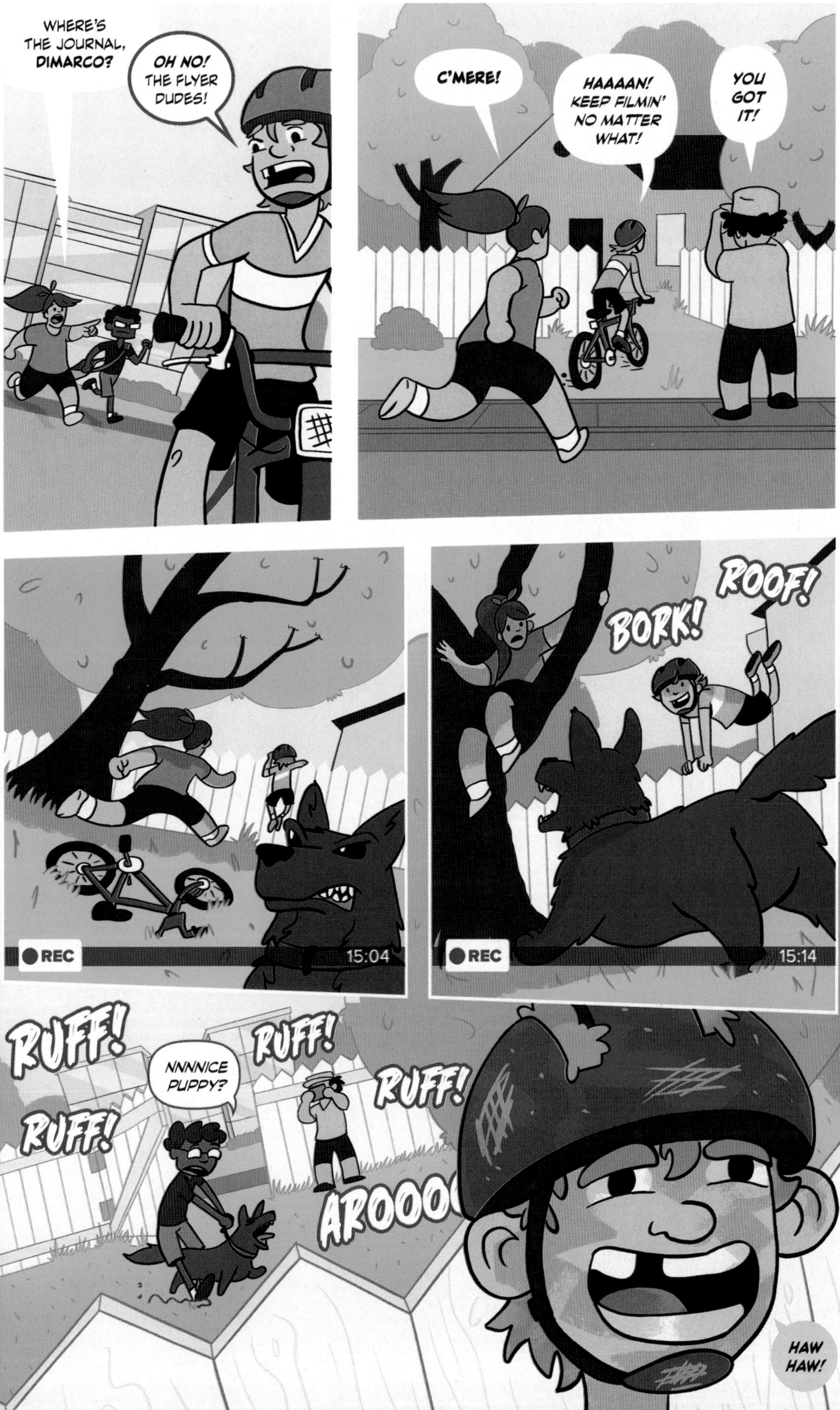
WHERE'S THE JOURNAL, DIMARCO?
OH NO! THE FLYER DUDES!
C'MERE!
HAAAAN! KEEP FILMIN' NO MATTER WHAT!
YOU GOT IT!
REC
15:04
BORK!
ROOF!
REC
15:14
RUFF!
RUFF!
NNNNICE PUPPY?
RUFF!
RUFF!
AROOOO
HAW HAW!

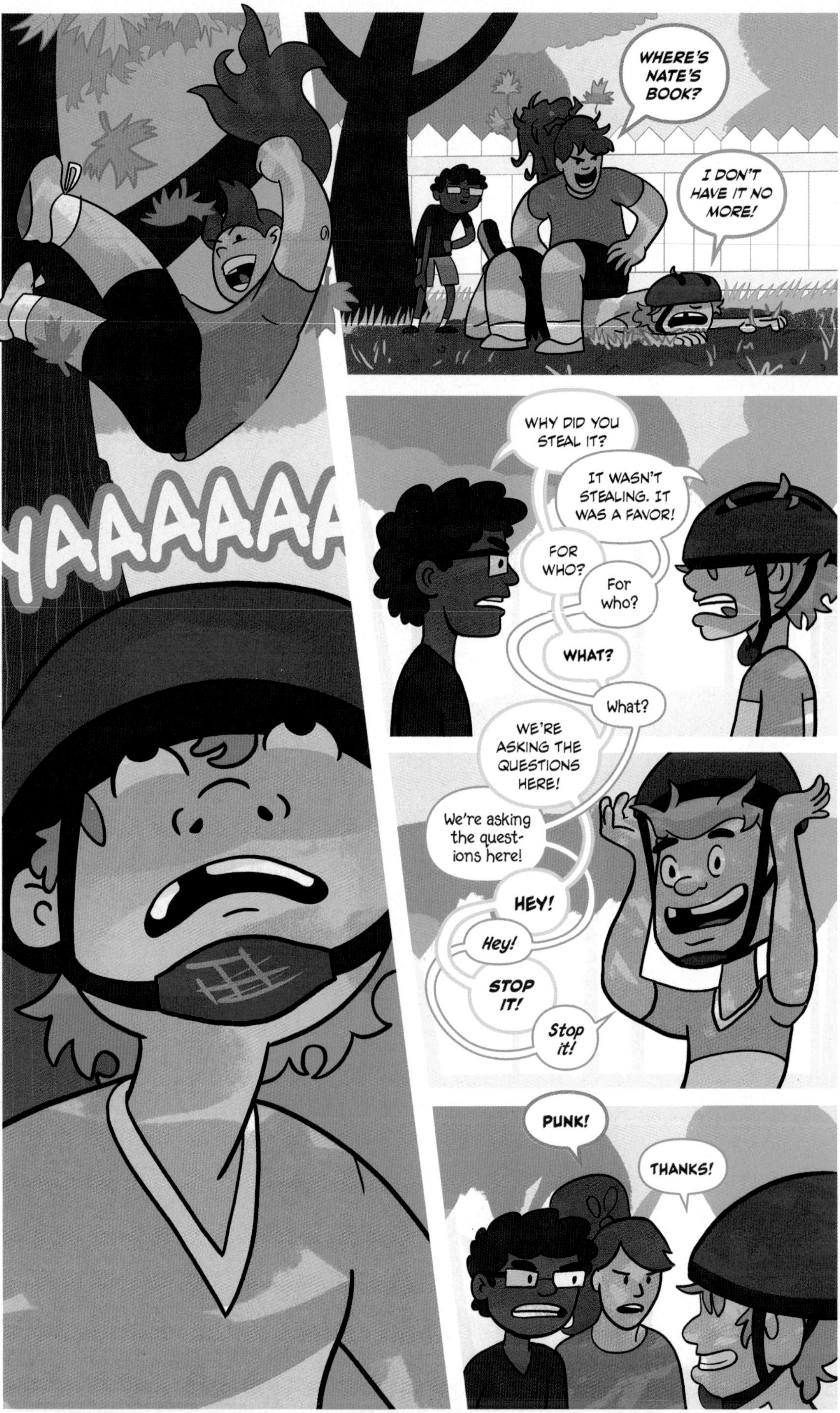
WHERE'S NATE'S BOOK?
I DON'T HAVE IT NO MORE!
HAAAAAA
WHY DID YOU STEAL IT?
IT WASN'T STEALING. IT WAS A FAVOR!
FOR WHO?
For who?
WHAT?
What?
WE'RE ASKING THE QUESTIONS HERE!
We're asking the quest-ions here!
HEY!
Hey!
STOP IT!
Stop it!
PUNK!
THANKS!

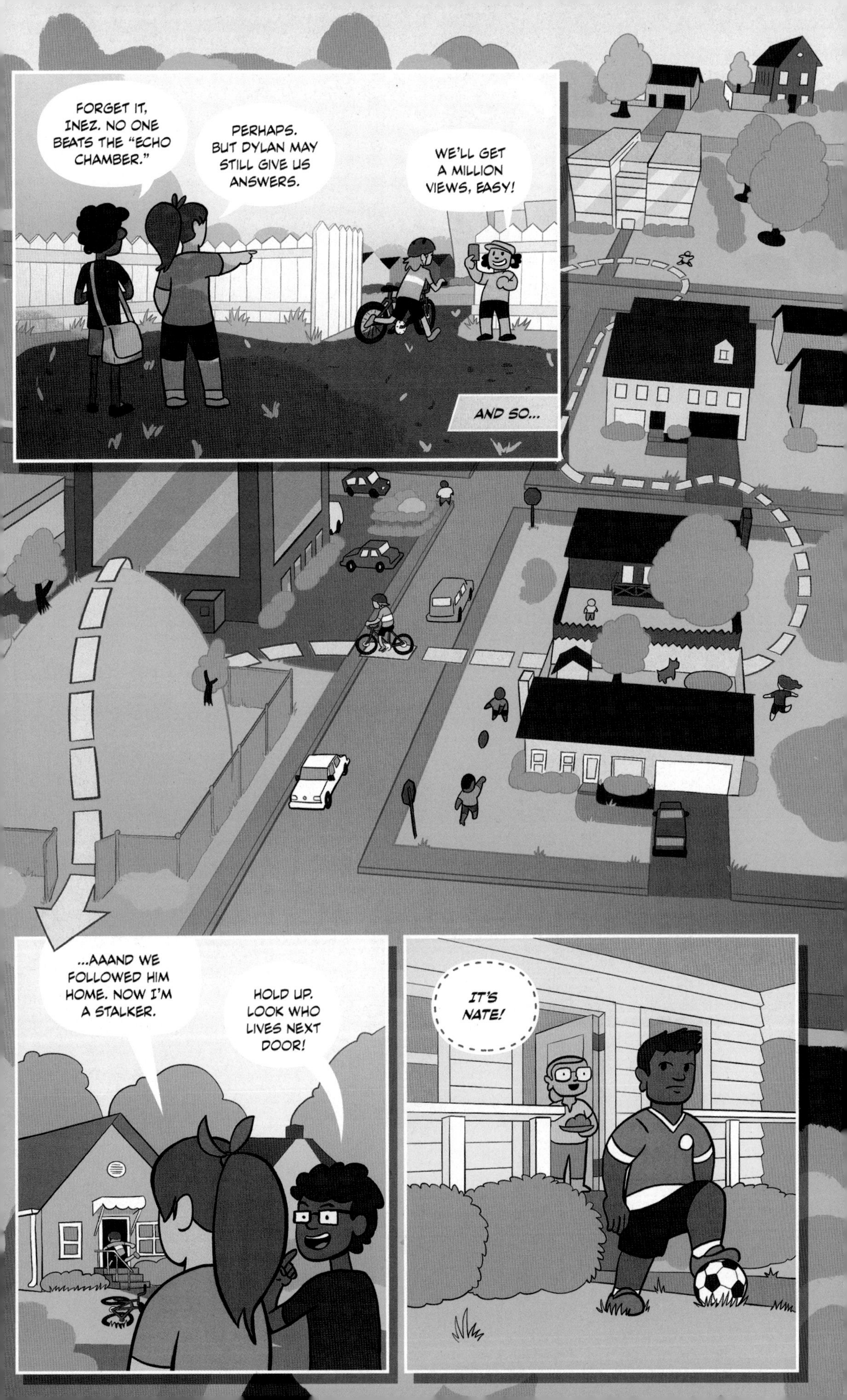
FORGET IT, INEZ. NO ONE BEATS THE "ECHO CHAMBER."
PERHAPS. BUT DYLAN MAY STILL GIVE US ANSWERS.
WE'LL GET A MILLION VIEWS, EASY!
AND SO...
...AAAND WE FOLLOWED HIM HOME. NOW I'M A STALKER.
HOLD UP. LOOK WHO LIVES NEXT DOOR!
IT'S NATE!

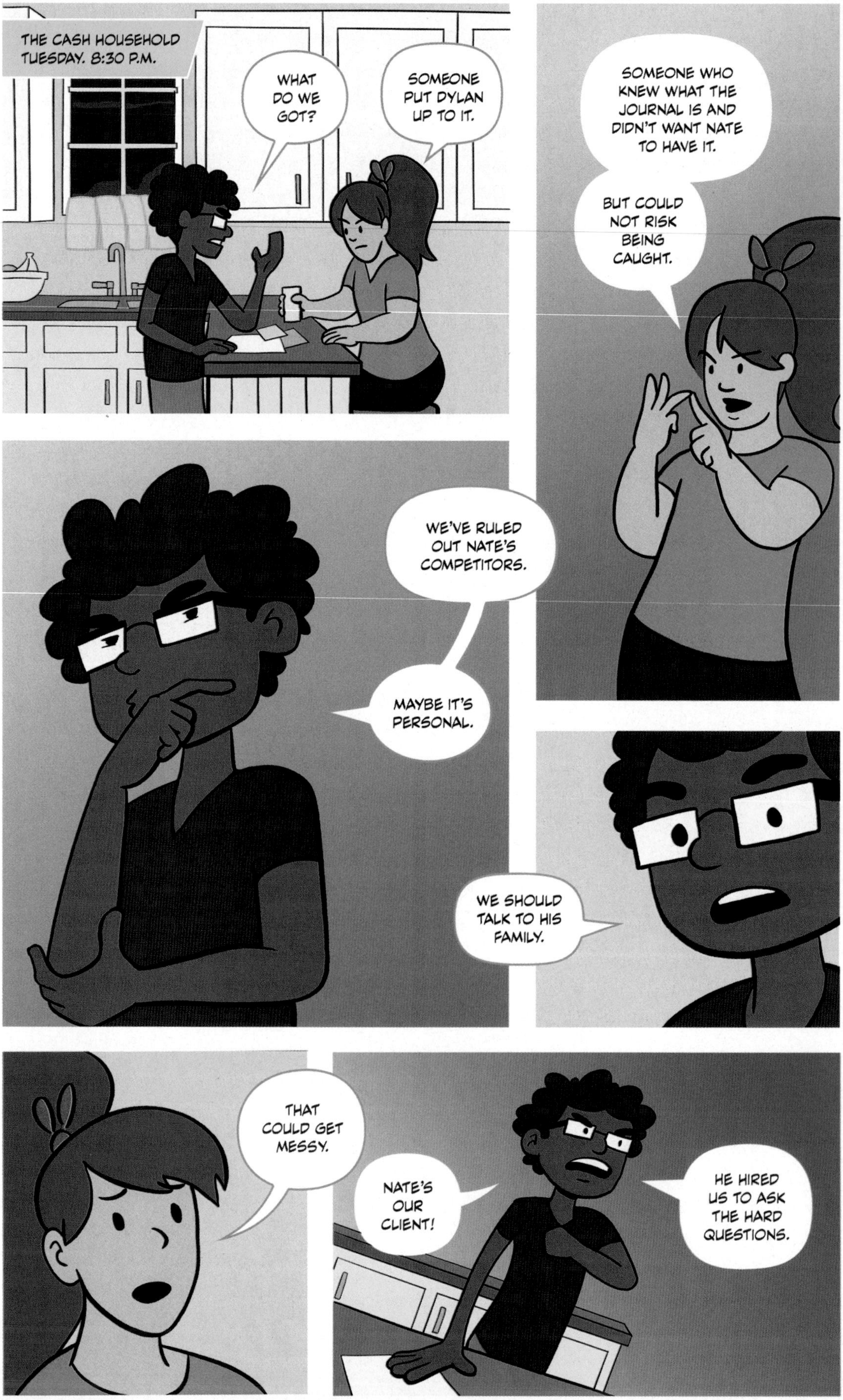
THE CASH HOUSEHOLD
TUESDAY. 8:30 P.M.
WHAT DO WE GOT?
SOMEONE PUT DYLAN UP TO IT.
SOMEONE WHO KNEW WHAT THE JOURNAL IS AND DIDN'T WANT NATE TO HAVE IT.
BUT COULD NOT RISK BEING CAUGHT.
WE'VE RULED OUT NATE'S COMPETITORS.
MAYBE IT'S PERSONAL.
WE SHOULD TALK TO HIS FAMILY.
THAT COULD GET MESSY.
NATE'S OUR CLIENT!
HE HIRED US TO ASK THE HARD QUESTIONS.

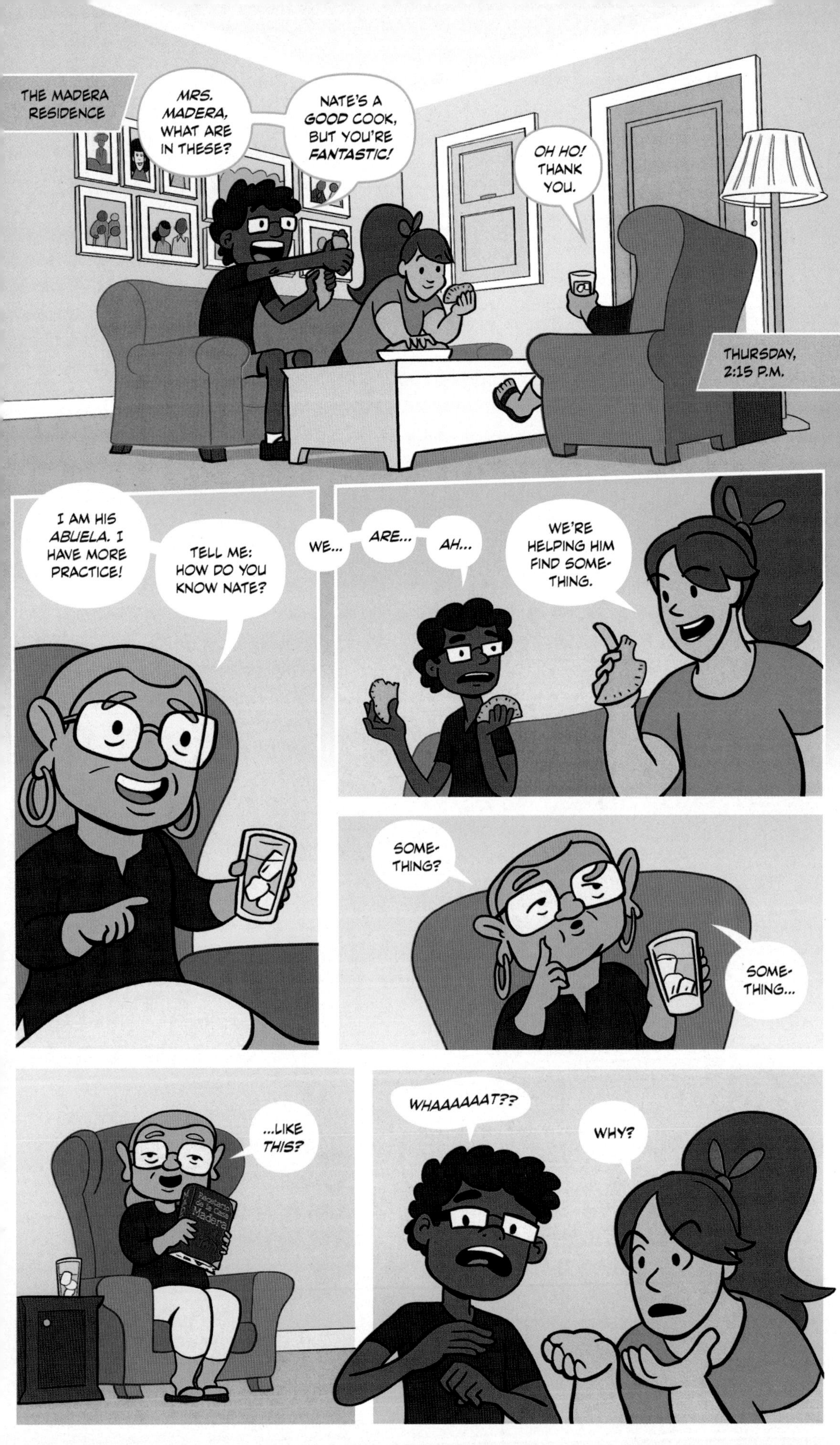
THE MADERA RESIDENCE
MRS. MADERA, WHAT ARE IN THESE?
NATE'S A GOOD COOK, BUT YOU'RE *FANTASTIC!*
OH HO! THANK YOU.
THURSDAY, 2:15 P.M.
I AM HIS *ABUELA.* I HAVE MORE PRACTICE!
TELL ME: HOW DO YOU KNOW NATE?
WE...
ARE...
AH...
WE'RE HELPING HIM FIND SOME-THING.
SOME-THING?
SOME-THING...
...LIKE *THIS?*
Recetario de la Casa Madera
WHAAAAAAT??
WHY?

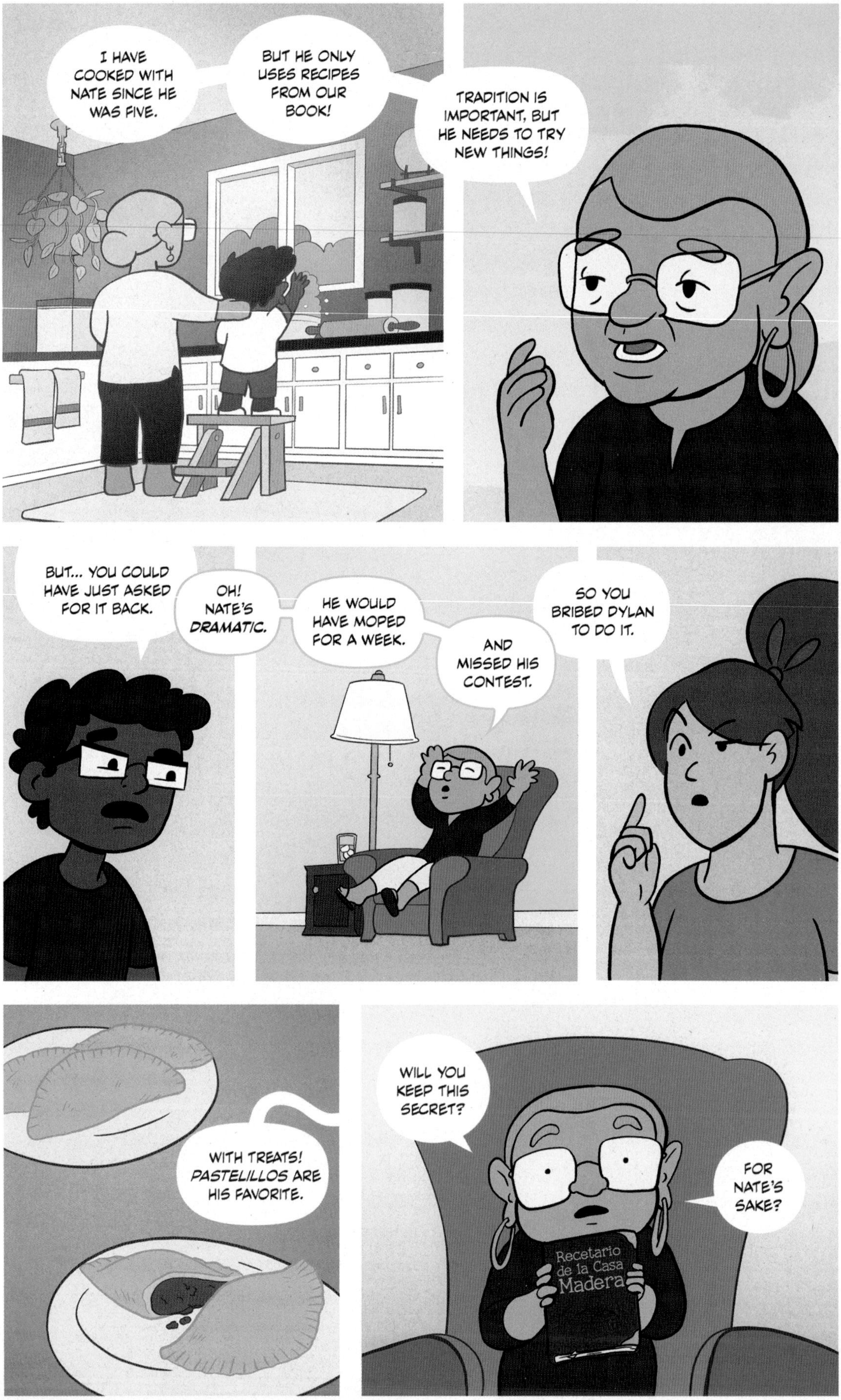
I HAVE COOKED WITH NATE SINCE HE WAS FIVE.
BUT HE ONLY USES RECIPES FROM OUR BOOK!
TRADITION IS IMPORTANT, BUT HE NEEDS TO TRY NEW THINGS!
BUT... YOU COULD HAVE JUST ASKED FOR IT BACK.
OH! NATE'S *DRAMATIC.*
HE WOULD HAVE MOPED FOR A WEEK.
AND MISSED HIS CONTEST.
SO YOU BRIBED DYLAN TO DO IT.
WITH TREATS! *PASTELILLOS* ARE HIS FAVORITE.
WILL YOU KEEP THIS SECRET?
FOR NATE'S SAKE?
Recetario de la Casa Madera

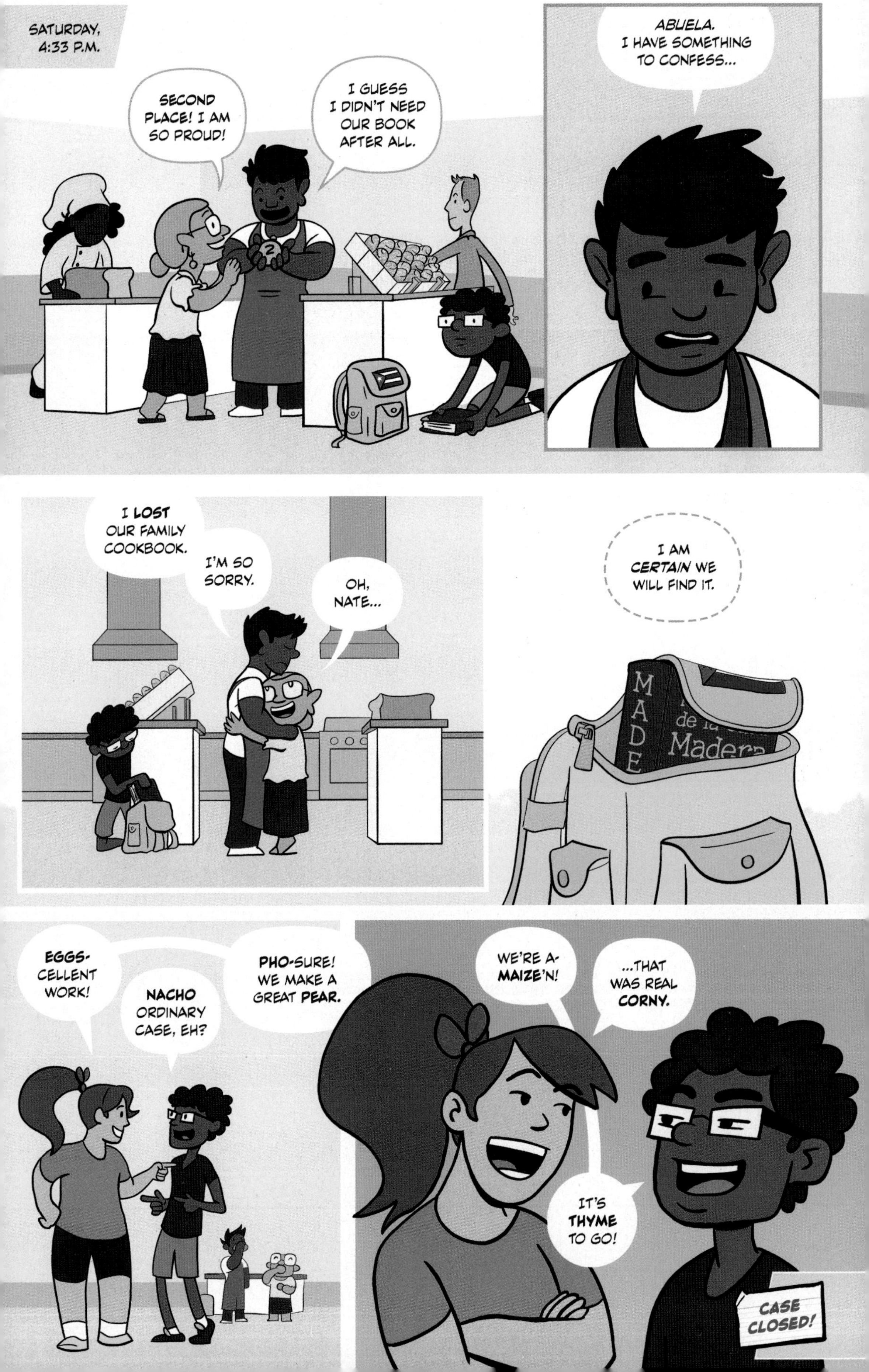
SATURDAY, 4:33 P.M.
SECOND PLACE! I AM SO PROUD!
I GUESS I DIDN'T NEED OUR BOOK AFTER ALL.
ABUELA. I HAVE SOMETHING TO CONFESS...
I LOST OUR FAMILY COOKBOOK.
I'M SO SORRY.
OH, NATE...
I AM CERTAIN WE WILL FIND IT.
MADE
de la
Madera
EGGS-CELLENT WORK!
NACHO ORDINARY CASE, EH?
PHO-SURE! WE MAKE A GREAT PEAR.
WE'RE A-MAIZE'N!
...THAT WAS REAL CORNY.
IT'S THYME TO GO!
CASE CLOSED!

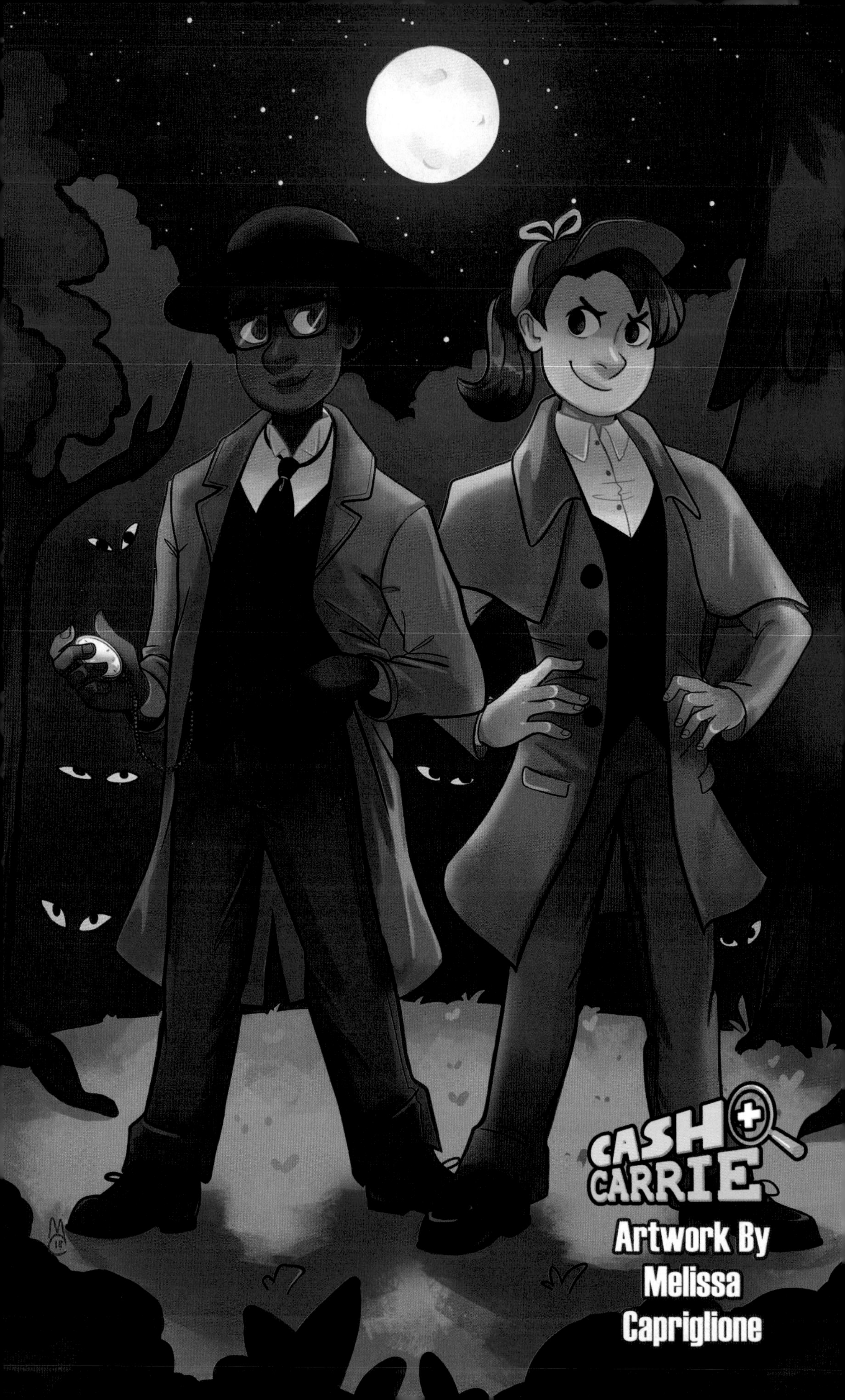
CASH + CARRIE
Artwork By
Melissa
Capriglione

The Mason Middle Messenger

Summer Edition!

NOW HIRING!

Mason Middle School is in search of a new principal.* Applicants can send résumés to hiring@mms.k12.edu

*Extensive background checks will take place.

CHAPTER FIVE

STORY CONTINUED ON PAGE A3

FUN IN THE SUN

Remember when you are out this summer to stay safe in the sun. Here are some tips for you and your family to follow:

STAY HYDRATED

STAY IN THE SHADE

SLATHER ON THE SUNSCREEN

KNOW YOUR LIMITS

Pinup by Pizzaface

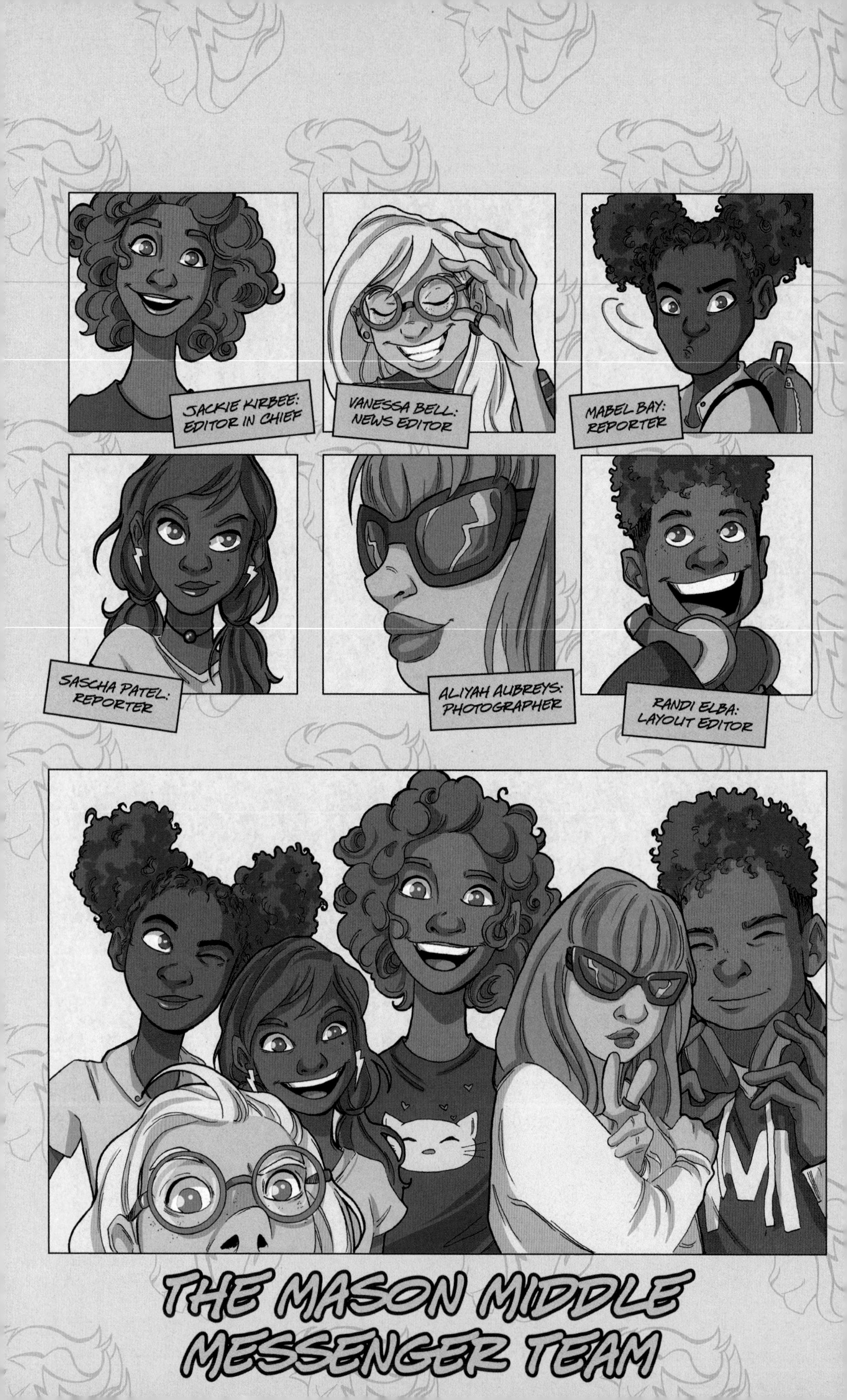
JACKIE KIRBEE: EDITOR IN CHIEF
VANESSA BELL: NEWS EDITOR
MABEL BAY: REPORTER
SASCHA PATEL: REPORTER
ALIYAH AUBREYS: PHOTOGRAPHER
RANDI ELBA: LAYOUT EDITOR
THE MASON MIDDLE MESSENGER TEAM

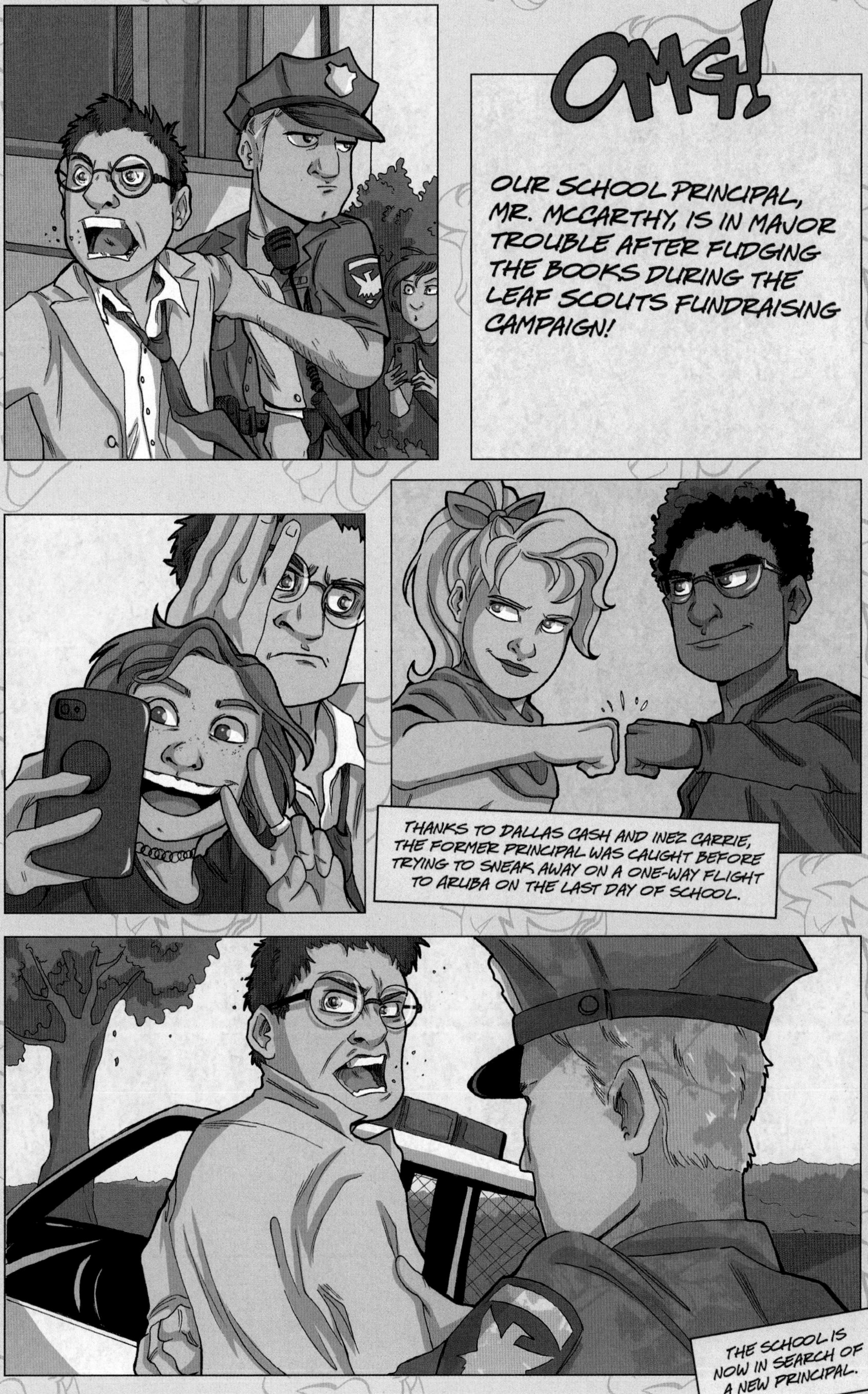
OMG!
OUR SCHOOL PRINCIPAL, MR. MCCARTHY, IS IN MAJOR TROUBLE AFTER FUDGING THE BOOKS DURING THE LEAF SCOUTS FUNDRAISING CAMPAIGN!
THANKS TO DALLAS CASH AND INEZ CARRIE, THE FORMER PRINCIPAL WAS CAUGHT BEFORE TRYING TO SNEAK AWAY ON A ONE-WAY FLIGHT TO ARUBA ON THE LAST DAY OF SCHOOL.
THE SCHOOL IS NOW IN SEARCH OF A NEW PRINCIPAL.

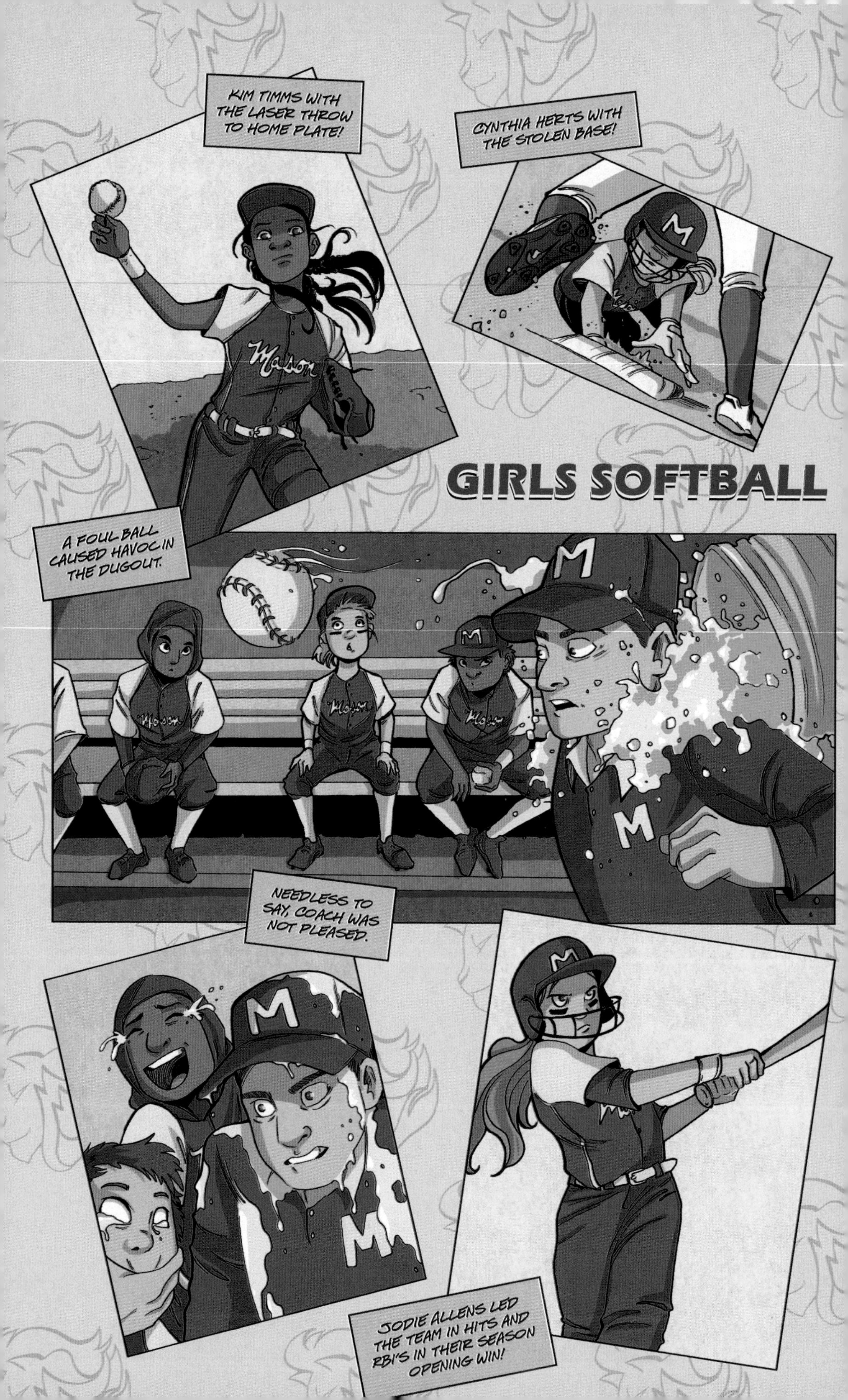
KIM TIMMS WITH THE LASER THROW TO HOME PLATE!
CYNTHIA HERTS WITH THE STOLEN BASE!
GIRLS SOFTBALL
A FOUL BALL CAUSED HAVOC IN THE DUGOUT.
NEEDLESS TO SAY, COACH WAS NOT PLEASED.
JODIE ALLENS LED THE TEAM IN HITS AND RBI'S IN THEIR SEASON OPENING WIN!

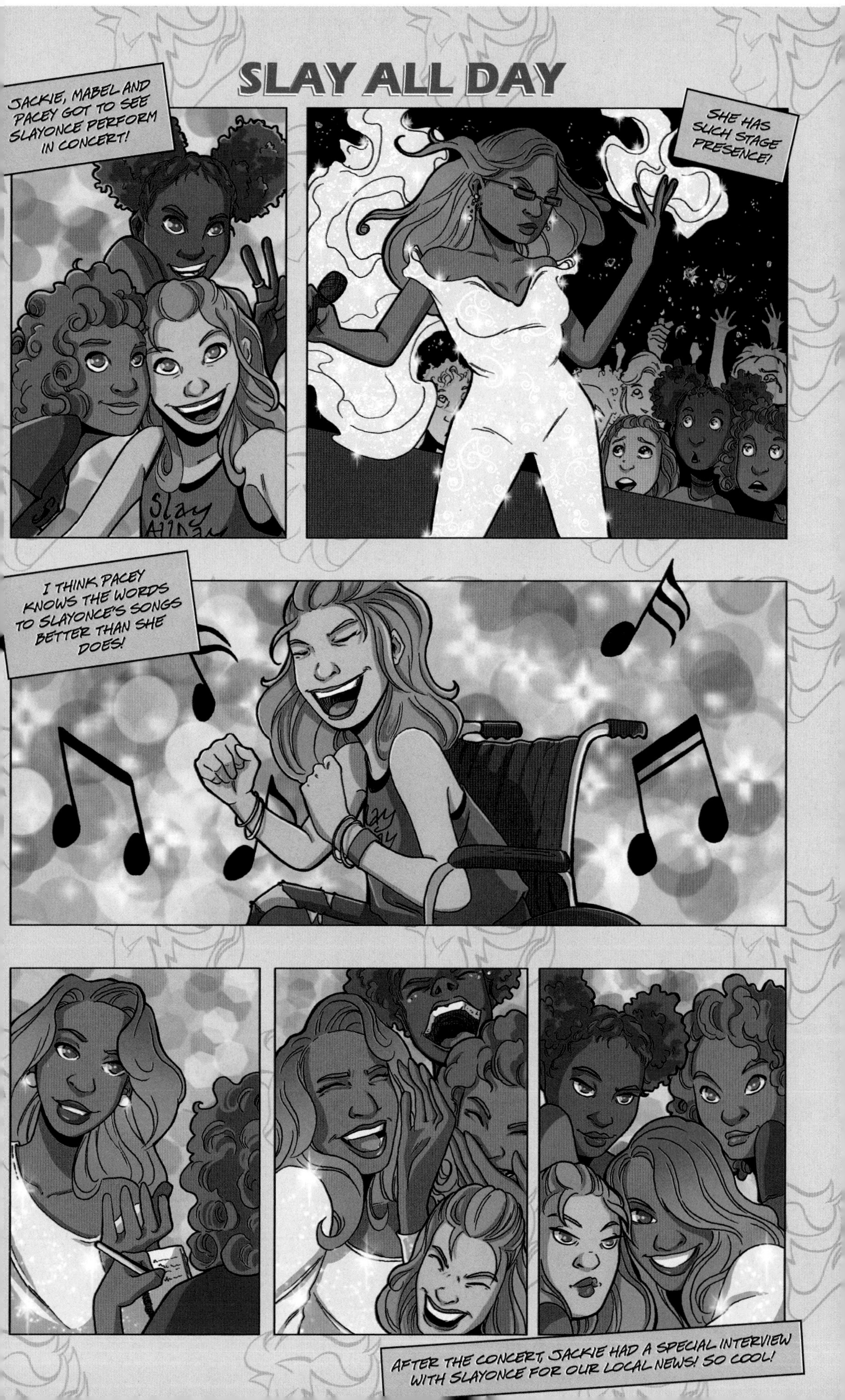
SLAY ALL DAY
JACKIE, MABEL AND PACEY GOT TO SEE SLAYONCE PERFORM IN CONCERT!
SHE HAS SUCH STAGE PRESENCE!
I THINK PACEY KNOWS THE WORDS TO SLAYONCE'S SONGS BETTER THAN SHE DOES!
AFTER THE CONCERT, JACKIE HAD A SPECIAL INTERVIEW WITH SLAYONCE FOR OUR LOCAL NEWS! SO COOL!

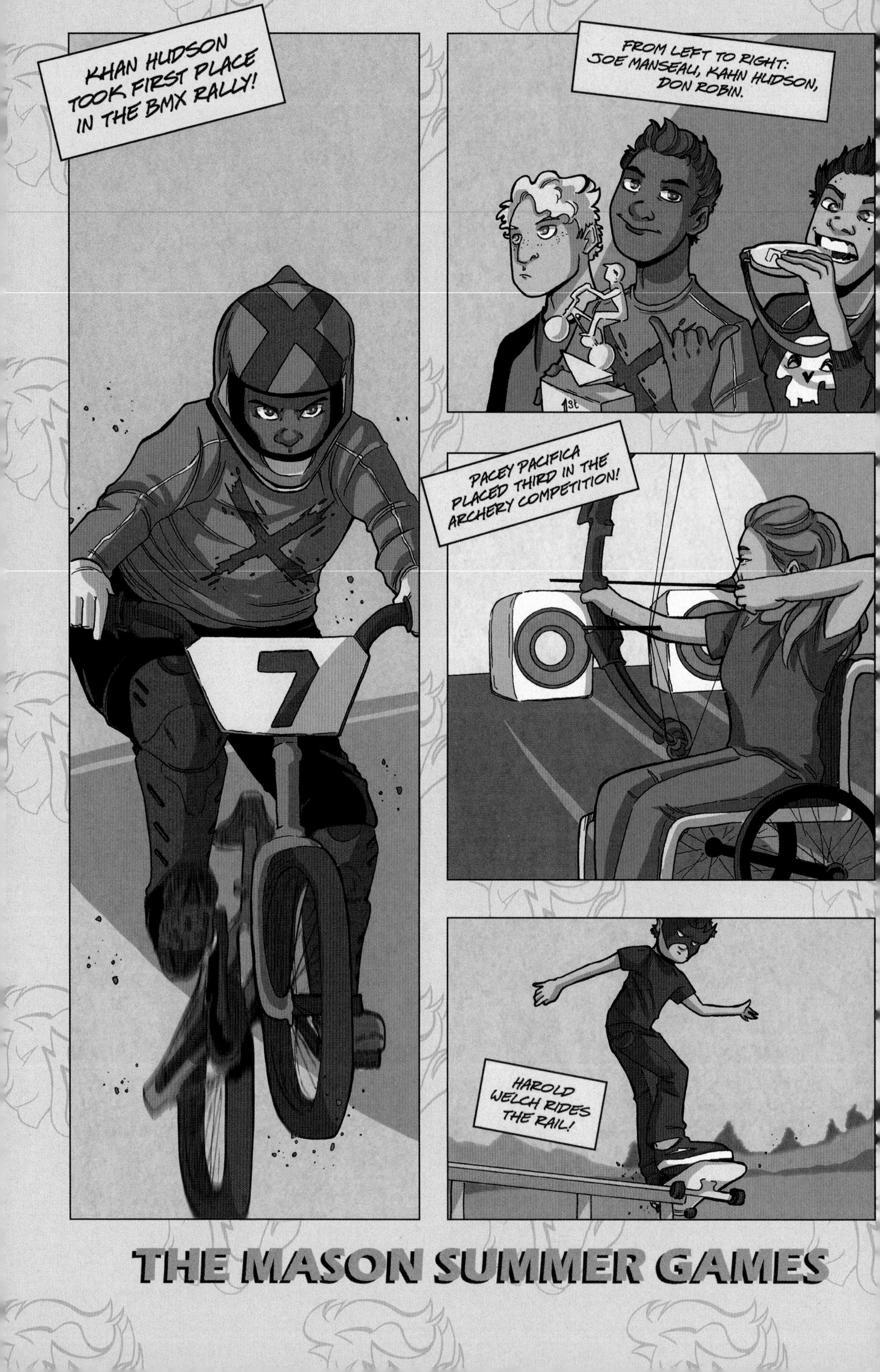
KHAN HUDSON TOOK FIRST PLACE IN THE BMX RALLY!
FROM LEFT TO RIGHT: JOE MANSEAU, KAHN HUDSON, DON ROBIN.
1st
PACEY PACIFICA PLACED THIRD IN THE ARCHERY COMPETITION!
HAROLD WELCH RIDES THE RAIL!

THE MASON SUMMER GAMES

HELPING OTHERS

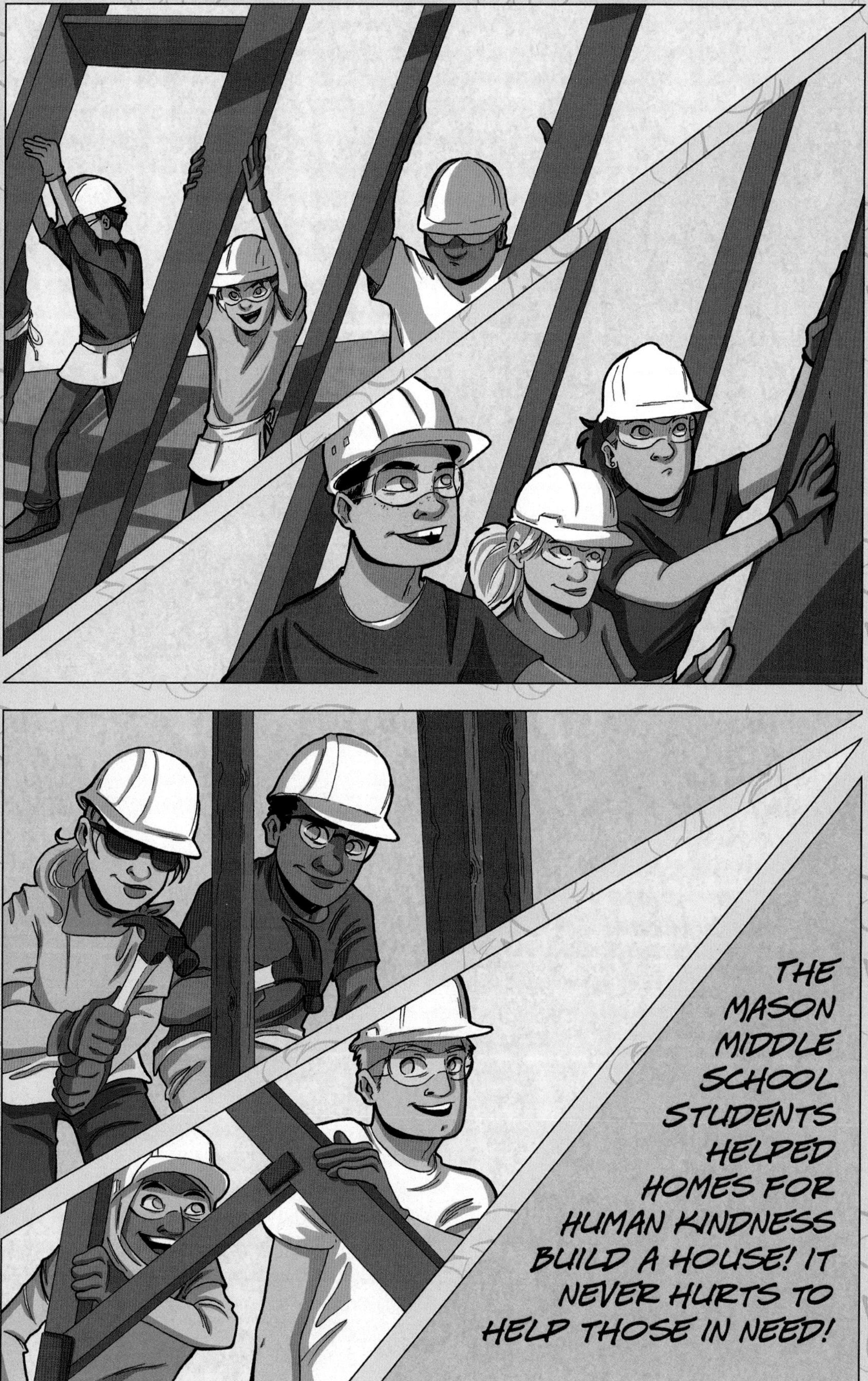
THE MASON MIDDLE SCHOOL STUDENTS HELPED HOMES FOR HUMAN KINDNESS BUILD A HOUSE! IT NEVER HURTS TO HELP THOSE IN NEED!

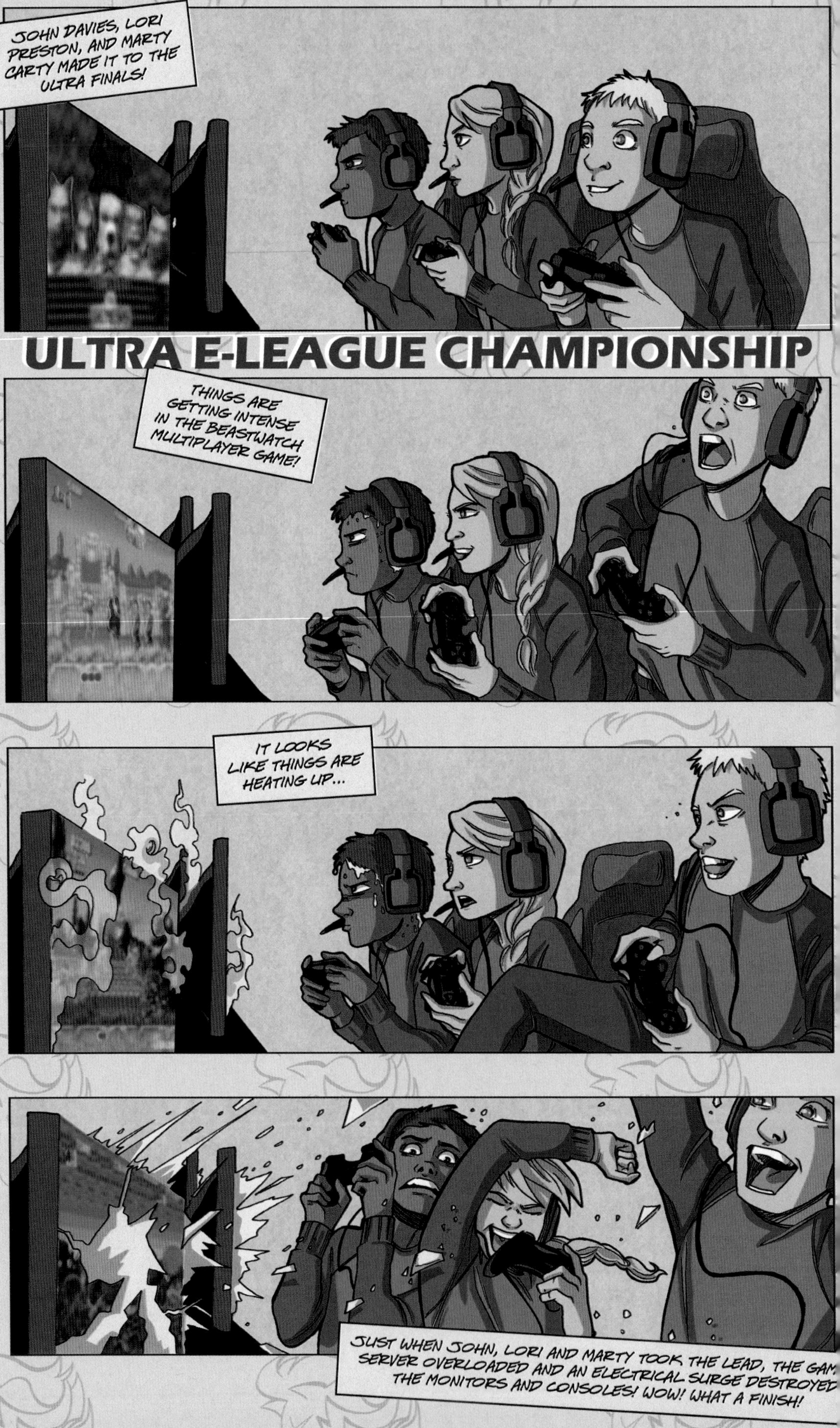
JOHN DAVIES, LORI PRESTON, AND MARTY CARTY MADE IT TO THE ULTRA FINALS!
ULTRA E-LEAGUE CHAMPIONSHIP
THINGS ARE GETTING INTENSE IN THE BEASTWATCH MULTIPLAYER GAME!
IT LOOKS LIKE THINGS ARE HEATING UP...
JUST WHEN JOHN, LORI AND MARTY TOOK THE LEAD, THE GAM SERVER OVERLOADED AND AN ELECTRICAL SURGE DESTROYED THE MONITORS AND CONSOLES! WOW! WHAT A FINISH!

WINNERS & WELCOMES

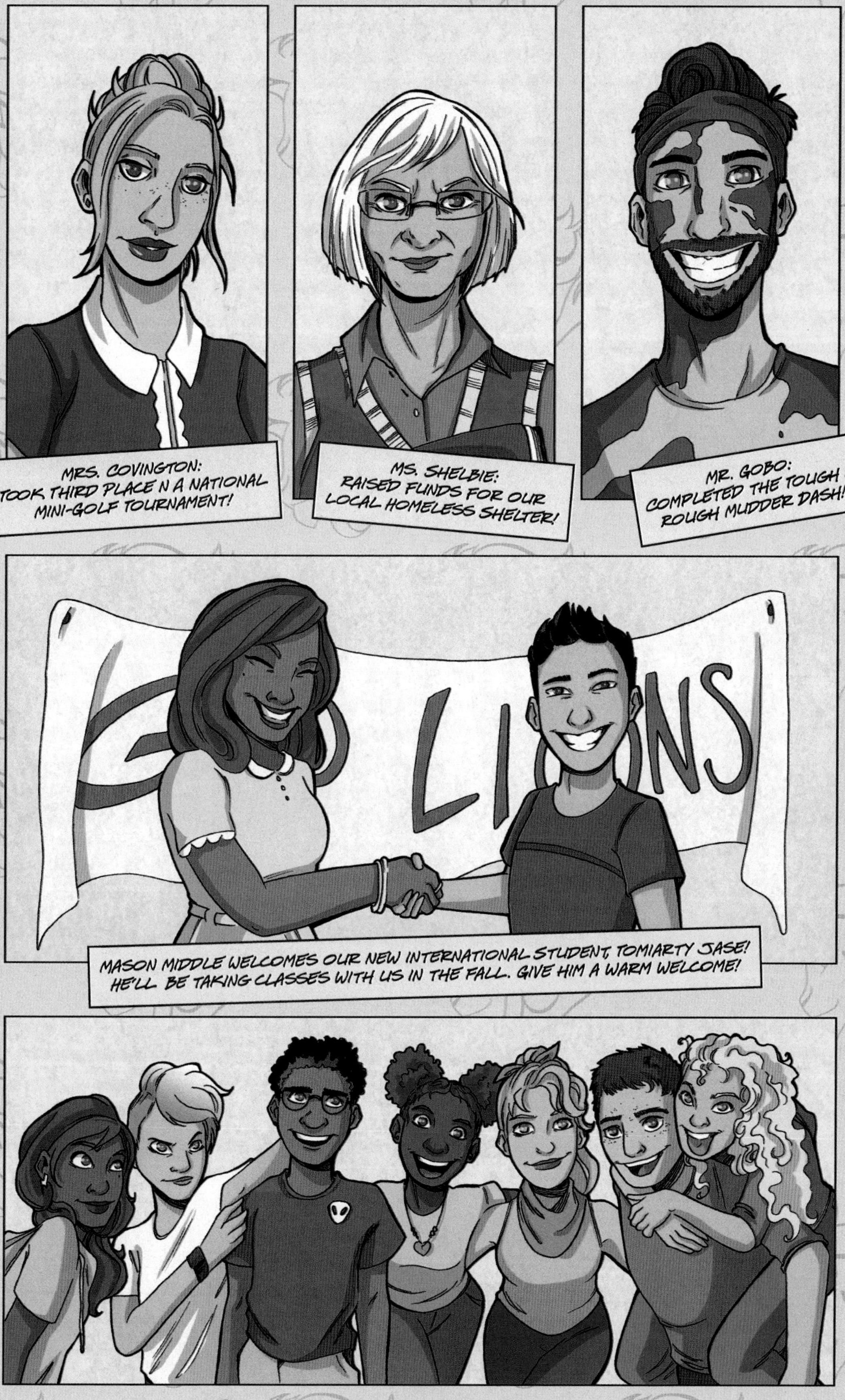
MRS. COVINGTON:
TOOK THIRD PLACE N A NATIONAL
MINI-GOLF TOURNAMENT!
MS. SHELBIE:
RAISED FUNDS FOR OUR
LOCAL HOMELESS SHELTER!
MR. GOBO:
COMPLETED THE TOUGH &
ROUGH MUDDER DASH!
MASON MIDDLE WELCOMES OUR NEW INTERNATIONAL STUDENT, TOMIARTY JASE!
HE'LL BE TAKING CLASSES WITH US IN THE FALL. GIVE HIM A WARM WELCOME!

ENJOY YOUR SUMMER!

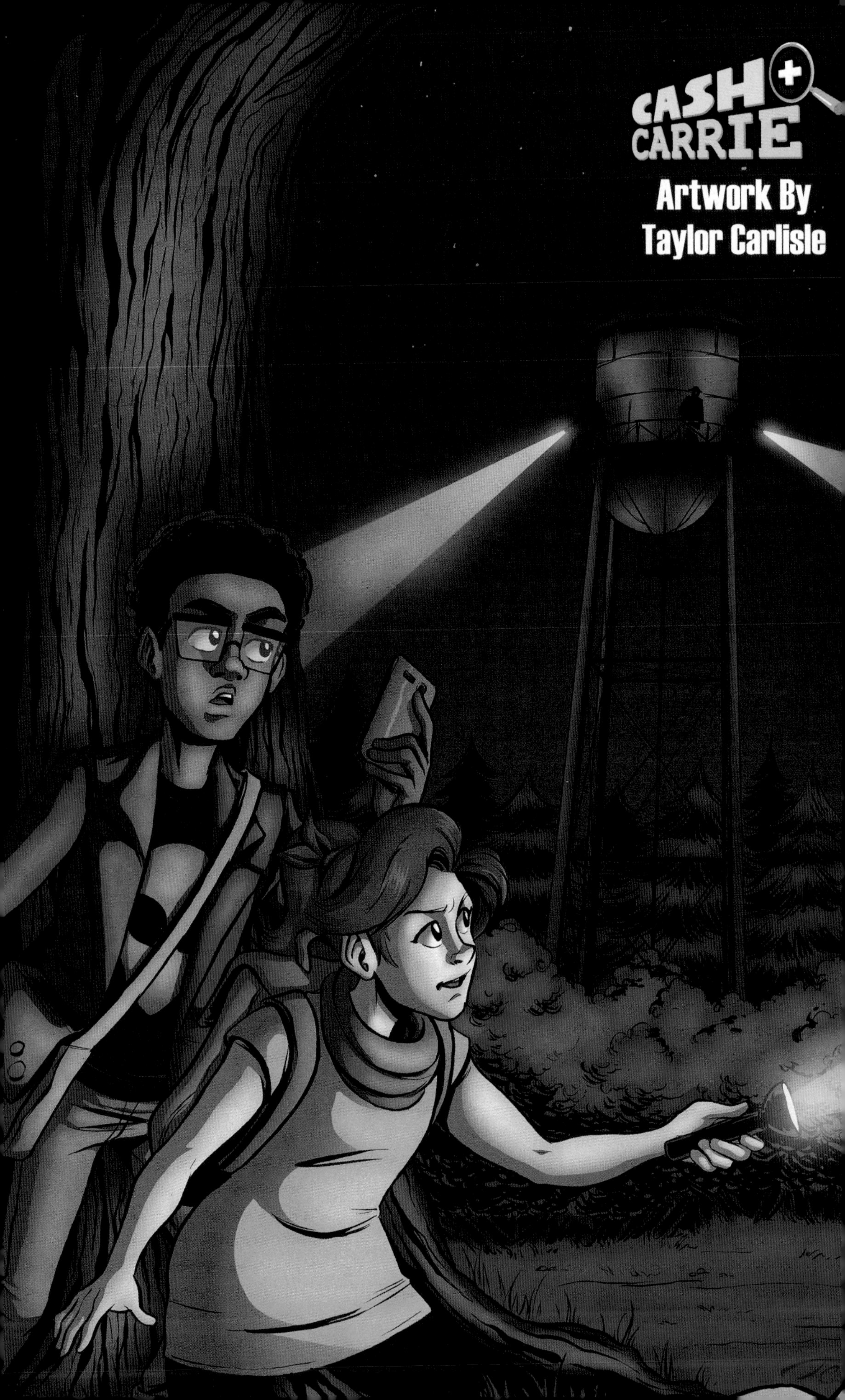
CASH + CARRIE
Artwork By
Taylor Carlisle

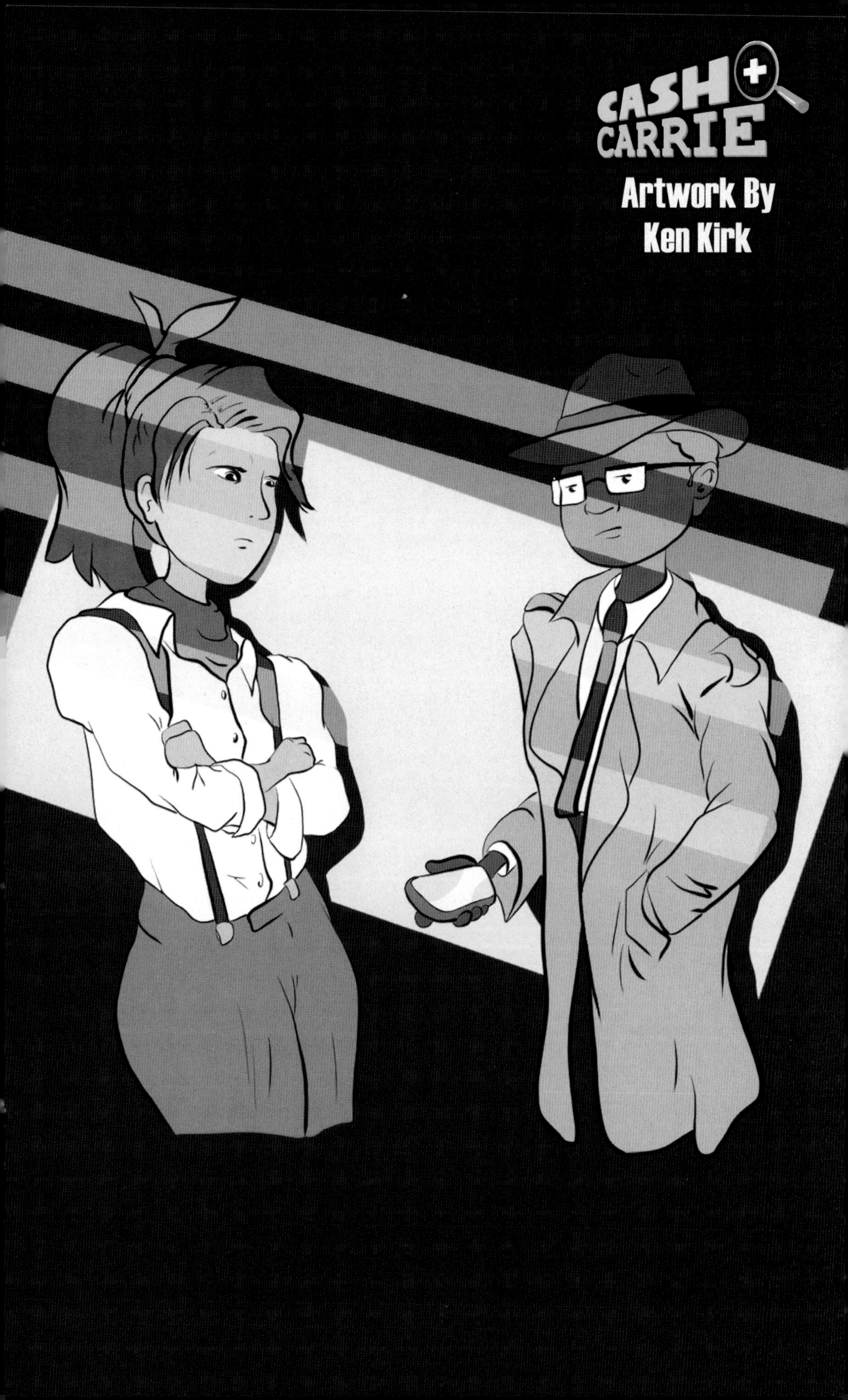
CASH + CARRIE
Artwork By
Ken Kirk

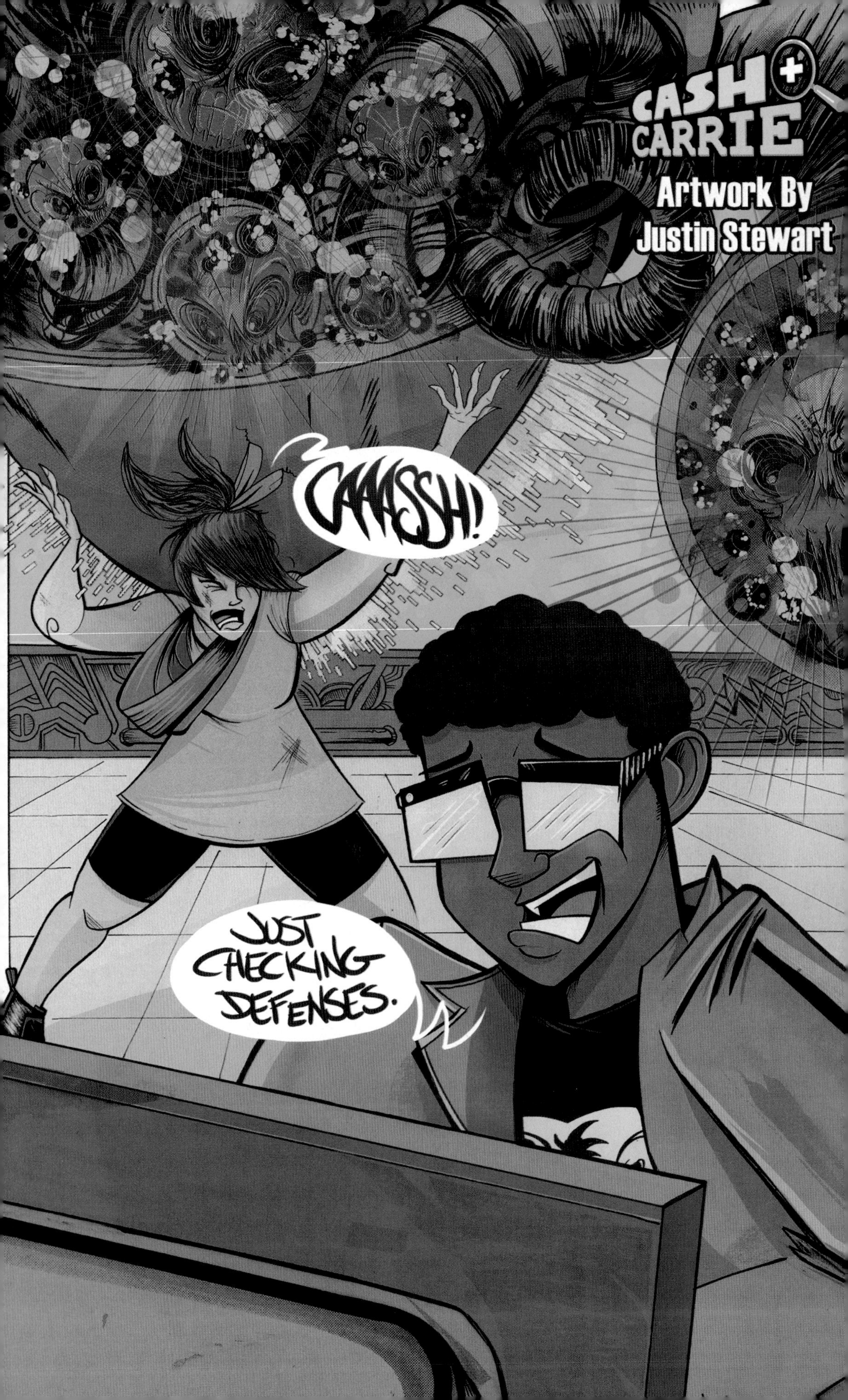
CASH + CARRIE
Artwork By
Justin Stewart
CAAASSH!
JUST CHECKING DEFENSES.

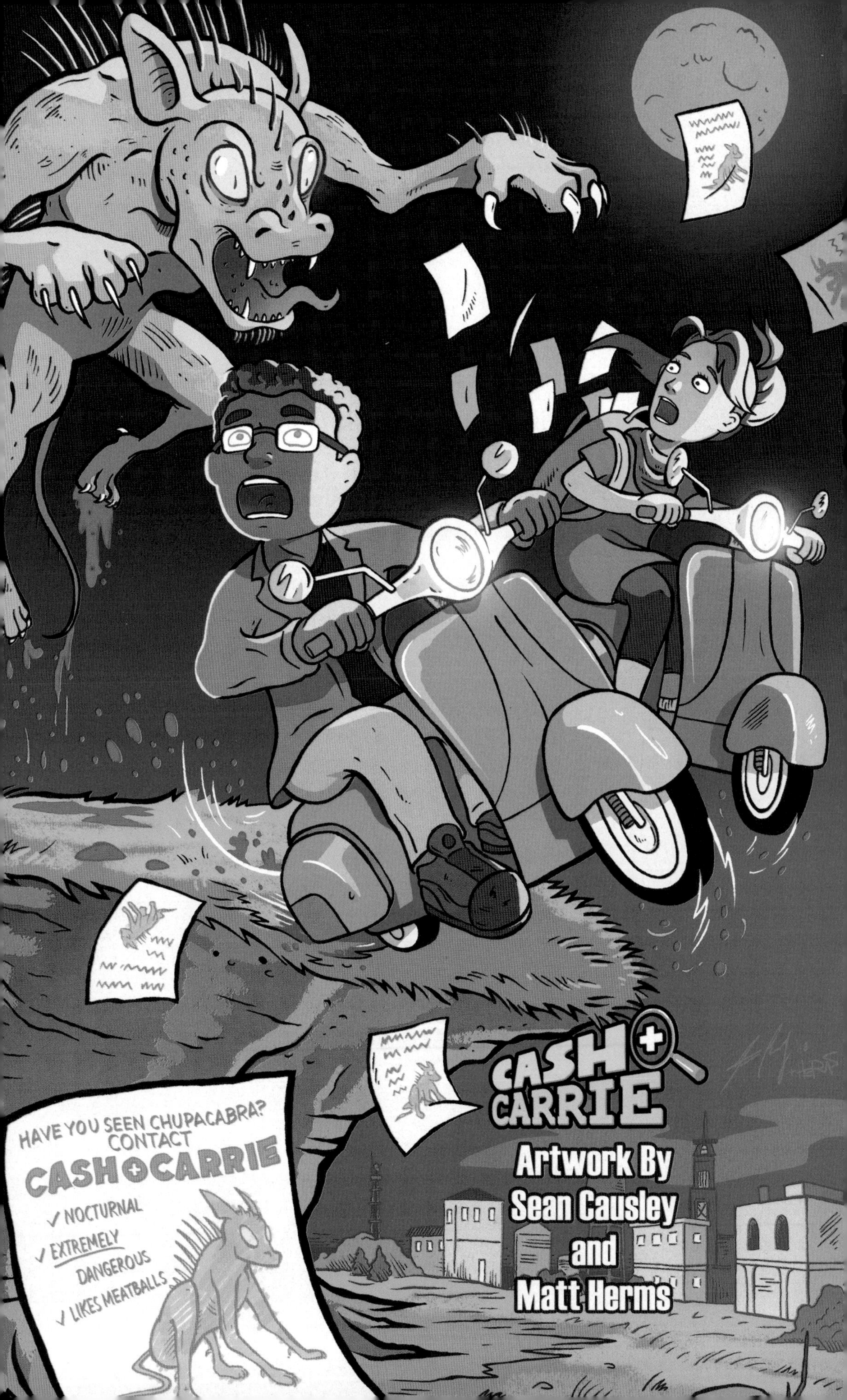
CASH + CARRIE
Artwork By
Sean Causley
and
Matt Herms
HAVE YOU SEEN CHUPACABRA?
CONTACT
CASH + CARRIE
✓ NOCTURNAL
✓ EXTREMELY
DANGEROUS
✓ LIKES MEATBALLS

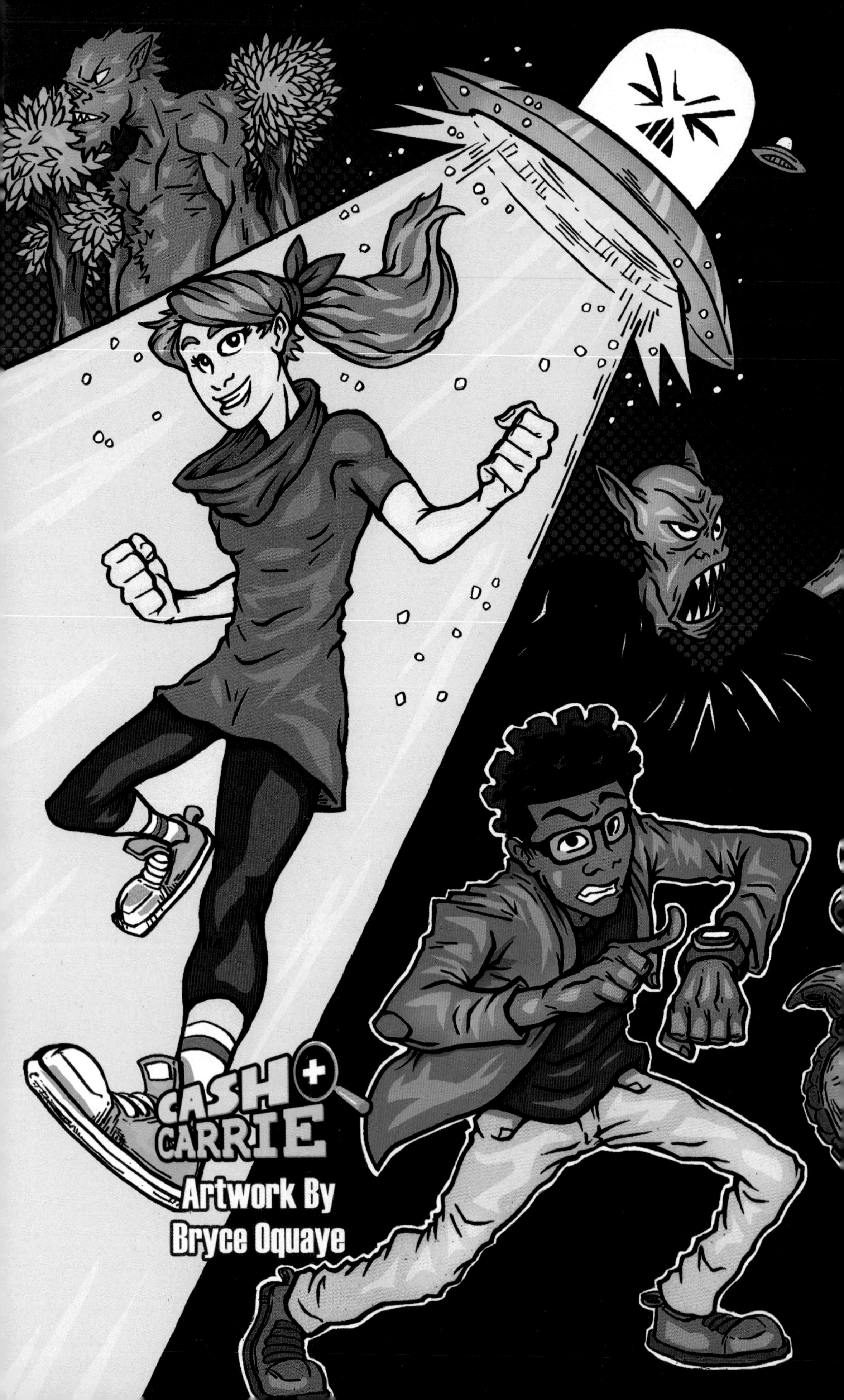
CASH + CARRIE
Artwork By
Bryce Oquaye